THE REQUIEM RED

BRYNN CHAPMAN

Month9Books

This book is a work of fiction. Names, characters, places, and incidents are either products of the author's imagination or are used fictitiously. Any resemblance to actual persons, living or dead, business establishments, events, or locales is entirely coincidental. The author makes no claims to, but instead acknowledges the trademarked status and trademark owners of the word marks mentioned in this work of fiction.

Copyright © 2016 Brynn Chapman

THE REQUIEM RED by Brynn Chapman

ISBN: 978-1-942664-85-7

All rights reserved. Published in the United States of America by Month9Books, LLC.

Month9Books is located in Raleigh, NC 27609.

Cover and typography designed by Deranged Doctor Designs

Cover Copyright © 2016 Month9Books

Month9Books

"And those who were dancing were thought to be insane by those who could not hear the music."
- Usually attributed to *Friedrich Nietzsche*

For Sherry
You are airidh *(worthy), in all things, my friend.*

THE REQUIEM RED

BRYNN CHAPMAN

CHAPTER ONE

1894, SOOTHING HILLS SANATORIUM
PHILADELPHIA, COMMONWEALTH OF PENNSYLVANIA

"*Jane!* Jane, where are you? There has been an accident!"

Nurse Sally's tremulous voice echoes down the sanatorium's hallway, ricocheting off the walls like mad bats in flight. I close my eyes, press my lips tight, and keep silent.

"*Patient Twenty-Nine!*"

I flinch at the use of my patient number and slide from the hidden window seat, snapping my book closed to bound down the corridor. The nurse's cry came from the direction of my room.

"Twenty-niiiine ... " a male, sing-song voice calls out through the bars. I swerve and dart out of his way, narrowly missing those yellowed, grasping fingernails. My heartbeat doubles as I spin and run faster.

What has she done now?

My roommate Lily is *truly* disturbed. I spend most of my time out of the room, out of her way, because of her howling, because of her—

I round the corner and skid to a halt, instantaneously shaking.

Lily's long blond hair spreads out on her cot like a coquette's fan. Her eyes are closed. Her chest appears … still.

"Nurse?"

"Jane, go for help. Now. Run to Ward 4 and fetch Dr. Grayjoy!"

I stand staring, blood frozen in my veins, feet frozen to the floor. Lily's head gives a violent jerk, and I gasp.

"For the love of heaven, *now*, you imbecile!"

I run. But not before I see the wall. Not before I see the message scrawled above her bed.

Help me. I know not what I do.

SOOTHING HILLS ASYLUM VISITORS' SALON

"Bravo! *Bra-vo*, Miss Frost!" Willis Graceling, my would-be-suitor, claps too loudly.

I wince, but curtsy all the same, deftly moving my cello behind me. I walk off the small stage and ease myself into the milling crowd.

Father claps as well, slow and deliberate. Everyone in the salon follows his lead, though truth be told, it is a *distracted* applause. These hospital patrons and philanthropists are more interested in donations and connections than what musical selection I have performed this eve.

The windows are fogged from the patrons' breath and the too many bodies in this too-warm room, despite the chilled fall breezes that whisper at the panes, reminding us that winter is coming. My eyes roam as I try to calm myself—to prepare for the onslaught of attention. I am unused to such large gatherings due to my largely sequestered upbringing.

Crystal goblets of rose-red flash by on a silver tray, just beneath my nose, close enough to catch the fragrant bouquet. I snatch one and the waiter raises an eyebrow, but says nothing, hurrying back into the fray. I am used to the whispers of virtuoso, but the outright attention I do not prefer. I would rather wield the pen and music and have another perform it.

Colors now dance behind my eyes. I picture them weaving in and out of the wrinkles in my brain. Notes appear in color for me. The color-note correlation never alters, like my own multi-hued, musical alphabet. This ability allowed me to learn to play at a very, very young age. As a child, I merely wished to see the rainbow in my mind.

Papa strides toward me, black eyes narrowing as his substantial arm slides about my waist, shuffling me into the crowd.

He whispers, "That was very good, Jules."

His eyes shift through the patrons, nodding and smiling, but out of the side of his mouth, he says, "But I have heard it played better. In your own chambers."

Willis trails behind us like a bounding, oversized puppy. I can almost see the leash from his neck to my father's belt. Or perhaps an invisible chain from his coin purse to my maidenhead.

I am to be sold, *er*, married within the year.

Father vacates my arm, and I sigh in relief, but he is quickly replaced by Willis's eager face. "Shall I fetch you some punch, Jules?"

"Thank you, that would be lovely."

I ghost to the window and wrap my shawl tighter about my shoulders to guard against the draft sliding beneath its frame. Outside, a vast cornfield dies a day at a time. Remnants of green poke through the blackened leaves—as if hazel-eyed fairies play hide-and-seek, peeking out of the gloom-colored stalks.

I turn to watch Willis's retreating form, disappearing into the society crowd, and cannot stay the sigh.

It is not so *very* terrible. He *is* handsome ... and kind. Better than many other prospects I have had forced upon me. If people were flavors, Willis Graceling would decidedly be vanilla. Though nothing is decidedly wrong with vanilla, it is predictable, and quite often a filler.

I bite my lip.

I always dreamed of sharing my life with more of a ... curry.

A gaggle of what my mind has deemed *society women* descends. Women with whom I share no connection, no interests, but for the sake of reputation, I must politely endure their inane conversation.

"Jules, it was *so* lovely. Did you truly compose it yourself?"

"Yes." My stomach contracts.

Despite the low din of their prattling voices, *I hear it.*

A trickle of fear erupts in a violent shiver as gooseflesh puckers my arms.

"Whatever is the matter, child?" Lady Bennington's face pinches with concern.

I shake my head. "Nothing."

But I hear it ... *louder*. Growing louder every second. The *music*, wafting in with the draft, as if the dying corn laments its own demise.

I curtsy. "Please do excuse me. I am feeling a bit faint. Perhaps the night air will set me to rights." And without waiting for their reply, I make my getaway to the back of the salon, toward the door.

I slip out to the darkened porch and lean the back of my head against the door, closing my eyes. A multitude of covered lanterns cast a yellow haze over the myriad of rocking chairs, which now move in time with the breeze. As if the hospitals past invisible inhabitants sit, waiting in other-worldly expectation. *Listening*. As I listen.

It has been so long since I heard *this* music. Childhood experience has taught me only *I* hear this music. It seems to live only in my mind.

Maeve, my governess, forbade me to speak of it.

When I was but three, I first told her of the music. Of the *words* I hear in the music. Not in every song ... only very specific melodies. Not lyrics, precisely, but intonations ... like a whispered message. The harmonious voice whispering promises between the notes. She made me promise never to mention it again. Especially not to Father. I heeded her warning, the terror in her round, dark eyes forever etched in my memory.

The notes now pull and tug at my chest, as if sawing through my sternum, managing to wrench my rib cage open, as the tones grasp my heart and *squeeze.* The music elicits unwelcome tears.

A single phrase repeats over and over, embedded in the sound, like a musical Morse code.

Save me. Save me. Save me.

I bite my lip, then whisper, "From where. Who *are* you?"

CHAPTER TWO

"You know *something*, Jane. What happened to Lily?"

Dr. Frost's eyes are abnormally round—wild and wide as his livid mouth.

The leather straps tighten around my wrists, and I thrash against them. I smile ruefully. Three burly orderlies are necessary to contain me. Once a panic hits, I am as wild as any mountain cat.

My thoughts cloud as the familiar mental-mist descends.

I see the events as if through another's eyes as my mind prepares to escape.

My dirty bare foot strikes out, connecting with the young one's face, leaving a sooty streak. "You little—"

"Hold your tongue, James."

The doctor stalks back and forth before me, his eyes boring

into mine as the remaining three *white coats* firmly affix my ankles to the chair. I thrash and strain, but it's futile. Tears made of fear and anger bead and stream down my face.

My teeth grind and gnash. I *detest* this room. The very smell of it gives birth to the raging panic.

It is gargantuan, once an airing yard—with a glass roof that cranks open and closed. My mind has labeled it *Frost's playground*, where he has used his giant intellect to fashion every type of device—all designed for therapeutic torture.

To my right, the sloshing of a dunk tank. A woman, barely conscious, hangs limply from the seesaw as it plunges her once and *again* and *again* into ice-baths. To my left, three women, strapped to gurneys, retch into chamber pots—all undoubtedly have consumed the *crème of tartar*—its sickening mixture shall roil their guts and have them vomiting until their ribs cry out for mercy. Behind them, a second set of gurneys—these residents with black, writhing polka dots peppering their alabaster skin. *Leeches.*

I stare straight forward, panting, licking my dry lips.

But *this* … he has saved the worst *for me*. As is his custom. Frost detests me above all others.

"Please. Not this *treatment*," I wail, channeling as much sarcasm as possible into the word. "I *tell you*, I was in the common room. I have no idea what happened to Lily."

Or to Faith. Or to Candace. My two roommates before her.

Or the other three women who had disappeared off the women's floor, as if into the ether, over the past two decades.

I hear the whispers among the staff, a killer is loose—either a patient as skilled as Harry Houdini at slipping his restraints, or a deranged staff member.

I am a suspect. After all, three of the missing were my roommates.

"You *lie,* Jane. You always lie." Frost's lips retract to reveal white, straight teeth. Teeth that remind me of white-washed tombstones.

Indeed, he is very handsome. A handsome, dangerous, deranged jackal, with complete and total power as to whether I live or die.

If you can call asylum life living.

I have none to speak for me. An orphan. I have been here, behind these towering walls, as long as I can remember. I know not even my last name. My only home is this land of divergent reality.

The clanging sound of cogs grind to life as the smell of oil hits, my nostrils instantly flaring; I break out in a sweat, retching. A learned response. The contraption shudders as my chair whirls into the air, my stomach dropping as I soar into the cathedral heights of the asylum.

The windows are open wide, the night wind battering my upturned face. I register the first droplets of rain before the machine veers, plunging me downward. Lightning flashes in the sky-windows overhead, and I shudder, my teeth clacking together like a skeleton's song. My mind fills with music—sorrowful, weeping chords of self-pity.

I soar into the heights again, nearly striking the glass ceiling. The chair revolves slowly now, but as I am easily sickened by any circular motion, my head buzzes, thick with panic.

I gag, crying, pleading. "P-please, Dr. Frost. *Pray, have mercy.*"

I whiz past and see the manic gleam in Frost's eye. "Up one notch, Nurse Sally."

"No, *pleeease! I shall speak! I shall speak!*"

The revolutions increase again, and I close my eyes, my mind sloshing back and forth in my skull like wine trying to vacate the lip of a goblet. I feel my soul slip inward, preparing to depart. I was once mute for an entire year.

There were no words worth uttering.

"Slower now, bring her to me."

The contraption slows, spinning toward him.

His face, the wall, the nurse, the other patients. His face, the wall, the nurse, the other patients.

"I *said*, Jane. Did you see anything?"

"Yes!" I lie. "Yes!" I will tell him I am bloody Queen Victoria if it will stop the revolutions.

The chair halts, and I double over, sobbing, heaving, and expel my breakfast onto my bare feet. My arms are still tethered so that I hang from the chair like a swooping crane in flight.

"*What* did you see?"

"Release me," I bark. "Not till you release me." I try to revive my courage.

To find my rage.

Rough hands loosen the buckles, and I crumple to the floor, my face drinking in the cold stone of the flagstones, ever so grateful for the pull of the earth and gravity.

"I-I saw her sneak out," I pant. "The night before she died. She ... she was meeting someone."

"Who?"

"That is all I know, I swear! She swore me to silence."

The idea is ludicrous. Lily barely recognized her name, let alone possessed the cognition needed to plan an escape. The asylum is locked tight with two hundred acres of vast forest surrounding it. A veritable fortress. The only way people depart are in body bags. Or the crematorium.

My mind whispers, *Or they go to Ward Thirteen. And vacate in spirit.*

I shudder. That would be a fate *worse* than death.

A tight grapevine of information passes from loose-lipped staff to indiscrete patients. *Ablations* are performed in Thirteen. It is *supposed* to be the fate of *only* the most violent, the most uncontrollable—but there were rumors.

Rumors that the missing girls perished *there*—doomed to walk the halls at night like shuffling, aimless cadavers. Not dead, not alive. No more than animated corpses—the remnants of their personalities let loose to fly away by the holes drilled in their skulls.

"Take Patient Twenty-Nine to her room."

Hands thrust under my arms to haul me off the floor, and my cheek is pressed against the new orderly's chest. The smell. He has the most inviting smell. Not at all like the others. I automatically burrow my face into it like a child.

Pain. With each and every breath, as if nettles have overrun my chest. Dr. Grayjoy says my mind changes worry and fear into physical pain.

Times like this, life seems too difficult to endure.

The specter of mutism lingers, threatening to crawl up my throat and squeeze my vocal cords to dust. It has happened before. To ward it off, I begin to hum middle C, over and over.

Often fear overpowers me, and I begin calling on a God I am unsure hears my prayers.

Consciousness fades, then returns as I hear his footfalls echo through the halls. I fight to concentrate on the turns, to focus on where he is taking me, but my consciousness flares and dims.

Humming. His chest vibrates against my ear, and I struggle to remember what happened.

Mason. Praise Providence, it is the new, kind orderly.

His footfalls echo, and the sound ricochets throughout the high hallways as he carries me.

I instantly recognize where I am as the scents alter from urine to lavender. Plants I have picked myself are strewn about my room in scavenged containers to ward off the asylum smells.

I am home. My room.

I feel my cot depress beneath me, and his large, warm hands cradle my neck.

A cool cloth presses to my forehead. "How did you come to be here, Patient Twenty-Nine?" he whispers, thinking me asleep.

I try to open my lips to speak, but—

"Shh. Rest. Sleep now. I will watch over you. I will be out in the hall, not far away. No harm shall come to you."

His accent is Scottish. And nearly musical. I fervently wish he would keep speaking. About anything, about nothing. I find his intonations calm my heart.

He squeezes my hand, and the warmth of it is replaced by the cool rag. I raise it to my face, like a child would a familiar doll, and breathe deeply. Its scent, *his* scent, brings an unfamiliar feeling. It takes me a moment to pinpoint the feeling … Security. It sends me directly into a blissfully dreamless slumber.

"How was it, Miss Jules? The ball?" Abilene, my lady's maid, inquires.

Maeve, my one-time governess, raises her eyebrows, feigning an interest in the fall gardens outside, her long fingers twirling my lace curtains.

I shrug. "Fine."

Her shrewd, gray eyes narrow as Abilene gathers the sheets from my bed, rolling them into a ball. "And your arrangement was well-received?"

"I believe that will do, Abilene. Leave us now," Maeve directs.

Abilene huffs, but she and her dirty bundle stomp out into the hallway.

I stand and walk to the window. The same vast cornfield stretches between our lands to the music hall. Our hamlet, on the outskirts of Philadelphia proper, is known for corn, an overabundance of yellow and green at every turn.

Maeve clears her throat, demanding my attention. "How *did* your recital go, Jules?"

"Well enough, I suppose."

Her eyes scrutinize, as they have since I was old enough to toddle.

She walks over to regard me, resting her hand lightly upon my shoulder. "What is it? You can tell me, *ma colombe*." Her French accent increases, as is her custom when she is vexed.

What is it? I should be happy.

"Father and I have finally come to an agreement on my suitor. I will soon be free of this house. Of his rule over me. But … I am anxious. As if I am leaving something behind, but I have forgotten what it is."

I stare at Maeve's pretty face; wrinkles are just beginning to show in the corners of her bright gray eyes.

I've had the best tutors and governesses, finest clothes and meals. But no *friends*. Only Maeve.

Since my mother's passing, the woman has been my rock, my voice of reason, my … protector. Thank Providence she shall accompany me when I leave the estate. She is the only friend I have ever known.

Father finally presented me to society this year, after nineteen years of keeping me neatly tucked away from the world. My only contact with those outside of this household was when I accompanied Father to faculty functions or the rare social outing to play my music—for him to gloat over my talents.

I see my childhood self, playing hide-and-seek with the wind in the corn. Though I was specifically forbidden to do so.

My heart swells with pain and gratitude for Maeve.

Maeve now clears her throat. She has asked me a question. She repeats it. "What are you forgetting?"

"I am not sure. I have dreamt of leaving all my life." I cross to the window to stare out at the corn. "It's a shadow, lurking just outside my memory."

Her eyes pinch. "Perhaps it is your mother, *ma colombe?*"

A pang stabs my heart, but is an old pain; once excruciatingly sharp, it has dulled to a low, persistent throb.

My only memories of my mother are here in this very room.

I was so very small. What I *do* remember are arguments, between her and my father. And Maeve's cool hands pressed to my ears, shuttling me out of earshot.

I also remember strange bits and pieces of my mother, like the feel of her hands, soft as petals against my nape as she arranged my hair atop my head. The tilt of her head as she played the violin. Bits of memory that are so hazy, I am now unclear whether they were fantasy or reality.

I remember another little girl. With dark hair. But how can that be? I am an only child.

I cock my head. This is not the first time I have posed this question. "You are *certain* there were no other children in the nursery besides myself?"

Maeve's eyes cloud. Or it could be my "extravagant imagination"—my father's favorite designation for my mental flights of fancy.

"No. Not unless it vas perhaps servants' children, visiting your classroom." Maeve's French accent intensifies once again.

I sigh. My mind hums a symphony.

And her music. Always mother's music. It was she who gave me my gift, but she did not live long enough to see it realized.

I turn away from the window and shrug. "I do not know. This is, no doubt, where she is most real to me."

Maeve squeezes my hand. "You best go down to dine. Himself will not hold his temper much longer." Her face flushes as she turns to gather my remaining bed coverings that Abilene forgot in her huff.

"Yes. I will see you later."

I walk into the hallway, squaring my shoulders. Father is a

tempest—a man capable of showering me with love and gifts, and other times … it is as if I do not know him.

He becomes cold and distant, angry and volatile. The change comes unbidden, like stone-gray clouds marring the bluest of skies.

The signs are always the same: He ceases to look me in the eye, the light in his eyes dimming as he slips further away. Becomes so single-minded, I, and all others, cease to exist. Only responds to every other sentence. Becomes more and more engrossed in his work as I slowly disappear from his consciousness. Even the tone and timbre of his voice changes. He disappears into his laboratory for days, sometimes weeks, at a time.

Now, I know the signs—know how to spot the change. But as a child …

Gooseflesh tears up my spine. Me, crying, begging for him. He … screaming. Refusing to see me. It is then that I hide in my room, grateful for the estate's many wings as we begin the familiar game of hide-and-seek.

I never know with *whom* or *what* I shall dine each eve—and it is only he and I and the servants. Not a soul to diffuse the tension. Maeve hovers in a world by herself—not high enough to dine with us, not low enough to dine with below stairs staff.

I smile as I think of her. She is my talisman against the darkness of the estate. She is a very handsome woman. And clever. Tall and willowy. She reminds me of the tree outside my window: beautiful, dark, and strong. So very strong.

She says she doesn't mind, but sometimes I see it in her face—what she has given up to remain here with me. Her own home, her own husband and children. Her French homeland. All she has abandoned, given up for me. She was my mother's very best friend. And is now mine.

My boots echo on the hallway's polished wood floors as I approach the massive double doors that lead to the dining room. I peek through the window in the door.

The dining room's deep jades and scarlets feel claustrophobic and dark … too dark. I long for openness and light. When I have my say, I shall have all walls painted white—in celebration of my freedom from this stifling, opulent place.

I think of the abnormality that is my life. That I should dread such a normal occurrence as one's dinner. That I dread residing in his company for a mere hour.

The realizations about my father's personality are new—only conceived upon my entering society. As I watched, listening to others, I saw no signs of Father's volatility in any others I met, which only made me feel more isolated.

I peek again, mastering my breathing as I stare at the flickering candelabra through the tiny, beveled glass window. I inhale a final, cleansing breath, and push the swinging doors wide.

"My goodness, my dear. You are breathtaking tonight. Willis truly is a lucky young man."

I stare down at the dress, the royal blue with white lace. It is Father's favorite.

"The color, with your dark hair. Striking. Magnificent."

My breath exhales in relief. It is jovial Father, even *good* Papa, tonight.

I feel the hot sting of tears and quickly blink them away. Because deep down, I do believe he is *good*, and I wish everyday could be the same, so that I might return his love daily. And not *hate* him other nights.

"I think everyone loved your arrangement, my dear. It was lovely. Are you ready for your impending nuptials? There are still many matters to be discussed." He gestures for me to sit.

The next quarter hour is filled with talk of flowers and chapels and dresses and dates. When he finally stops to take a bite of his tart, for we are now on dessert, I seize the opportunity of his good mood and blurt: "Have you decided on a day I might accompany you to the sanatorium?"

His features instantly blacken, and I recoil, my hands instantly sweating.

His voice restrains the rage, but its tone lurks, rumbling like thunderclouds beneath his words. "You have not yet given up that notion? Jules, you know of my misgivings. It is not proper for a woman of your station to—"

Do not cower. I bend to his every whim, like a sapling in a hurricane.

I clear my throat. "That is untrue. I have been reading. Many women, even royals, have ministered to the poor, sick, and needy. I can show you the references."

His teeth grind together, and I am certain he is wondering *where* I found such information. Maeve, of course, is the answer. She smuggles many "unapproved" works into the house—newspapers, references, and *world-be-cursed* novels.

I make my eyes wide, my only feminine wile that seems to pierce his hard bubble. "Please, Papa. You act as if I wish to join the circus. It shall make me feel useful. Besides, Willis has already given his permission that I shall be allowed once we are wed. Better to begin now, under your expert tutelage."

Father's face flushes dark red. The idea of another controlling my life is often a sore spot. I know it will be the hardest thing he has ever endured to let me go. To pass my reins to another.

"I see."

I hastily add, "And Dr. Grayjoy says I am welcome at any time. I spoke with him at the recital."

It is a dirty blow to mention the younger doctor—a man with whom he perpetually seems to be locking horns. Since his appointment, it appears Father's hold on the sanatorium's board has lessened.

Staff and residents have embraced Grayjoy—he and his more humane treatment methods, on which Father casts a disparaging eye. Truth be told, I only saw the man from afar. Indeed, his looks are impossible to disregard. I was far too shy to introduce myself—but Father need not know that.

Father's eyes flick to stare at a portrait—two turtledoves holding pieces of ribbon, which intertwine about a red cardinal, above them the phrase, *Youthful gift from God.*

Father's gaze ticks back to me, and he folds his hands, pressing them to his lips. I know I have won. Were he not in his present state, I would not have dared broach the subject.

The servants bustle in to clear the plates, and he bridles his tongue, the sound of his deep breathing filling the room. When they exit, his dark eyes stare intently at mine. I am told I have my mother's eyes—blue with a yellowish-hazel center, near feline.

"Fine. You may attend one day per week. You must follow the directions of the nursing staff *precisely.* I want you with Nurse Sally, and Sally alone. There ... have been problems of late. Excessively so, and I will not have you exposed to possible danger. Am I making myself clear?"

I nod, tethering my excitement, forcing my lips not to smile. "I shall be the model of good behavior." As I always am. I detest myself for it at times.

"Might I go tomorrow?" I prompt.

He stands, smoothing his waistcoat, conceding defeat. "If you must."

CHAPTER THREE

The sanatorium bell rings, calling me out of my dreams—where bluebirds and ravens fly in undulating, endless black and blue waves over the corn.

It is a familiar dream, coming most every night since I turned nineteen.

I roll to my side, clutching my middle, trying to relish the last moments of relative warmth beneath my coverlets. I exhale, and my breath rises like the steam from a dragon.

I stare around my room.

Lightning flashes in my mind, a specter of the previous night. Frost's face ... the vertigo of the revolutions twirling vomit up my throat.

I blink repeatedly and banish the images, breathing deeply as Grayjoy has instructed me. Letting the smell of the lavender calm my beating heart.

"Control your thoughts, Twenty-Nine. Do not let them control you," his voice commands in my head. I know he fears I shall return to the laudanum.

I breathe slowly, eyes ticking about the room.

I have done all in my power to make it my home. And it is luxurious when I compare it to most patients'. But most patients have lived outside of these drab gray walls, at least for a time. A rocking chair, with a forlorn rag doll. A threadbare rug over freezing stone floors. Curtains I have sewn myself, of eyelet lace, framing my barred windows. And my sketches and music, plastered over my side of the room, so that barely any paint shows through. I live in the world of my head, through the stories I tell myself and the music that is a constant inhabitant of my every thought.

But this room ... has secrets.

For one, my window opens—not so very far, but far enough. Also, the walls hold secrets.

I swallow, not even wanting to imagine the voices.

I hear voices sometimes. Only in this room. My name, whispered over and over.

Chills erupt at the thought.

For years I struggled—was it in my head, was I truly as mad as they say? But as I think of others here—others who clearly know not where they are, *who* they are ... many incapable of speech or reason ... *that is not me.*

When I plug my ears, which I do each and every time my name is whispered, the voices recede.

So they cannot be *inside* my head, can they?

The block walls and thin bed coverings make for a very long, exceedingly cold winter. My body shivers as if in agreement with the notion.

I force my eyes to stare at the wall above Lily's bed, painted the ever-festive institutional green. The staff scrubbed the words clean, but the ghost of them remains, vaguely visible if I squint.

Help me. I know not what I do.

My eyes dart about the room. The very same words have been scrawled on my wall three times. Three times my roommates have either disappeared or ended up ... *Is* Lily dead? Or perhaps now one of the shuffling dead of Ward Thirteen? Not one of the staff will confide her fate to me.

The madman, nay, the murderer, seems drawn to this room. Why else would so many have disappeared from between these walls?

How have I *escaped the murderer?* It seems I am the cat with nine lives.

I breathe deeply, and it shudders out. "My time will come. I am certain of it."

I suddenly realize the day, Wednesday, and my mood soars.

Wednesdays, I no longer feel like me.

Me, the patient.

Me, the pathetic.

Me, the future-less.

It is the one and only day I allow myself to consider *a life outside of these walls.* As if feeling my countenance shift, sunlight streams in through the hallway through the only window in the common area—its glass as thick as bricks.

I finger my smile, this foreign stranger on my lips.

Rap-rap-rap.

A knock at my door makes me jerk, and I scurry backward, arms splayed out in defense.

A bronzed head pokes round the door. My breath intakes, my mind seeming to stutter at his presence.

Mason's blue-green eyes widen as he takes in my posture.

His warm voice is melodic. "Easy, Twenty-Nine. It's only breakfast."

I nod, letting my arms drop to my sides.

My chest is still heaving as I ease myself back onto my bed, clutching my sheet beneath my chin to stare over it.

I have seen precious few *beautiful* men in my nineteen years, and I find to be in the presence of one makes me nervous. Most orderlies at Soothing Hills are old enough to be my father, and the younger ones are outcasts like myself, unremarkable. *But him …*

A tousle of dark-copper hair above matching thick eyebrows, poised over eyes the color of the sky at sunrise. Deep, thoughtful eyes. Intelligent eyes.

And, he does not *behave* as the other orderlies.

Their typical personalities being two: the cruel—the type that thrill in exacting punishments—or the bored but harmless—constantly checking the time, eyes pleading for their shift to end, to off them to the local pub.

He is neither.

Mason has a questioning gaze, with a blazing spark of intelligence, more the countenance I have come to associate with a doctor than an orderly.

He licks his full lips, gingerly placing the tray on my cot, eyeing me like I am a jungle cat. "You really must eat somethin'." Those perceptive eyes rove over me, and I feel exposed and naked. "You are little more than skin over bone."

I sit, slide the tray onto my lap, and stab the eggs, carefully placing some into my mouth.

He should not linger. It is forbidden. However, my door is ajar, giving him leave to depart quickly at a moment's notice.

He stands, leaning awkwardly against the doorjamb. He chews the side of his cuticle. "Might ... Might I ask you something?"

I dab my mouth with a napkin, then rest it ladylike in my lap. "Of course."

"Have you always been here? Pray, excuse my forwardness... but your manners, your demeanor ... *your use of words.* They indicate someone high-born. And I cannot help but wonder—"

"How I came to be Patient Twenty-Nine?" I laugh harshly but resume stabbing the runny eggs. There will be no food till midday, and I have learned never to skip a meal.

I speak around the food, twiddling my fork in the process.

"I have *always been* Twenty-Nine. I have no memory of anything other than Soothing Hills Sanatorium. I am told there... is nothing else. Nothing before here." I shrug. "Perhaps I was born here, to another patient."

"Perhaps you suffered an accident? Have merely forgotten anything else, forgotten your past?" His eyebrows are raised.

His voice is near musical. His *anything* sounds like *anytin* to my Continent-ears. He is decidedly Scottish; I no longer have any doubt. He seems to be able to mask it, but the colorful accent shines through.

I cock my head at this notion. "Not that I am aware of. But if

I had hit my head, I would *not* be aware, would I?" I laugh quietly.

His eyebrows pull together. "No family? Your manners—"

"Strangely, the physicians insisted I have tutors. Tremendous tutors. I know of places I've never seen and people I shall never see." I tap my temple. "I am a fountain of useless knowledge. That shall gurgle and flow through these dreary halls till I dry up and die. Right here." I pat the cot.

I am being morbid, and I care not.

His face is all revulsion. It is quickly replaced by anger. My stomach tightens. I do not understand his reaction.

"What is your *name*, Twenty-Nine?"

He pulls on the wooden post on the end of my bed, the top of which comes off in his hands. He stares at it, looking alarmed, so I say, "No need to worry. That happens all the time."

I get to my knees and take it from him, placing it back onto the bed frame.

I smile, coquettishly. Or at least what I *imagine* to be so. I have only seen nurses flirt with doctors. And I have read of this societal dance in novels. In the bowels of this wretched place, in the deserted catacombs beneath the sanatorium, I discovered a library, fallen into disrepair and forgotten.

There I have read of love. Of Austen and Bronte. Of feelings and people and situations I cannot fathom and, truth be told, do not think on often, for I cannot bear the pain.

Cannot bear the possibility of these things I will never have.

Mason clears his throat, one eyebrow cocked at my delay.

"I shall not tell you my name. It will spoil the mystery."

His smiles, and my breath abandons my chest.

"I assure you, Twenty-Nine, you are naught *but* mystery."

When it is clear I am not going to budge, he steps out into the hallway.

My heartbeat quickens. "What are you up to?"

Mason looks up and down the corridor. When he is apparently satisfied no more staff roam the halls, he reaches inside his white coat to produce a bottle.

I shoot to stand, backing away, fear flushing my cheeks. "I shall not drink it. I shall scream."

I have heard the stories—orderlies drugging patients, having their way with them.

Horror colors his features, his mouth twisting. He casts the bottle to the bed, his hands raised palms up.

"It's not a tonic. It's ... " He blushes a violent red from the top of his five o'clock shadow to his hairline. "Your hair. Forgive me, but *your hair* is beautiful. I have never seen such a shade on so young a woman."

I self-consciously twist my snowflake-colored locks around my fingers. Stark white.

"And I have seen what passes for soap here. And you were in that wretched, fetid dunk tank for so long. I ... fear you will catch ill."

He is right, of course. The soap is horrid, coarse and lumpy without any scent. I smell the nurses and have often longed to possess what they take so readily for granted.

"It is shampoo. From the town. I ... " He opens his mouth as if to say something else, but shuts it, nodding and giving a little formal bow. "I will take my leave. I do hope you enjoy it."

And before I might comment, he is gone. For a moment I stand, staring at it, waiting for it to disappear, a mirage on the desert of my threadbare covers, a figment of my longing imagination. But it remains, hard and solid in a crystal-stoppered container, snuggled into my bed sheets. My shaking fingers pluck it from the bed.

Tears bead, and I press it to my chest, carefully removing the stoppered lid.

The smell of summer hits my nostrils—visions of violets in bloom and the one bit of beauty this place affords: Soothing Hill's full, luxuriant gardens. Used to allay the guilt of well-to-do families as they drop off their problem child, spouse, or lover. Always they say it is temporary. Always it is permanent.

We are the forgotten.

A kindness. I have never known a kindness. My heart *soars,* but quickly plummets. This is very dear. Thievery is a way of life inside the walls.

I must hide it.

I walk into the hall, to be sure I am not watched, then return to the wall behind my bed.

I found *the peculiarity* many years prior—when I was a lass of about ten. A large clump of stones, hewn together, readily pops from my wall to reveal a wooden hidey-hole beneath.

It contains my few meager treasures: a china doll from when I was very small; a singular earring dear, eccentric Mrs. Balfe gave me; an expensive pen and parchment—gifted in secret by Dr. Grayjoy, for my compositions. A bundle of rags, for my secret cat's bed.

I just manage to slide my bed back into place when I hear the footsteps.

I stand, just in time to see Big Hugh—a very gruff, very

awful orderly—arrive at my door, and praise Providence said cat is nowhere in sight.

I back against the wall and stand rigid. He eyes me, picking up my tray, and is gone without a word.

But I ... I am ... happy. The word and feeling are so unfamiliar that I close my eyes and let it wash over me, relishing every skipped beat of my heart. I wish upon all wishes I could bottle this feeling and slip *it* inside the stoppered treasure behind my wall.

What a tremendous day. I shall play my music *and* I have had a kindness. And perhaps ... this man ... Could a man see me for more than just ... Twenty-Nine? My hope *slams* closed. I flinch.

"No. Do not think such. It is not for the likes of you."

I shall take what the day provides and relish it.

Smoothing my work dress, I stride into the corridor, trying to mask the spring in my step.

GRAYJOY

"Gentlemen, this is the future." Frost stands before the boardroom. Behind him, an illustration of two brains—one canine, one human.

"I fail to see how this shall impact our more intractable patients, Dr. Frost," dares Dr. Gentile, his white eyebrows disappearing beneath a thick shock of equally frosted hair. He is the only physick, or board member, for that matter, to ever question Frost.

I allow my eyes to rove around the table. Three men, all impeccably dressed, with identical pencil-moustaches, identical cowardices, cower to Frost's every whim.

The board are philanthropists, with only a passing interest as to whether the asylum survives or perishes. More than one is using it to further his political agenda, showing him to be a "man of the people." Of late, however, with the most recent disappearance of Lily, they are finally listening to Gentile's dissenting voice, and my own.

"I am reluctant to begin any new treatments. Lily's family was not estranged. They were livid that their only child first became catatonic and then disappeared altogether. They have threatened to go to the authorities, to close the asylum," Gentile says, calmly, as if discussing the weather.

I bristle, staring at Frost. I am younger, smarter, and more restrained. Many balk at my silver-spooned upbringing—hold it against me—but no one understands these patients as I do. Especially not this untethered, whirling dervish—

"The science comes from our German colleague, Friedrich Goltz." Frost taps the illustration of the canine brain, his long fingers lingering over the pre-frontal cortex. "Once Friedrich performed his ablations on the dogs, they became docile, with no trace of their previous violent tendencies."

Gentile's wise, contemplative gaze flicks to me and away. It is but a second, but I grasp its meaning—

Perhaps Frost himself might benefit from ablation.

Last fortnight, we had to forcibly drag him off a young physick for deviating from his treatment plan. I would smile, were the situation none so grave.

Gentile speaks up. "Surely there is risk? Not to discount what Herr Goltz has proposed, but I, for one, would like more evidence. What about your visitation to Dr. Burkhardt in Prefargier?"

I lean forward. Frost had only just returned from a European tour, to study ablations—first in Germany, then to Switzerland, where Dr. Burkhardt has been pioneering the procedure on his own patients.

"As of today, they are all docile. All traces of aggression removed from their persona."

His eyes gleam with mania. I recognize it, but have no power over the board.

I swallow. "I would like to see the canines, and the results, prior to allowing it to be performed upon my own patients." *On Jane, you mean.*

My face heats. I must rid myself of this obsession. She is a patient. It is not possible. Not ever. I imagine the expressions of my highborn family as I proclaim my infatuation and nearly shudder.

Frost's gaze narrows, and his face flushes. Every man around the large table shifts their attention. Gentile's lips press together, but we are of one mind when it comes to Frost.

"Fine, Dr. Grayjoy. If all of your years of *experience* require it, I shall permit you to see them." His voice drips with sarcasm. Any attempts to question his judgment result in mockery or outright aggression.

"Fine. I shall wait for your word, then."

Gentile presses his gnarled hands to the table. "Gentlemen, our meeting is adjourned."

JANE

I nearly glide down the hallway as I return from the recital room. It is the highlight of my week, to play with other musicians. At times, they even bring in professionals from the local orchestra.

"Twenty-Nine. Twenty-Nine. T-t-t-twenty-Nine." I sidestep the younger woman and press myself against the wall as she moves closer, so close I smell the cloying stench of her breath on my face.

I gently lay my hands on her shoulders and push her back. "Twenty-One. How are you today?"

I slip past her, not waiting for a response. She is unable to formulate one.

It has been a major breakthrough that after two years she now is able to place numbers with faces.

No sign of Alexander. No sign of Big Hugh. This may turn out to be the best day in a fortnight.

I smile as I push open the door to Twenty's room and gently close it behind me.

The sunlight streams in through the dirty window to shimmer off the graying strands in her hair. She has been here as long as I. Her wooden wheeled chair has seen better days, but the wear and tear is from use. I often push her outside, through the topiary maze.

She too was abandoned, but by husband, not by parents.

At two score, a mysterious illness left her legs paralytic. Her well-to-do husband, a politician, could not be bothered with such a cumbersome wife.

I was very young but shall never forget her voice as she told me, "Left me for dead, he did. I had no family. I am barren, gave him no children. So he dropped me off and proceeded to wed once again." She sighed heavily, reaching out to touch my cheek. "I suppose I should be happy he still pays for my room and board. Otherwise, I should be out on the street."

I step on a loose board and it creaks, and her head snaps up. "Come around to the front, Twenty-Nine. My neck is powerful sore today, so I can't yank it round to see ya."

I walk to the window seat and sit, allowing the warm sun to hit my back.

I stretch my arms high, and her eyebrows rise. "You look like the cat who swallowed a nest of canaries. Have you been playing, then?"

She nods to my violin, hanging loosely from my right hand.

"Yes ... but something has happened. Something wonderful."

She laughs, showing yellowed, cracking teeth. "Here? Something wonderful. This I must hear."

I lean forward and reach inside my pocket. "Close your eyes."

She rolls her eyes but complies.

I unstopper the crystal bottle and wave it once beneath her crooked nose.

She smiles. "What is that scent? Have you brought me a bouquet of your dried lavender? Funny, I didn't see it when you came in."

Her eyes flutter open. Once dark brown, a milky shadow progresses across them, dimming her sight.

I thrust the bottle forward for her to see.

Her white eyebrows pull together. "Where did you get that?"

"A present."

"A present?" Worry pinches her mouth. "What did you have to do for that present?"

My face instantly heats. "Nothing. It isn't like that." Anger flickers. "Why ... am I so very horrible that I might never ever know a kindness?"

Her hands shoot out, beckoning me to her. "Do not be ridiculous. But it is Soothing Hills, my love. Everything here comes with a price tag."

I shake my head. "Not this time."

Half of her mouth pulls up with skepticism. "I do not suppose you shall tell me who bestowed this treasure upon you?"

I shake my head. "Not a chance." I suddenly wish I would not have told her and hide it back into the folds of my skirts. "Would you like me to play for you?"

She cocks her head. "That is an obvious attempt at subterfuge, but ... of course."

I feel the bottle, heavy in my skirts. "After ... we shall wash your hair."

Her old face puckers, her bottom lip trembling. "I couldn't possibly. It is too dear. It is a gift—"

I take her hand in mine. "You shall. I shall keep some for me as well. So first the music, then the hair."

I begin to play Wolfgang Amadeus Mozart—her favorite piece no less—and for the next half hour, we speak no more of presents and admirers, allowing Herr Mozart's feelings to speak for us both.

JULES

"You may empty the chamber pots in the morning and feed the patients at lunchtime. If you wish to *return* to Soothing Hills, you must follow your instructions to the letter. Just because your father is an esteemed physician here does not mean you shall be granted liberties. Understand, Jules?" Nurse Spare's beady eyes narrow.

"Yes, mum. I understand."

I stand behind the rolling medicinal cart, drinking in every minute detail that is Ward 4.

All the wards have the same configuration: a large common room at the entrance, with sofas and chairs, where patients may paint, or sketch, or read. And accept their medications, the ones who are of the mind to remember their medicinals. To the others, the forgetfuls, we deliver their reorienting pills and tinctures to them. The hallways have five rooms on either side, with varying levels of restrictions.

For the docile, open doors that swing wide.

For the violent—bars and peepholes.

"Whatever are those? Why are the cots shaped like a rocker on the bottom?"

Nurse Spare's beady eyes roll. "Apparently you have not been to Wards Five and up."

My mind retraces my steps, and the rhythmic sound immediately comes to mind. "They rock while lying down, then?"

"Some of them are incapable of being still. So when strapped to the plinth, if they are able to manage the rocking motion, it calms their savage souls."

I bristle. None here are savages. Unfortunate. Ill, even. But not savages. My face colors with the effort of not telling her so. "Yes, Nurse Sally."

The nurse's eyes rove over me, and I self-consciously pat my bun to be assured all is in place. It is, so I shift nervously, wondering *why* I am the target of her scrutiny.

The older woman's expression is one of near fear, as if she has seen a long-dead relative or the like. She shakes her head, and her face hardens to its normal faux-iceberg façade.

"I will return in one hour to collect you."

A scream echoes from a nearby hallway, and gooseflesh blazes a trail beneath my sleeves. Her cold eyes flick toward it and then narrow.

Her lined face puckers. "This place is not a ball, nor a salon, Miss Frost. It can be dangerous." Her eyes rove to my neck, and her fingers slip beneath a necklace, barely visible beneath my uniform. "You see this?" She gives it a sharp tug, and I feel the burn in a circle about my neck. "Strangulation device. Take it off. Have you given a thought as to why your hair is in a bun? Why *everyone's* hair is piled upon their heads?"

I shake my head, a cold chill licking my neck.

"*So it cannot be ripped from your skull.* Last month, a nurse who was late for her shift arrived with it down about her shoulders. In two minutes, they took hold of her hair and shut it in the door—left her to dangle from her roots, screaming till an orderly interceded. Heed my words, girl."

And she is gone in a flutter of white. A great, wrinkly, flapping bird of prey.

My eyes trail after her receding form. I pull gaze away and take a deep breath to assess the ward.

I walk forward, the cart rumbling before me, intent on delivering my mind-altering tinctures of bliss. In moments, I have delivered my first medicinal and head back to the hall, walking toward the end. The very last room.

I arrive at the first door, which has a number on it.

The patient's identification numbers, I have been told. The nurses and physicians refer to the occupants by number rather than name so as to maintain a professional distance.

Except for Ward One. Here, the wealthy or the almost-ready-for-discharge are afforded luxuries unheard of to the others—such as rich meals, preparation classes to re-enter society, and the use of their given names. Nurse Sally says precious few regain their senses to return to society at large.

I catch a whiff of urine from a nearby chamber pot. "They aren't going to clean themselves," I murmur.

I walk into room Twenty-Nine, squaring my shoulders. I head toward the chamber pot, but I halt in my tracks, my mouth gaping.

Drawings litter one side of this room from ceiling to floor. After a moment's consideration, I decide they seem to chronicle a life in sketches. They halt directly at the center, as if respecting the other patient's wall space and taste. The images first are childish, immature, but still inspired. I see the latent talent in the scribbles. Then the images grow greater and greater, assumedly with each passing year, if the tiny signature at the bottom is an indication.

No name. Only a number. *29.*

My eyes trail to the ones closest to the door, which are truly magnificent. Watercolors of every season—fall in gold, green, and red; spring in a multitude of wildflowers; summer in a tumult of green, a massive field as a cat stalks through tall grass. And winter. Many, *many* scenes of winter. They somehow convey sadness and hope and the mind directing every stroke of the brush.

Sunrises, sunsets. Children frolicking with pups.

A gray, striped cat, staring out the window, the shadings so perfect I can almost feel the texture of his fur beneath my hands.

Snow on the spires of the sanatorium, its usually foreboding façade made breathtaking by the black and white contrast, the candlelit windows, and the swirling crystal flakes around the panes.

And …

Gooseflesh rips up my arms. *Ravens.* Their pointy beaks split wide to allow a cascade of notes fall. As if their birdsong has been *replaced with music.* I begin to hum the tune, but another picture calls.

My heartbeat goes wild as I rush to stare at a very small picture, partially hidden amongst the collage of immature drawings.

A beautiful woman, with long-flowing hair, her fingers poised on the strings of a cello. Three small girls gather round her—no faces, merely the backs of their heads. Two with dark brown hair, one with a deep, flowing auburn.

I shake my head, feeling the tears bead. A flicker of recognition. "What? It cannot be."

That is silly. A lonely girl's longing for friendship.

"Jules! Where are you, girl?" Nurse Sally's voice echoes down the hall, clanging in time with her approaching boot falls.

I snatch the paper from the wall and carefully fold it, hiding it in the pocket of my skirts, and whirl just in time to meet Sally's flushed face.

My face colors with guilt, and I walk toward her, praying she doesn't notice.

She is breathing heavily—as if the old crow has been running. That sight twitches my lips. It's one that I would love to see. I picture a scrawny, flapping, flightless bird.

"There has been a mistake. You are needed on Ward Six. Ward Four is, from this day forward, off-limits to you." Her eyes dart around the room but then seem strangely satisfied.

"What? Whatever for?"

Her face colors, as if she has said too much. "I mean, we have enough staffing here. Your services are more needed on other floors."

She exhales, as if she has been holding her breath. Her bony finger juts toward the chamber pot. "Finish this one, quick-like, then off with you to six."

I curtsy, hurry to collect the pot, and risk one more glance back, trying to commit the drawings to memory.

CHAPTER FOUR

JANE

"Wednesday, thy name be blessed," I murmur quietly. I got word of it whence I sat for lunch. Whilst mired in the usual flingings of foodstuffs—I had, in fact, just ducked a flying treacle tart—a tiny new nurse arrived, bearing the news.

"You are Twenty-Nine, correct?" the sweet-looking slip of a nurse requests.

My heartbeat doubles despite her benign appearance. Being singled out is never advisable. Not here.

I nod, carefully blotting the tiny dab of confection that has landed on my shoulder.

She clears her throat, and formally squares her shoulders,

"Patient Twenty-Nine, you are cordially invited to attend a tour of Ward 1."

My eyes widen as she thrusts the much-coveted, legendary silver-sheet into my sweaty palms. It was the formal invitation to Ward 1.

No one may enter without one, the doctor's official seal pressed in blood-red wax—like a passport to sanity. Ninety-five percent of patients at Soothing Hills shall never lay fingers to one.

I stare at it, dumbfounded, afraid it may be a hallucination that will dissipate to mist should I move or breathe.

"Hide it," she chastises, hastily closing my shaking fingers around it. "Come down when your lunch is finished."

"Today?" I look down at my drab day dress—as grayish-green as the depressing walls that surround me. I have seen the comings and goings of the folk streaming in and out of that ward. Well-heeled ladies and gents—far, far from what is my daily institutional frock.

"Oh, you needn't worry. It is just a tour. If the need arises, we will find you appropriate clothing."

You mean if I can appear normal. Pass your tests.

I open my mouth to reply, but already she is hurrying out of the dining amphitheater, her clipboard pressed primly against her chest.

The lunch hour seems to stretch and elongate, as if the clock's hands tick through an invisible quicksand as I stare fixedly, waiting. Unable to touch my food for the roiling anxiety in my guts.

Finally, the hour arrives. I push out of my chair, waiting for one of the monitors to notice. I flick up the silver card to depart the cafeteria, and to my amazement, I am permitted to depart alone. No escort.

The only other moments I roam free are fraught with peril and risk, in the dead of night as the asylum sleeps. But this embossed silver paper is like my ticket to another reality. One I have only read of … dreamed of.

I am wholly breathless as I enter the final corridor leading to the elusive *Ward One*. I finger the magical silver ticket in my pocket, reassuring myself it is tangible, real.

Most good fortune in my life disappears. Frost always sees to that. I learned early to hide any and all happiness from him, lest he suck it out like some detestable, good-will-swilling mosquito.

The hallway seems to abnormally elongate as I draw close, and I shake my head, grinding my teeth, determined to appear completely in control. But the trembling rocks my body from crown to toe, and I place my hand on the cold brick walls to steady myself, breathing deeply till the swoon passes. I arrive at the door and hover outside, terrified to enter.

My eyes flick to the bottom of the document, and I spy the official signatures.

Grayjoy's first, and Frost's below it. Even his penmanship seems begrudging, as if the loops and scrawls scream in silent protest. My heart beats so fast and hard, I suck in more deep, steeling breaths, trying my best to calm it. Dr. Frost, obviously at the urging of Dr. Grayjoy, has granted me the status of entering for a trial—if the arguments over my fate, on which I have eavesdropped, are any indication.

Suspicion heats my cheeks. He must have an ulterior motive.

I find I care not. For the first time in my nineteen years, I shall experience something that is not Soothing Hills. To hear people address me *by my given name,* not my patient number.

I knock. A hole in the door, fashioned like a small window, opens.

"Ticket, please?" As if the woman is some surreal train conductor.

She is older, with graying hair swept up into a fashionable bun.

The ticket trembles in my hand as I flash it and quickly place it back into the hidden pocket within the folds of my skirt.

The face disappears through the hole, and I stand, cradling my arms around my waist, trying not to weep.

The throwing of a multitude of bolts. The door opens.

My mind explodes with music; cello, violin, and oboe scream a layered march of freedom between my ears, the notes falling in a kaleidoscope of corresponding color across the musical bars. My digits twitch, fingering the invisible frets of the violin.

"Come with me, dearest." The same pretty young nurse appears at the door, her perceptive eyes instantly comprehending my anxious expression.

She takes my hand and gives it a reassuring squeeze. Her nameplate proclaims her *Nurse Ginny.*

My head spins with fear and anticipation as I fully expect to wake at any moment from this too-good-to-be-true late afternoon.

Ginny shuffles me through the Ward One sitting area— overstuffed rose-colored wingback chairs and a copse of large, green potted ferns are reminiscent of photos of hotel lobbies I have seen in my hidden library's books. Ornate wood scrollwork climbs up the steps and are adhered to the window frames. The resulting incoming sunlight is cut into geometric forms, cast onto the hardwood floor in beautiful streaks, reminding me of the topiary maze outside. I blink.

On the other side of the room are plain windows.

Windows. Real, honest-to-heaven glass, not a security bar in sight, to overlook the late-blooming botanical gardens. Clusters of lavender, which I have picked with my own hands and placed in my room, line the brick walls framing the garden. They stand straight and tall outside, like familiar purple friends awaiting my return. I stand on tiptoe and see stone paths cutting through puffs of maroon, orange, and yellow chrysanthemums.

I smile, remembering my childish rendering. *Chris-ann, the mum.*

"Jane?" Ginny's voice rises in question at my inappropriate mirth.

"Nothing. Sorry."

My toes squish in carpeting so plush I resist the urge to drop down and purr, to rub against it like a cat.

Ginny greets all we pass with a nod and a smile, until we mercifully reach a set of stained-glass double doors. My fingers lift of their own accord to trace the patterns of gilded black roses so lovely, my throat constricts at their beauty.

Another novelty. So many things to see.

I could stay right here, sketch and stare at the colors for hours. If Ward One holds so many unfamiliar sights, I shudder to imagine the originality of life outside these bleak stone walls.

We step through, and I am astounded at the instant warmth

enveloping this ward; was it really mere hours ago when I shuddered, my teeth chattering violently beneath my multitude of tattered coverlets? It is truly another world.

"In here, *Jane*, isn't it?"

I swallow, my ears seeming to ring.

Hearing my own name, for the first time in years, brings wetness to my eyes. I nod.

I enter a large, sprawling office. Skeletons, human anatomy charts, and beautiful countrysides and landscapes cover the walls. I blink again. There is a tank of fish. I have never, ever laid eyes to such, only read of them. Flashes of silvery maroon and blue dart to and fro, hiding behind waving green plants secured to the bottom.

"Wait here, he will be in soon." Ginny gives my shoulder a quick squeeze before departing.

I nod and grip the arms of the chair till my joints protest, trying to force my focus on the fish, not on the next very, very important few moments of my life.

The door reopens, and an older, portly man shuffles in. His white lab coat proclaims him a doctor. He moves slowly past my chair as woodsy cologne fills my nostrils. His name badge reads *Dr. Gentile*.

He stares at me; bright blue eyes pierce from beneath bushy white eyebrows, white as my hair. His gaze lingers on my hair. "Good afternoon, Jane. How are you?"

"Fine, sir."

"You know why you are here, then?"

I nod. "I am to have a trial of Ward One."

"And what is your definition of Ward One, my dear?"

"A place where patients are tested to see if they might re-enter society. And if found acceptable, to help them find suitable employment."

He smiles. Not like Frost's smile. It looks genuine, and somehow familiar. Grandfatherly. "And … "

"And to determine if they are a danger to themselves or others."

His blue eyes narrow behind the half-moon spectacles but remain light. "And are you either of those, Jane?"

I shake my head. "No, sir." A sudden, inexplicable rage heats my cheeks, but I keep my voice even. "I have never been such, sir."

He nods. "I believe you, Jane. I was present … when first you arrived."

My heartbeat stops for a breath, then stutters fast. I have never met anyone who knew *anything* about my past. Or at least who was willing to admit it.

A plethora of questions surge through my head, but I press my lips tight. If I allow them out, I may shatter my chances.

My insides shake, and I fight to steady my hands.

He shuffles papers on his blotter, signing them with a flourish.

"Ginny!" His voice is loud and commanding, and too soon Ginny is in the doorway, as if she were eavesdropping.

"I proclaim Jane to be ready for Ward One visitations. She may play in the orchestra for the public. If all goes well, we will discuss a more permanent transfer." After a moment, he adds, "Send my report to *Grayjoy*, won't you?"

He tries to conceal it from me with his placid demeanor. But his words all but scream, *Not to Frost.*

In moments, I am whisked from the exam room, Ginny chattering away so fast, skipping over so many subjects, I scarcely discern a fraction of what she says. I nod and smile, trying to keep my eyes from darting like the frightened little animal that I am.

When we re-enter the ward, her steady stream of words dries up, and she directs me wordlessly down a hallway. We arrive at ornate double doors, and she indicates I should enter.

Heat and scent lambast my skin, and my nostrils flare.

Large, luxuriant copper bathtubs fill this room. I recognize two other young women from neighboring wards, eyes closed, already submerged, toes poking out from beneath the frothy bubbles concealing their bodies. Inviting spirals of steam corkscrew into the air, and the intoxicating smell of lavender tightens my throat again, bringing renewed tears to my eyes. It is as if my dreams have vacated my mind and been breathed to life.

A full bath is granted only twice a year.

I swallow and blink to drive back the tears. They are an indulgence. Here, tears mean weakness, mark you as easy prey to the opportunists ever-ready to pounce.

My eyes tick across the room to three dresses hanging on an armoire. Evening gowns, the likes of which I have only ever spied on paper, hang waiting.

I clear my throat. "Is one of those … "

"For you?" Ginny's eyes shine and dance in the candlelight. "Yes. The sapphire blue one. We thought the contrast with your hair would do well. Despite the fact you shall not technically be seen."

I cock my head but do not question, afraid to say anything that will pierce this reality's fragile bubble.

"Come."

I follow Ginny to the tubs, and without a word she assists with my buttons, slipping off my day dress.

I shyly cover myself—though the other girls' eyes do not even flutter, let alone open. They are presently entrenched in their own daydreams.

My toes split the warmth, sinking down into the copper tub, to find purchase. I step in and ease my body down and allow the sensations to swallow me; I pretend for a stolen moment in time I am somewhere else, *am someone else.*

The flicker of the candles reflects off the bath's surface, as if it is somehow infused with sunlight. The warm, oiled water slips up my toes, knees, thighs, and reaches my belly, till I am wholly submerged. The nurse's warm hands touch my neck, and I flinch, but she merely gathers up my hair as I feel the pleasant tug of a hairbrush combing through the length of my hair, scalp to ends.

Footsteps behind the door intrude on the daydream, and my mind replays the people we passed on Ward One. A woman with a pinched but hopeful face, most likely a mother of one of the other submerged musicians. Hopeful her poor, wayward daughter will make her way back out from behind these walls.

And beside her, a man. A man who is interested in me as a person.

Not in controlling me, not in torturing me. Dr. Grayjoy has always taken a particular interest in me. Indeed, since his arrival four years prior, his belief in me has kept my hysteria at bay.

I hear Ginny, somewhere in the dark, murmur to another unseen nurse, "She didn't speak for a full year," and know she speaks of me.

I swallow. It is true. I have fought to keep the silence at bay. Mutism.

It is my nemesis. As is the laudanum. 'Twas Grayjoy who helped me vanquish the laudanum.

Frost gave me too much, too young. It took years to shake its familiar, mind-numbing draw. I swear he did not wish me to banish my addiction, preferred me riddled with confusion. The slosh of water rouses me and my eyes flick to see one of the other women slip out of the tub and into a plush white robe. "Let's ready you, deary," a small nurse murmurs.

Too soon I am whisked from the warmth of the water.

The Ward One nurses are not finished.

I blink again and again in disbelief as my skin is plied and massaged with a creamy lotion; hands begin at my feet and work the entire length of my body, ending at my neck. My fingertips lightly touch my skin, now soft as a child's.

Nurse Ginny's expert hands pile my snowflake-colored hair atop my head. She slides a sapphire comb at the back.

"There. Perfect. What do you think, Jane?" She swivels me to have a better look.

I stare at the creature in the mirror, blinking madly, trying not to muss the perfectly applied makeup.

I ... *am beautiful.* Two words I never thought would inhabit the same sentence when applied to me.

But I am.

"I am speechless."

The royal blue gown does indeed accentuate my hair and fair skin, and the feline yellow-blue of my eyes.

She gingerly pats my hand. "It's time to go, love. Deep breath, now."

Nurse Ginny ushers the three of us into the vestibule outside the music room. The three of us follow her like perfectly coiffed ducks in the proverbial row. The other two refuse to meet my eye. One has a tremor in her hands. She self-consciously rubs them together, over and over.

Ginny turns me to face her, smoothing my hair like a mother. "Oh, darling. You truly *are* magnificent."

Dr. Grayjoy saunters into the room. He tips his hat to me; his eyes flick away and then widen and jerk back.

"Why, Jane, I confess I truly did not recognize you. Are you ready? Do not be nervous." He tips his hat to the other girls. "Claire. Susan."

I nod, not trusting my voice. I follow him, unspeaking, into the next set of rooms. Here, wallpaper lines the hallways in festive pinks and browns, reminding me of boxes of chocolates on the nurses' stations. My vision is accustomed to plain, institutional green so that the sight of the busy pattern gives me vertigo.

I steal a glance in one of the nearby patient rooms and spy large, pink poof chairs and something nearly unheard of at Soothing Hills: *carpeting*. A long, plush area rug with an oriental design.

My hands shake, and I press them together, fighting the urge to wipe the sweat on the gown. Panic whispers, *This is not for you. You* are *mad.*

"Right through here. There shall be a screen between you and the audience." Dr. Grayjoy gestures toward the open door. "All you need worry about is the music. I shall handle the rest. I will stay nearby, behind the screen as well, but out of the way so as not to distract you."

I follow my fellow musicians; the chairs and sheet music seem to float past, dreamlike, as I feel Ginny's directing fingers at my elbow, tugging me to sit.

Then I spy it, and all else fades except its polished, dark wood surface.

A violin.

I have been permitted to play every Wednesday since I was old enough to speak, and as much as I wished in my room.

Often, a gaggle of employees would gather outside my door, listening. At best, a scolding would result, at worst, a few dockings of pay for their extended loitering. I played as best as I could on the hand-me-down instrument they provided.

But tonight … there is something *familiar* about this instrument. As I pull the bow across the strings, the resonance sings—it is of higher quality than my usually provided one. Something in the curves of its dark wooden body ticks my memory, but it is hazy, out of focus, like a poorly constructed dream. I tuck it beneath my chin, and it settles in, seeming to belong there, like some long-lost musical appendage.

The two other women sit, their beauty adorned and arranged to a fervor sufficient for English Court—one at the pianoforte, the other with a cello.

I stare at the sheet music, and in moments, it is memorized, the notes dancing behind my eyes—each with a blazing, corresponding color in my mind.

A translucent screen is assembled between us and the patrons. Patrons who have paid dearly to hear us—the *nearly rehabilitated*—play. The almost ready to re-enter polite society, we are a freakish spectacle. Do-gooders, philanthropists, and the well-heeled come to donate out of their excess to the asylum.

This is a test.

Crowds of candles flicker behind us and in chandeliers above, making our silhouettes shimmer and undulate, giving them a life of their own.

Murmurs and gentle laughs rise up and over the screen, descending on us like wordy butterflies. I see a familiar outline through the divider, and my stomach clenches. His jaw, the ruff of unmanageable hair. *Is it him?*

Dr. Frost pokes his head around, his eyes first narrowing on Grayjoy, then flicking across us all.

His gaze halts, naturally lingering on me. "Are you ready, Twenty-Nine?"

I bristle. The purpose of Ward One is to use our given names. But *still* he refuses. *Why does he despise me so?*

I nod. "Quite."

Frost disappears to stand in front of the screen, his shadow evident before us as he addresses the crowd. His arms outstretched like a preacher to a congregation.

Grayjoy passes by, heading for a room in the back. He squeezes my shoulder. "Good Luck, Jane." And he too, disappears.

"Gentle ladies and gentlemen, I welcome you to the Soothing Hills Sanatorium evening recital. All of the proceeds collected tonight shall benefit our patients … "

I stiffen, my head inclining toward the window. *What was that?* My breath stops, a cold chill licking my nape.

No, not now. Please not now.

The corn music. It has returned.

My palms begin to sweat as I readjust the bow in my hands.

"I hope you will enjoy our production—"

The corn music swirls into the room, demanding attention, words riding the melody like the four horsemen of a musical apocalypse. I shiver convulsively as the notes explode in my head in a kaleidoscope of color and sound.

She is near. She is near. She is near.

The refrain repeats over and over in the melody. The notes, normally multi-colored and radiant—each note with its own hue—are red. All are red.

It is a test. I must not speak of it. I mustn't. I mustn't.

I close my eyes and through pursed lips release a shuddering exhale.

It is the reason I am here. The words in the music. No one ever believed me.

Hmm. Hmm.

My heart skips a beat then surges forward with a staccato beat. Someone in the front row, directly behind the screen, hums a middle C. My heartbeat instantly slows.

Middle C is my safe haven. The sound of it produces the feel of warm blankets and soft cotton on my skin. The tone has soothed me since childhood. I hum it each and every night to lull my frantic brain to sleep. *Why would someone here hum that singular note? Pick it above all others?*

The girls begin. Their music a living, organic creature, pulsing against me on the tight, narrow stage.

"Jane," Claire hisses. "Jane you must play. Play!"

I shake my head and force the music out my fingertips, my other hand sawing across the strings.

The middle C has stopped. The corn music is mercifully waning.

I breathe deeply, minding the rise and fall of my chest.

I give myself over to my violin, letting the music pour from my soul, saturating it with my sorrow.

Silent tears roll down my face, as is my custom. I only give myself over to feeling when I play.

Emotion, feeling, sentiment—all deadly inside the fortress that is Soothing Hills.

Better to stay alone, be the proverbial island in a mad, mad sea.

Care for no one, and they have no ammunition for pain.

My cheeks burn as the hair on the back of my neck prickles and rises. Someone watches. I turn my head in time to catch sight of Mason, just beyond the screen. *It was he. He is here.*

His wide eyes, deep and full of wonder, watch me play, flick back and forth with every movement of my fingers across the violin's fragile neck.

I shift my attention back to the music for a second, and when I look back—he is gone. And with him, the corn music.

All too soon, I am back on the Ward Four. As I approach my room and step across the threshold, I picture it a great, orange pumpkin coach shall now disintegrate at the customary midnight, to resume its guise as a gourd. My happiness is transitory like the many Cinderellas before me.

Nurse Ginny bustles into my room. I immediately turn my back, awaiting her assistance to slip off the gown—to return it to its rightful world. Its sapphire undulations are too magnificent to reside in the dark, gray shadows with me.

Her fingers unbutton it, and as I step out, I thrust it into her hands. Dropping my gaze.

She cocks her head. "Whatever are you doing, deary?"

I shrug. "Well, the gown. I am returning it, naturally."

Her smile is wide. "It is yours to *keep*, my love. My father is the town haberdasher, my mother a tailor, and they fashioned these specifically for each of you. Soothing Hills paid him."

My throat thickens for the third time in a day, and I permit my fingers to play across the fabric.

They stop stroking as I think of all the wanderers roaming the halls, pilfering and stealing anything they might barter or sell with the outside. A regular black market operates within these barricaded walls.

"Might you keep it for me, on Ward One? I obviously will have no occasion to wear it until next I play."

Ginny's eyes are soft. "Of course I will, Jane. I will keep it safe." After a moment, she adds, "Put it with me own effects."

I turn away so she shall not see the tears. She chooses to use my name, despite the fact we are back on Ward Four. A small, warm light blooms in my chest.

She sees me as a *person*, not a number.

I walk to my armoire to retrieve a drab day dress and slide my arms into the sleeves, the fabric scratchy against my skin. I decide the grayish-green is the precise color of vomit.

Ginny's nimble fingers are at my back, buttoning. Her hand on my shoulder bades me turn.

"Jane." She pauses, as if unsure what to say. She begins to smooth my shoulders instead, not meeting my eyes.

"Yes?"

Her hands drop as her shoulders square, and she meets my gaze. "You are quite talented. And I know it is ... " Her eyes wander about my room. "It is *hard* here, on Ward Four. Mind your manners, and I hope you will be transferred to Ward One soon. I am the nurse responsible for helping patients find shelter, employment. You can *trust me,* Jane. If you need help, just send word."

I nod, unable to speak.

By the time I compose myself to murmur a thank you, she is gone.

Hours later, I lie still in the utter blackness, awaiting the physicks' final rounds.

Please do not let it be him. It is not often I see Dr. Cloud, whom my mind has labeled the night physick, but when I do, each exam and conversation is yet more disturbing and bizarre.

Muffled voices rumble out in the hall.

I slip out of bed, shooing Sebastian out the open window. He gives me a disgruntled feline look before his puff of a tail disappears beneath the slit above the sill.

I pad quietly to the door and incline my ear, careful not to touch it, should it creak and give away my eavesdropping. I recognize the first voice instantly. *Frost.* Frost is arguing with someone.

"I care not what you say, I shall do as I please," he says. But I hear something in his voice. Something foreign.

Gooseflesh springs up on my arms. *Fear. Frost is afraid?*

"You are soft where she is concerned. You know what must be done with her. And not the course of her elder, either. That, too, was—"

A deep inhale. "I shall decide what happens within my own household."

"What are you doing here? You know it isn't safe! You mustn't be seen!" Nurse Spare has arrived.

"I ... I ... " Frost sounds befuddled, as if waking from a dream.

"I, I," she mocks. "You should not bloody well be here. Go. Go this instant."

My mouth hangs agape at the way she speaks to him. And that his sharp tongue does not cut her down. And Cloud. He has gone silent.

The shuffling recommences, and I bolt back beneath the covers, trembling all over. I wait, holding my breath, but the footsteps recede down the hall.

What happened to ... my elder? I am an orphan.

Who could possibly be my elder?

I lie still, hearing Sebastian re-enter, his warm body curling up on my chest.

Even with his comfort, it is a very long time till sleep finds me.

CHAPTER FIVE

JULES

"I cannot bloody well believe it!" The woman's hands slap the table before her.

My head snaps up from the charts I am sorting.

A beautiful older woman stands, her hands shooting out to grasp the table as her body quivers all over, sending her chair clattering to the floor.

I stand alert. Is she having a seizure? What is happening?

Three elderly matrons cower by the *Ward One* sign. One snuffles into a handkerchief and begins to cry in earnest. Alexander, the burly orderly, is on the beautiful one in a flash. "Mrs. Smith, you must not excite yourself. Sit down."

But the matron's eyes are blue fire—her perfectly arranged

bun falling in large blond clumps as she disobediently shakes her head. "I shall do no such thing. How *dare* he? Who does he think he is?"

Nurse Sally bolts from my side, sliding herself between Alexander and the disintegrating Mrs. Smith. Her eyes scan the table and narrow. A local society page lies open to an obituary.

The nurse's lips press into a grim white line. "How did she get this? Who gave it to her?"

She scans the room, spinning in a circle, her beady eyes impaling every staff member—a scrawny bird of prey.

Her spindly neck muscles pull tight, reminding me of a rabid snapping turtle. "You all know the rules. No contact with the outside, and that includes publications."

My face flushes with anger.

The feeling is too familiar and my skin dots with gooseflesh. Like Father and his endless rules. These patients are like me— suffering loss of freedom. Others dictating what they can and cannot read, say, and do every blasted moment of their days.

The ward is tomb-quiet under the glare of Nurse Turtle, save the sniffling of the elderly matrons in the corner.

The nurse's beet-red face rivals that of Mrs. Smith's as she says, "If no one confesses, I will dock everyone's pay. I expect it in writing by shift's end—or so help me, I shall do it."

Mrs. Smith's chest heaves, hitching with a crying fit. She seems to disintegrate; her eyes look everywhere but see nothing. "I hate him. I *hate him*."

She lurches, springs away from the orderly and hitching up her skirts, leaps a settee to bolt directly for the open door.

"Seize her!" Nurse Sally commands, tearing toward her drug

cart. Her shaking hands snatch a syringe. In what appears a singular movement, she bites off its cap, bolts, and covers the space in seconds.

"Let me go! You *know* I do not belong here!" The patient's fists pound Alexander's chest again and again like rapid rifle fire. He catches them in his meaty paws, twisting them behind her back. "Unhand me! Someday I shall make you all pay! Pay!"

"Jules! Fetch the white jacket! Hurry, girl!" Sally ejects over her shoulder, wrestling with Mrs. Smith's writhing limbs.

I sweep up the jacket and hurtle back to the grappling trio.

Alexander's arms now encircle the woman like a muscled vice. She jams her foot down *hard*, smashing Alexander's toe.

"Oh, *you* shall pay for that one." He leers through the pain.

I shudder. He is a *horrible* man. I have no doubt she *will* pay.

"Slide them on, *now, girl*. Make yourself useful."

I grit my teeth and thread the woman's hands into the straitjacket. I am mere inches from her face; her sour breath puffs across my lips.

"Dear girl. Help me, please. Do you not know who I am?"

Our eyes meet; her pupils so large they block out the sky-blue that surrounds them.

"I am not who they say."

"Quiet!" Sally shrieks.

I slide the sleeve up to her shoulders, and her body jerks as Alexander tugs the jacket hard, securing it behind her.

She shrieks, eyes wild, spittle hitting my cheek, "I am—"

Sally plunges the syringe into her thigh, and her eyes roll back to reveal the whites—her entire person slumps, giving way like a life-size rag doll to hang in Alexander's arms.

Sally stands, her head whipping back and forth, instantly assessing the room for an uprising. She confided on my orientation, *"They are like pack animals. When a rebellion begins, it often whips others into a frenzy."*

But all is quiet on Ward One. I suspect, if it were any other ward, we might be in danger.

Turtle-bird nods to me. "Well done, Nurse Frost."

Nurse Sally nods, heading immediately back to her med cart.

Indeed, the rest of the nursing staff looks shaken. I suspect these incidents rarely occur on the well-mannered Ward One.

The only two unaffected are Sally and Alexander. They are floaters—traveling from ward to ward. Their presence is dreaded and indicative of the board's displeasure, as they are the reconnaissance squad, sent to root out and subdue any and all problems in staff and residents alike. They are lifers—asylum employees till they quit or die, whichever occurs first.

I picture Nurse Sally, decrepit as dust, her chest finally still, her bony hand refusing to relinquish a syringe despite death's rigor mortis.

My heart hammers for the better part of an hour as I finish cleaning the chamber-pots and delivering medications and tinctures. I try to make my way over to the table to see the obituary, but *Nurse Rigid and Efficient* has already disposed of it, plopping it in the center of the roaring fieldstone hearth.

I make a mental note to ask Maeve to try and find a paper from today and smuggle it into my nearly-as-sheltered world at home.

Making my way back to Nurse Rigid, I wind through well-dressed men and women, many playing whist or checkers. Only a few telltale signs show something may be awry—such as the man without trousers or the woman proclaiming she is Cleopatra. "Come, Marc Antony. Do obeisance to your queen!"

I sidestep her cane-scepter to return to the medicine counter.

"How are you getting on then?" Sally prompts.

"Fine," I reply. I swallow and muster my courage. "That … woman. Mrs. Smith. She seems so *sane* … Who is she?"

Sally's eyes narrow. "She is no one. Half the patients in Soothing Hills claim to be a king, queen, or the almighty himself." She gives an absent gesture to Cleopatra behind us.

I nod, defeated. "I have completed all my tasks. Do you have anything else I might do before I depart?"

The nurse cocks her head, her beady gaze roving over me once again. Her bun is pulled so taut her eyes seem fixed in a permanent slant. Her stare is intense, and purposeful, as if she is trying to remember something. She seems to decide and replies, "No, Miss Frost. You are dismissed. Do not miss the carriage to town." She opens a patient's chart, pulls out a parchment, and quickly seals it with a wax emblem. "Might you take this across the campus to Dr. Grayjoy on your way?"

She whips out the campus map, drawing the route I should follow with her pointy finger. Really, everything about the woman is pointy.

"Do not dawdle. Do not deviate from your course. Go directly to Dr. Grayjoy, then directly to your carriage. The danger doubles at night here."

I curtsy. "Yes, mum. Might I return next week then? On the same day?"

She eyes me up and down. "I suspect so. Your father will tell you for certain."

I open my hand, and she places the parchment in it.

My heart beats lightly in my chest. I have only met the good doctor twice, during asylum recitals, but if I am honest with myself, I was quite taken with his looks—dark, curling hair and the frame of a longshoreman, not a doctor, broad and powerful.

I turn without another word, glancing down at the map. The campus is sprawling—domiciles for staff, a full working farm, and a variety of wards. The higher the number, the greater the history of violence.

I reach the door to the courtyard and halt, staring up into the dark, brooding sky. The stone path through the center of the yard is the quickest route to Dr. Grayjoy.

Rain pelts the panes, lambasting the windows so that they vibrate, the whole of the building seeming to shudder in the late fall wind.

My destination, Building Seven, is barely within sight. The asylum grounds are almost a mile, all told, in addition to owning the surrounding two hundred-acre woods. Nurse Turtle proclaimed if you walked each ward from end to end, the entire asylum is four square miles.

It is indeed its own dark world.

"You don't have to go out there, deary."

I jump, my heart hammering in my chest.

I turn to stare at an elderly man, a mop grasped between his gnarled fingers, his bulgy eyes adhered to my map.

"There is an easier way. No need to dowse yourself through."

"*What* other way?"

He shuffles forward and I smell the day-old spirits on his

breath. He points toward a door, dead center in a long hallway. "There."

I cock my head, thinking him clearly mad. Perhaps he is a patient. Often patients earn the right to do labor within the grounds, as a trial before being reintroduced to society.

"I don't understand."

Why are you encouraging him? You are to reorient the deluded to reality at all times.

"Go and see," he says, a long finger pointing to the door

I reluctantly walk down the hallway, partially to put space between us. I reach the door after a very long moment, and it whines as I grasp the doorknob and push it open.

Stairs. A very long flight of stairs, the bottom bathed in the yellow glow of a sconce.

"What is it?"

"Tunnels. 'Em connects all the buildings. They all have their numbers affixed to the walls. They follow the same course as your map there."

I wait, conflicted. "Are we … permitted to use them?" I had never heard Father or Nurse Sally-turtle-bird utter a word about hidden tunnels.

His face is like stone. "Precious few do. But I won't tell if you don't. I am good at keeping secrets."

I shudder. I bet he is.

Footsteps echo in the corridor nearby. "Hurry up now. Make your choice." He quickly begins to mop once again, his eyes strategically avoiding me so that whoever may be approaching shall not be drawn my way.

I take a deep breath and descend.

JANE

I cannot sleep. Truth be told, I almost never sleep.

My dreams are a place of torment rather than comfort, oft filled with bizarre images and such sharp sensations, they might well be memories.

Birds fill my dreams. Bright bluebirds, and black leering ravens. Circling, pecking, and singing. The notes spiraling from their mouths alight with their corresponding colors.

Always, it ends the same. One bluebird, poised in the corn, humming middle C. It takes flight, disappearing down a darkened, leafy path.

They might well be memories … but I cannot trust my mind, as I have had my fair share of treatments—shocks, dowsing, isolation.

My mind is not to be trusted … even by me.

I lie still, staring at the empty bed beside me.

I have never had a bunkmate to whom I might talk. As a child, I used to dream, weave myself stories about her. How we would become fast friends, share all our joys and fears. A makeshift family.

Frost made sure that wish was never realized.

He ensured my roommates were either profoundly impaired or so entirely melancholy no amount of cajoling, empathy, or pain could pull them back from their despair.

I roll to stare out at the snow, falling in huge, white flakes, instantly melting as they hit the pane.

I began speaking to myself when I was five, most likely to fill the silence. I oft find the words slipping out even now, without my permission. Perhaps that is why I hum and compose; it is more socially acceptable to sing than to mumble.

Wrinkling my brow, I slide out of bed to shut my door. I shove my chair over and wedge it under the doorknob. It will not keep them out, but at least slow their entrance.

I slide open the window, and the cold snatches my breath.

A fire escape runs along beneath the windows, but the ladder to the ground is chained with a padlock.

I stick my head out the window and hum, loud as I can. Nothing. Just the sound of the wind rustling through the trees, the icicle-covered branches clinking together in a natural symphony.

"Where are you?" I whisper.

It is much, much too cold for Sebastian to sleep out of doors this eve.

My eyes steal to the sky, dread weighing down each cautious blink.

Many *somethings* come to my window. Ravens. They perch on the wrought-iron scrolls about my window—sometimes only one, sometimes as many as ten. They are quiet when they visit. *Unnaturally* quiet, as if frightened of capture. Cocking their twitchy heads back and forth, as if posing some unspoken question.

Indeed, if Frost saw them, he would accuse me of either witchcraft or yet another reason to be "treated" for my affliction. As if tiny little leeches could actually suck out and right any abnormalities swirling through my lifeblood.

I hear it. A tinny echo as something approaches on the fire escape.

A big, brown-striped tabby, with eyes quite similar to my own, leaps onto my windowsill, and I quickly whisk him inside and slide the window down with a *thud.*

I bury my face in his fur, inhaling the clean scent of snow, and place him onto my coverlets. "Sebastian, I have missed you so."

The big cat purrs, winding his body around my legs, till finally collapsing onto my knees. To have him here, to not be alone, has been a relief I cannot put to words.

I found him five years prior, injured and near death on the escape. I stole for him, sneaking milk from the kitchens, giving him half of my own meals. I even managed to steal the bandages and liniments necessary to heal his paw. From that day on, he has been *mine*, returning each night to my window. Indeed, he is the first real friend I ever had. I blush. I speak to him as I would a person. I know it to be abnormal, but to have a creature not reject me, to accept me, no matter what ... It comforts me.

I sit up in my cot and tug up the rough covers to my face to muffle the sound of my humming. *Middle C.* I allow the warm, calming sensations to wash over me and close my eyes. This note in my mind is red, always in red.

Normally, each note holds a specific color. Except for the special music. *The Requiem Red*, I call it.

It is the *corn music.* When it calls to me, whether by day, or in my dreams, all notes falling from the birds' beaks blaze in a fiery red.

As a child, I believed Frost. That is was part of my sickness.

But now ... I know them to be real, not created in my mind.

The ravens. Their music. It means something—something I am certain will alter my life. It is as if they *want* something from me. But I cannot discern what.

I banish the thought as the gooseflesh erupts across my skin like a tactile brushfire.

Instead, I picture a field filled with flowers and sun. Picture finding it, hiding there—never to return.

A shriek slices through my reverie as my eyes fly open wide and Sebastian's claws sink into my flesh. He drops to the floor, slinking to hide under my bed. I shiver hard and cock my head to listen.

Another wail. Feminine. Close.

Our ward is directly next to the ablation ward. More aptly termed *the torture ward*. The place where minds are lost.

The scream again, this time, long, drawn out, as if the pain lingers. The hairs on my arms rise. The voice sounds familiar. My chest balls with panic, and a gush of fear floods my legs.

Tears bead, and I blink and press my lips tight, grateful I cannot recall who suffers.

"No tears. No tears, Jane." I hastily wipe them away.

Fear is as much a part of me as my beating heart. I cannot imagine a life without it.

Of late, a woebegone, familiar shadow threatens to return to my heart. Hovering, longing to adhere itself to my soul, to snuff out my will. Or at the very least, to drag my lips back to that wretched bottle of laudanum.

The shadow is more loathsome and dangerous than the fear. With fear, one may fight. But melancholy ... Its tentacles creep around the soul, crushing and smothering, until all desire is choked out.

I grow tired of being brave.

I used to be certain, if I was good, so very good, and followed the rules, helped others in need—one day my life would change.

There are days I no longer believe such.

Once in the tenacious grip of laudanum, I spent *days* in bed. Which was never my custom in childhood. One year in particular seemed to be swathed in muslin. I passed nearly a year in my mind. Mute. Unmoving.

Catatonia, they called it. *Escape*, I called it.

It took another year to regain my body.

Another scream to curdle my blood.

"Help. Dear merciful Providence, help her."

The shuddering begins, chattering my teeth, shaking my hands. I slide out of bed and, gritting my teeth, trying, fumbling, to dress. I drop to my knees to remove the loose chunk of stone behind my bed, to conceal Sebastian should any enter my room. He eyes me from beneath the bed, tail swishing madly.

The screaming continues as I skulk from my room into the hallway. My door is rarely bolted. I am not deemed an escape risk, which is so very foolish. I am thankful for the thousandth time these doctors cannot read minds.

The doors between the wards, however, are typically bolted.

No sounds. Our ward is mercifully quiet.

Tim, our typical night orderly, is no doubt in a spirits-induced near coma, as is his custom. My ward is filled with quiet young women. Young, sad, demented women. Requiring little attention or muscle.

I sneak down the hall, ending up at the nurses' station.

There's only Tim, slumped in his chair, his head resting on the nurses' counter surrounded by a pool of highly flammable, foul-smelling drool.

I crouch and head to the converted supply room. Once inside, I stand still, leaning against the racks, catching my breath, listening. When no other sound ensues, I jam my shoulder into the small chest of drawers, sliding it across the floor.

It conceals *The Hatch*—the name I have given to my gateway to another world. A world of relative freedom.

I found it many years prior. It is very, very dangerous but enables me to go to the abandoned library—and perhaps one day will be my means of escape.

The trapdoor creaks, the warped wood popping and cracking like an old man's bones as I open it and slide carefully in, allowing it to swallow me whole. For a moment I grapple in the dark, clinging to the cold metal.

I scurry down the ladder and leap the last few rungs, dropping to the tunnel. The screams have given way to moans as I pass beneath the ablation room.

The shadows whisper, *"You have fought long and hard. Time to give in, give way to me."*

I know if I do, it shall be to Ward Thirteen, with no hope of return.

There, the lobotomized shuffle in endless circles, with unseeing eyes. I wandered in there once as a girl. I will never, ever forget the glazed eyes, the drooling mouths, the broken bodies, devoid of spirit. Just empty husks of once humans.

Once someone's lover, wife … child.

I place my hand on the tunnel wall, hurrying along as fast as I dare in the gloom. There are few sconces, and one out of every three is lit, leaving very long seas of inky black between. So black, anyone or anything might be inches away without one's knowledge. Someone or something uses this tunnel.

I have encountered odd smells, the occasional footprint. But I have thus far avoided running into staff.

I halt as the moaning increases directly above me.

Footfalls.

My heart panics. *Think, think.* My mind spirals in revolt, picturing solitary confinement—my toes, my only free members, drawing on walls as they have in the past to keep the demons of insanity at bay.

I cannot lose this meager freedom. The library is my only means of sanity. Without the escape of the books, the shadows will close and win. The footsteps are much too close.

I bolt back from whence I came.

Mercifully, a laundry cart has been abandoned, shoved into a nook in the tunnel. I bound behind it, cowering, peeking through the piled linens.

Humming. A singular note. C. My breath hitches sharply, and I hold it.

A cascade of warmth. The flashing note of red.

Bootfalls. Loud. Right here.

A girl steps into view, bathed in shadow. Long, dark curls bob. Her profile portrays a turned up nose.

Chills explode down my spine. She halts, listening.

I grasp the cart as my knees fail. My eyes squint as I struggle to discern her form in the dim sconce light.

She turns to face the corridor down which I am hiding, head cocked as if sensing my cowering presence.

The tunnel careens, pitching in time with my mind's revolt, and my head strikes the corner of the cart in time with a blinding pain to the temple.

The world shrinks, a circle going smaller and smaller, like a noose cinched around my eyesight. My last thought as my cheek hits the rock is *Eyes*. Blue with a yellow inner ring. Feline eyes.

CHAPTER SIX

JULES

I finger the letter in my hands and look over my shoulder for the fifth time. I swear I hear footsteps, scuttling, but so far, no man or beast has revealed themselves.

My forehead dampens with sweat, and I mutter a curse under my breath, my eyes darting around in the dark tunnel.

I should've ignored the old man and just endured the downpour.

I pass low-lit sconces, each with a number nearby, reciting the wards and the functioning levels of their residents in my mind. The recitation calms me, drawing my attention from the noises in the shadows and the fleeting sulfur smells that somehow lurk in the darkness. I keep moving, walking swiftly toward my goal.

Ward One—where the nearly well are given the opportunity to work, to be embedded in community gatherings like the asylum recitals.

Wards Two and *Three* are tuberculosis wards. Father has forbidden me to go near them. And for once, I have obeyed.

Ward Four—the women's ward. Sad, demented women of every state of confusion meander up and down its yellowed hallways.

Wards Five and *Six*—the men-only wards.

Ward Seven—a special place indeed. Where the foreign-tongued are housed—till it might be determined if they be sane or mad. Nurse Ginny relayed the ward to be a creation of Grayjoy's after encountering an elegant, elderly gent who was considered demented and housed at Soothing Hills for a year, only to discover *he merely spoke French.*

The Frenchman had lost most of his ability to speak, but when spoken to in his native tongue, he suddenly followed every command and showed the appropriate emotions, proving he was not entirely mad, merely lost, unable to communicate his situation, his way back home.

His distraught family came to collect him within a fortnight.

I pass the rungs for *Wards Three, Four* and *Five* in tight succession. The children's wards. I'll admit, I have not been able to muster the courage to step foot inside.

A scream dances down my nerve endings from the topside hole as I pass by *Six*. A shuddering cry with chest-rattling gasps of masculine pain. I shudder, wrapping my shawl tighter and nearly run.

My eyes flick down the tunnel, where Wards *Eleven* and

Twelve house the criminally insane. One for women, one for men. Violent patients—the most highly guarded wards. Where the vast majority of injuries occur.

And *Thirteen*. Where patients are taken for experiments. Patients without families to speak for them. Patients who are deemed uncontrollable.

Father calls them animals.

But I have heard the rumors among the nurses—by eavesdropping—that if one should cross my father, Ward Thirteen should be their fate. Another shiver wracks my body, rattling my teeth, and I snap them together.

I know my father to be stern, but is he … capable of such atrocities?

I halt and stare. The number seven sits before me, waiting for me to scurry up its ladder.

At last, Dr. Grayjoy's ward. I reach my hand up and touch the cold rung and freeze, my mouth going dry.

Several portholes down the corridor, what seems a great, white bird flaps awkwardly down from the topside hole. My heartbeat pounds in my ears, the world slowing as I squint in the gloom. I peer closer and, to my growing horror, realize it is a woman.

A dead woman. Her body dangling from the porthole above as an orderly below angles her lifeless form toward a gurney. I estimate the distance to guess that is Ward Thirteen.

Nurse Sally descends from the hole. My father is never far behind. I vaguely wonder if she might be a dalliance. I avert my gaze and scurry up the ladder, intent on not letting the nasty woman catch sight of me.

My conscience plays devil's advocate. *Of course, patients die. The tunnels would be a sensible way to take the bodies to the morgue.* But the hairs on my neck rise in warning. Warning to stay out of her way, out of her sight.

Just keep moving. Just keep moving.

I open the next hole to yet another hallway, the ward number blazing right before me, just as the old man said. I scramble out and dust off my uniform, straighten my cap, and step forward to rap on Dr. Grayjoy's door.

I wait for several moments, my heartbeat accelerating. Nurse Sally was quite insistent I deliver it. I stand still for several very long minutes, waiting. Every shuffled stone and scuff of boot of the corridor seems to scream of my presence.

I sigh impatiently as my pulse escalates; its rhythm of vexation pounding in my ears. I shall miss the night carriage back.

My face burning, I jiggle the handle. The office is unlocked, and the door swings open, as if inviting me in. I slide inside. Other than the off-putting skeletons in each corner, it is mundane. Precisely the office one would expect of a respectable physick—dark woods, a myriad of reference books and papers towering on a gargantuan mahogany desk with a nameplate that proclaims, *Jonathon Grayjoy, M.D.*

The room smells of lingering leather, fire, and tobacco smoke.

Pinpricks of red embers remain in his hearth. He has not been absent long.

I slink to his desk, afraid of disturbing the loud silence of this room, and slide the letter onto his desk, in the center of his blotter to assure he will see it. I turn to go, but something in the periphery catches my eye. Something on the top of his desk.

A sketch. In watercolors, no less.

I blink. My heart sinks to my knees as a river of fear pumps out, weakening them. I grasp the desk to keep erect.

Eyes. Just a set of eyes. Decidedly feminine. Nearly feline. Blue with the yellow-hazel ring around the iris.

"My eyes," I whisper.

I trace my finger over the lashes. The lashes are the wrong color. White-blond, not dark brown-black like my own.

They cannot be mine. Dr. Grayjoy and I have only met in passing at the recital. I lied to Father about him encouraging me to come to volunteer. I merely know him through Father's ravings and Nurse Sally's instructions, and his handwriting on charts. And my admiring him from afar.

My face flushes.

The titter of nurses passes the doorway as they walk past in the hall.

I drop the sketch and hurry behind the door. *Why am I hiding?* Something inside urges, *Keep still.*

I wait till they have passed and then skulk into the hall and quickly out the exit—intent on stopping for nothing till I sit safely in the hansom, my mind and heart racing.

Darkness. And an ever-loving pain in my temple.

I struggle to recall my surroundings. My back and neck provide the answer. Rough rocks grind into my flesh with each movement. The tunnel.

Humming again. Masculine humming this time.

The now familiar smell draws near. Woods and pine and musk. "Jane." Big hands grip my shoulders and give a little shake. "*Jane*, are you hurt?"

I force my eyes to flutter open, and I flinch at a piercing pain in my cheek. My vision is blurred, and I squint, trying to discern who kneels before me. But I recognize the smell. The abnormally appealing smell, a solitary anomaly in this land of smell-horror.

"Mason?"

"Yes." His hands slide under my arms, assisting me to stand. I stumble, so he props me against his side. "What happened? Whyever are you down here?"

My breath quickens, and I frantically look around—stupidly, because in the tunnel, time seems to stop, no light from outside ever penetrates its inky fortress.

"I imagine it is close to dawn."

I grip his shirt tight. "Mason. *Please.* If they catch me out of bed, all my privileges of visiting Ward One shall be revoked. I only played the one time."

"It was marvelous—"

"*Please.*"

He nods, bright blue-green eyes tightening. "Of course. Hurry. Lean on me now."

"If you are caught aiding me—"

"I shall be let go. You doan' worry about tha." His face is calm, but his accent has intensified—meaning he is worried as well.

We shuffle our way down the tunnels toward Ward Four, not speaking for fear of drawing attention should anyone up top, near a hatch, be listening. I am far too aware of his arm around my back, the warm touch of his hand steadying my forearm.

Time seems to stretch in the dark. But finally, mercifully, I see it. The ladder, looming ahead.

The footsteps again. Gooseflesh races like wildfire down my neck to my spine.

These are more of a shuffle than footsteps.

I feel Mason's heart quicken beneath my hand, which desperately clutches his shirt.

He presses a singular finger to his lips. "Shh." His eyes dart left and right, then finally up.

He points to another ladder, labeled *Ward Six.* Then he points upward, signaling me to climb.

I obey, and he hurries behind me. I have never exited here. We may be throwing ourselves into the middle of a common room or dead center of a nurses' station.

Vomit and fear rise in my throat as I throw open the hatch.

Relief instantaneously floods my limbs, leaving a residual weakness. This hatch, too, is mercifully in a supply closet.

Mason scurries out of the hole, closing it just in time. We hunker on all fours, ears pressed to the floorboards, listening. A sweat breaks on my brow.

Footsteps slow beneath us.

Our faces are inches apart as I watch his eyes tighten with fear. *Steady*, he mouths.

I swallow, press my lips tight and hold perfectly still.

Our breathing becomes one for a very long moment, our wide eyes searching one another's as we lay frozen, our cheeks pressed to the floor.

The footsteps shuffle, then move slowly past, and I exhale and become acutely aware of his proximity. My stomach contracts with a foreign emotion.

He sits up gingerly, our eyes locked in a slow, meaningful dance. His fingers, which still encircle my wrist from whence we collapsed to the floor, now seem to burn against my skin.

The sensation of touch.

I have had so very little of it. It's why I have clung to dolls, well beyond when children give them up. Comfort. *Any* sort of comfort. His eyes are bright with hesitation, but he gently pulls me toward him. His eyes flicker with emotions: fear, pain, and *longing*.

A door in my soul wrenches open, one previously secured with nails borne of grief, fear, and horror.

His lips brush mine, and the whole of my body shudders.

His eyebrows arch, concerned, as he pulls back, searching my face. His expression turns guilty. "I should not do this. You are a ... "

I grind my teeth. "A patient." Anger incinerates all other emotion. I stare at him. "A *freak?*"

He is breathtaking. More beautiful than any picture in any of the books in the abandoned library. Arched eyebrows, deep-set eyes, thin lips. His thick shock of hair is a dark brown; his impending beard holds highlights of red. I saw it glimmering in the skylight's sun the day he presented me with the hair elixir.

"You think because I am a patient I do not *want*? Need? Wish? Condemn?" My voice catches. "Hurt?"

His chest rises and falls, faster and faster, keeping time with mine. His eyes dart back and forth, trying to decide.

He lurches forward to grasp me with two hands and folds me into him, his warm mouth covering mine, his tongue velvet and plush. I feel the fever in his kiss. That he does, indeed, want me. Despite it all. Even if he never admits it.

I slide myself into his lap, and his hands stray up and down my back, stopping to knot my dress in his hands in a needy frustration.

Footfalls. The closet doorknob jiggles.

He casts me off, hauling me to stand in a single motion.

Our eyes scan the room. Only two routes to escape. Back into the tunnels or …

This closet has a second door which leads into another corridor, another ward. They share this supply room.

I am flying, or so it seems. His hand clasps over my mouth to quiet me as he pushes me, ushering me out the adjoining door. The neighboring corridor is quiet. But it shan't be for long. This is not my ward. We must move.

Our eyes fall outside. My ward is visible, running parallel to this one. To walk to it through adjoining wards and halls, we would absolutely be caught.

In the space between, in what was once a courtyard, grows an overflow of corn.

He whispers, urgency coloring each word, "If we are discovered … Our only chance to make it back before light is out there."

I follow his gaze, and I swallow. He gestures outside. Out into the corn.

CHAPTER SEVEN

"Run, Jane."

Mason crushes my fingers between his as we barrel into the stalks. The texture of the light has changed but a fraction. But it is enough to know morning is on its way.

Dawn is breaking. The asylum looms above us, its windows like the blackened eyes of an overbearing orderly. The corn grows very close to the building. Should the sun rise, any who happen to be standing near a window will witness our flight.

Mason's breath comes hard and fast as he cuts a straight line through the stalks, heading directly for my ward.

I hear it. Orchestral music blasting to life, embedded within its notes a wailing scream of despair and torture.

I fall to my knees, pressing my hands hard to my head, clutching my temples. "No-no-no-no."

Mason whirls.

I hold my breath, await the accusations to end any hope of happiness.

What is wrong with you? Await the inevitable pity, which quickly turns to fear at any sign of abnormality.

I squint, trying to discern his expression, but he is frozen, stock-still, a desperate sort of fear crossing his ashen face.

I peer up, blinking at him, the wails filling my head like a water-siren's call. But he is looking around, *not at me*, staring, eyes wide, at the stalks of corn as if they blaze with fire.

"*You hear it.*"

It is not a question. The horrified expression on his face proclaims it.

His gaze drops to meet mine. "Aye. I hear it. What the devil *is* it?"

I swallow as the screaming reaches a crescendo. "Can you hear ... the message?"

Now, he does cock his head. "I hear no words. Only music." He reaches down to grasp my hand and hauls me to stand. "We must away, Jane. If they catch us, I shall not merely be let go. I shall never see you again—they will never grant me entrance. They will make you disappear before I am able to fight my way back in."

I nod and let him pull me behind him, running flat out, doing my best to keep his pace.

Light. It casts a golden glow across the corn's silken heads. Our enemy has arrived. The sun releases dim red rays onto the horizon.

"Mason. They shall see us for certain."

His only response is to run faster.

Suddenly a *rrrrumble* cuts through the orchestra. At first I think it thunder, the fluttering, rolling timbre of it.

But it is a flock of ravens, so thick and deep, I mistake it for a locust swarm, flying low to the corn. I cover my ears—their squawking is deafening.

"They are blocking our view."

The black bodies cluster in a racing serpentine, matching Mason's weaving path through the corn. Mason skids to a halt, his boots sliding in the thick mud. We have reached the entrance. We need only bolt across a small patch of grass without the cover of the corn.

He pulls me tight, pressing his lips so hard against mine, I sense his fear.

"I will return to see you," he says, giving my shoulders a little shake. "No matter the cost."

I nod, wincing. The odds of us making it across without discovery are almost nil.

Suddenly, a great, black ruckus erupts at the other end of the field. What seems a thousand ravens dive-bomb one another—fighting, gnashing, flashing beaks in aerial battle.

I stand, dumbstruck.

"An unkindness of ravens."

My jaw drops. "What?"

"That is what a flock of them is called. An unkindness."

"It is anything but. They have created a distraction. Let's go."

We join hands and bolt across the patch, wrench open the door, and hurtle down the lonely hallway.

"Through here."

He fumbles, jamming open a side door, and we are in a parallel hallway I have never seen prior. I quickly surmise it is reserved for staff.

We fly up a back stairwell, our footsteps echoing eerily, like unseen bats in the dark.

We slip out into the hallway; the familiar smell of my lavender is not far ahead. My room is near as we walk as quickly as possible without trying to draw attention. Our panting is synchronous as I spy the number matching my room. My wretched, numerical name.

Twenty-Nine.

My heart stutters. The door beneath the number opens.

I lurch sideways, into the open broom closet, but too late—the orderly has spied me.

Mason has beaten me inside, one hand trying to yank me in, the other fumbling to open a hatch on the floor—our only escape.

The orderly bolts forward, his footfalls growing louder and louder. I hear his ragged breathing.

I shake off Mason's hand and, with my boot, kick with all of my might. He tumbles down into the tunnel shaft, the hatch shutting after his disappearing frame with a *whuump*.

Just enough time for me to shut the closet door behind me as I slip back out into the hall to face the proverbial music. My eyes raise slowly, my heartbeat so wild it flushes my face, to meet the murderous stare of a red-faced Alexander cracking his knuckles.

His smug smile sours my stomach. "Oh, my pet. How I will enjoy this."

His fingers reach out, maddeningly slow, and with a relish, he rings the alarm bell.

"You *lie,* Twenty-Nine!" Frost's lips curl back from his teeth, his voice a near snarl.

"Dunk her again!"

I hold my breath.

The sensation of falling, then a *freezing* cold. It sloshes past toes, knees, to swallow breasts, and then ices my face. The ice seeps through skin to freeze my very bones.

A convulsive shudder rocks my body as the dunking machine plunges me *up and down, up and down,* like a frigid, heart-stopping seesaw.

I break through the surface, slumping over, ice-water torrents spilling from my hair. I hear his voice, marred through the ringing in my ears. "Tell me the truth, Twenty-Nine. You know how I detest liars."

I manage a whimper and plunge down again. My heart skips, once, twice, and *again-again-again.* Fear opens my mouth at the unfamiliar sensation in my chest, allowing the water to rush in. Pain from the bone-chilling cold seeps into my teeth, making them ache. Blackness looms like a dark creature, scurrying up my legs with a deadly tingling, ready to wrap round my head and claim me.

I lurch upward again on the seesaw, coughing and sputtering, stars flickering in black and white explosions in my vision. My weak body hangs limp. Were not I tied to the dunker, I would slip off and plummet back into the ice bath. I would breathe deep, and it would end. It would all finally, mercifully end.

I hear the door open, and several sets of footsteps echo through the heights of the antechamber.

The dunker shudders, preparing to plunge, and my muscles tense in anticipation.

"Dr. Frost, *what precisely* is going on here?" Grayjoy's voice is grave.

The machine grinds to a halt, and a whimper slips from my lips. As much as I hate to let Frost view my weakness, I cannot stay the sound.

"Patient Twenty-Nine must be taught a lesson."

I watch through the wet curtain of my hair as Grayjoy's eyes narrow. His gaze rolls over me in doctorly assessment. "How so? What has happened?"

Mason is beside him, chest nearly heaving, his face a taut mask of pain. His hands clench and unclench with barely tethered rage.

Frost's lips part in a bitter smile, his knuckles whitening on his clipboard. He stalks back and forth, fathomless eyes flicking between Grayjoy and I.

"Firstly, she was caught out of bed last night, wandering the corridors."

Grayjoy's lips press into a line.

"Secondly, she knows something about her roommate's disappearance and, as usual, adamantly refuses to cooperate." His icy gaze halts, glaring, and my guts contract, as my eyes slam closed. I wish to never look on them again. They are dead, lacking emotion. A corpse's eyes.

"It is vital you assist us, Twenty-Nine," Frost goes on. "Why, a killer may be roaming our corridors this very moment." He paces, faster and faster, the words tumbling forth. "I find it curious three of the five missing happened to live in your very *room*." He bellows the last word, veins bulging in his neck.

I risk a glance at Mason. His expression is unreadable and impassive but his eyes burn with anger. His hands now shake. Our eyes meet for the briefest of moments, but it is enough. His eyes *blaze*. If he reacts, strikes out—even leaves—Frost will suspect us, will sense his attachment.

He must remain quiet or he risks expulsion—and never seeing me again.

Mason's lips press together as the shaking travels from his hands to engulf the whole of his limbs.

Grayjoy scoffs, his face reddening above his gathering beard. "Twenty-Nine is indeed adventuresome, at time deluded, but incapable of *homicide*. That is not what you're suggesting, is it, Frost?"

Frost shrugs, playfully tapping his lip. "Perhaps not. But she does deserve to be punished, all the same."

Grayjoy moves to my side to take my pulse. He pushes my hair back from my face, his warm hand comforting against my freezing, puckered flesh. Then he walks to Frost's side, growling low in his ear; I strain but am unable to hear.

Mason mouths the word *steady*. At great peril. Any orderly might see and report him straightaway.

Their conversation is a steady rumble until Grayjoy's voice suddenly rises, his stoic resolve shattering amidst clipped tones.

"See here, Frost. She is near exhaustion. You *do not need* another death at this asylum. Already the board threatens to shutter the doors." He gives Mason a small jerk of his head to free me. "She has had enough. Allow me to question her later. Need I remind you, she is, after all, now *under my jurisdiction*."

Frost's face flushes beneath his raven-black beard, but he nods. He quickly spins to stalk toward the exit.

"Take to her room."

CHAPTER EIGHT

JANE

My body shudders, a freezing convulsion rattling my teeth behind my lips. I feel a sudden pressure, and the cold mercifully recedes as I realize someone has added another blanket to my bed.

I open my eyes slowly, before blinking madly in the candlelight. I exhale in relief. Mason stands, hands deep in his pockets, staring up at the myriad of sketches and musical compositions that paper my walls.

I vowed when I was but a wee girl of five that I would cover each and every inch of the horrid institutional green color by my nineteenth birthday. I have nearly succeeded. My birthday came and went, and only a few spots of green remain, poking through my sketched memories like the asylum's morbid, probing eye—ever watchful, ever ready to sound the alarm.

Mason is transfixed, one set of pictures holding his attention.

"Do you like them?" I whisper. I clear my throat. It is hoarse from the purge of water and ice. I wish not to think of it, to speak of it—of Frost, of that room.

Anything else is preferable.

His eyes drop, as do his shoulders. He slowly turns, his eyes fixing me under their gaze.

"Jane, I am so very sorry. I wished to help." A sweat breaks on his brow. "It was nearly impossible *not* to help."

I nod. "I know. It was best you did not. If he suspects anything, anything at all, he will banish you. He has made it his personal mission to deny me all happiness. It has always been such."

His hands clench open and closed. His words are broken through gritted teeth. "I do not know if I could muster the restraint again."

I try desperately to change the topic. When he thinks on me, I do not wish it to be pity.

"Do you like the sketches, then?"

He raises his finger to trace a snowy sleigh ride. The carriage is decked in evergreens and holly, the woman's hands thrust into a wooly white muff and the man with rosy cheeks around a wide, white smile.

"Have … Have you ever ridden in a sleigh?"

I shake my head. "No. It is all from books."

His smile is sad. "Then I say, you have a very vivid imagination." He points to another set. "What about this one?"

A man and woman, hands linked, ice skating about a frozen

pond. Children and dogs lingering on the sides, frolicking in the powdered-sugar snow.

I shake my head again. "My experience with the out of doors has been limited to Soothing Hills' gardens. I will admit they have many beautiful trees and flowers in their season. And animals ... I have only seen what have been brought to the asylum."

He points to a cluster of dogs: German shepherds—their tan and black muzzles frosted with individual snowflakes.

"These are from imagination?"

I shake my head. "No." I slide from the bed, wrapping my shawl about me, and shuffle to the window. "See here."

Mason comes to stand beside me, and I point through the frosted pane, toward a kennel of shepherds far below in the courtyard.

One is particularly feisty. He lunges, pulling at his comrade's leg, and they tumble down into a rolling ball of snow and fur. "He is my favorite. Smoky."

Mason smiles. "You have named them?"

I nod. "There are ways to see them, if one is ... creative."

His eyebrows rise. "I see."

He turns, heading back to the sketches. "And these?" He points to paper after paper of compositions, the musical notes in colors as I hear and see them.

The effect is a staccato rainbow, weaving across sheet music like a musical trail.

Frost hated the pictures—telling me it was all a lie. It elicited such rage that I hid them when I knew he was expected to do rounds on my ward—as if they were a personal affront to him, somehow, that I create such fantasies. But since Grayjoy took over my case, he encourages every arrangement, encourages me to fill in the notes with the colors, to purge my mind. He went to great lengths to provide me with the necessary supplies—dyes from wherever he could find them.

"Why are they in color?"

I hesitate, not certain I should blatantly share the abnormal workings of my mind. But if I am to have a chance with him, there should be no secrets. I take a deep breath, and the words tumble forth.

"I hear the music when I see them. Notes and color always paired. I tried to cover the walls completely. So when I look around the room, I may live either in my imagination or within the music. The piece plays in my mind when I look at it."

He nods, his mouth fluctuating between awe and sadness. "I see. That is a lovely sentiment."

I swallow and cannot believe I am admitting it. "I … make up musical stories. Try to put myself in them. I know them to be fiction, but it … eases me through the day."

Mason's eyebrows knit, and he approaches my bed.

"Let me show you."

His mouth tightens, but he carefully sits, as if the bed were made of pin cushions. I reach for one of my compositions, colored notes sprawled on the music bars. I take his finger and trace the notes, humming the tune as I go. His chest rises and falls, faster with each bar.

"The colors, they appear in my mind, just as you see them here. Picture them like flickering, colored flames."

Our eyes hold, and my heartbeat soars. I swallow again and again, trying to quiet it.

"Astounding. It has always been such for you?"

I nod.

"May I ... ?" He clears his throat, looking supremely awkward. "I know it is forward, and nowhere in the bounds of polite society, but I haven't a choice. I cannot rightly ask you to take a turn with me. But ... will you? Take a turn with me?"

The ridiculousness of the statement makes us both smile. We are not in a parlor, nor near a park. We are in an asylum.

I smile anyway, playing along. "Yes, you may. But please be watchful. They will do rounds at sunrise. Won't you be missed?"

I picture us strolling down the asylum hallways, arms linked, commenting on the naked patients as offhandedly as if they were poinsettias in snow.

He looks sheepish. "I will admit my shift ended at eleven. But once I saw you in the dowsing room ... " He covers his face, rubbing it hard. "Why did you do that?"

"Do what?"

"You ... saved me. By pushing me down the hatch."

I shrug, my face heating with the truth. *I could not bear for any harm to come to you.*

Instead, I manage, "I ... never had a friend before. I wish to be able to see you still."

"I am grateful. I would've gladly taken the fall—but now, at least I might visit you. I brought you that coverlet. This place is bitterly cold. It is a miracle the residents do not freeze to death."

I swallow. "That happened once. We had difficulty with the heating system ... and four froze to their beds."

His eyes seem to sink further beneath his brows, as if recoiling, but his mouth stays strong.

A loud flapping sound erupts by the window, and we both turn. A great, black wingspan takes flight from outside my sill.

Mason stares from it to me and back. "Ravens … seem … drawn to you."

Hair rises on the back of my neck. People have been hanged for less. I keep silent, unsure how to respond.

"The other day in the corn … I have never seen birds act so queerly."

"I am not a witch."

His blue eyes widen. "What? I did not say you were." His gaze drifts back to the window. "Something odd is afoot in here, in the corn, but I am certain you are not to blame."

I finger the texture of the coverlet. It is woolen and so heavy and warm. I try to change the subject yet again. I want him to think pleasant thoughts when he thinks of me. *If* he thinks of me.

"I know not how to thank you for this, but I fear they shall notice. You see I have no family to speak of. So no one who would bring me such gifts."

Anger flits through his blue eyes, and they tighten. "You tell them it was from an admirer, left outside your door. Let them fret a little." His accent thickens, his voice gruff with emotion.

He takes a deep breath, letting the air whistle out through pursed lips as his eyes cast over the pictures again.

"So many sketches are in winter. Why is that?"

I shrug, fearful to admit the reason. "I suppose winter is the most memorable here. The contrast of the snow's beauty outside with the carnage it often wreaks inside makes it stand out in my imagination. Reminding me often what is beautiful cannot be trusted."

He cocks his head. "Do you mean me?" He smiles. "I mean, I know that sounds presumptuous."

I feel my eyebrows rise, and I shrug. "Perhaps. I ... trust no one. Each time I have tried ... it has been a miserable failure. Or, if one reaches out to be my friend"—my voice chokes on the word—"they always want something in return."

So much for pleasantries.

"I want nothing more than your friendship, I assure you." He moves closer, taking my hand in his. "Please tell me your full name."

I smile and whisper, "I told you, it is Jane."

He nods encouragingly. "I know that, *putan*. It suits you. You know your first name—have you ever found out your surname?"

"*Putan?*"

I wonder at the word he used for me, but he barrels forward. "Would you like me to try? I mean, what if you have relatives somewhere? Forgive me, but I do not think the staff here are eager to discharge any of their patients to the outside. It would mean less coin for this place, and the rumors say it is already struggling to keep its doors open."

This news strikes me like a hammer. "Where would I go, if they should close?"

"I am sorry. I should not have blurted that so plainly. I am sure they would help you—I mean, Dr. Grayjoy seems genuinely interested in you."

"Yes. It was he who arranged for me to play in the Ward One concert. He who recommended I be moved there. You called me '*putan.*' What ... What does that mean?"

His face colors. "Did I? I often lapse into me native tongue. I don' even notice. It means 'button.'"

"Why b—"

The sound of a shuffling footstep silences me. I hastily press my finger to my lips. Mason's eyes go wide. I gesture beneath the bed. His eyes shoot to the door, but I mouth, "*There is not time.*"

I know who approaches. Dr. Cloud, the night physick.

I gesture to the window. Mason's eyes widen, but he throws open the sash and scrambles out onto the escape, hastily shutting the window behind him. My window is without bars, due to the height. Only one who wished to end his life would attempt such.

I have never seen this physick by day. He often bypasses my room when doing his rounds. But tonight, I all but hear the intent in that *shuffle*-step as he slides his way toward my door.

I slide beneath the covers and leave my eyes open the tiniest slit. It should not bother him—many residents' eyes do not close whilst sleeping. I suspect from the many tonics administered that may be paralyzing their facial muscles.

Cloud's hair is a tousled mess. Dark blue lenses in horn-rimmed glasses seem out of place on his grizzled face. He still wears his traveling cloak, and his boots are covered with a splattering of mud, a stark contrast to the ever-prim, ever-proper Soothing Hills physicks. His walking stick, black with a serpent's head, shines silver in the candlelight.

His eyes dart around the pictures on the wall. His voice is no more than a low mumble. "Frost is going soft. He indulges you much."

My heartbeat accelerates, and I pray he does not have the notion to examine me. *Please. Please.* Sweat breaks on my brow.

He sniffs the air, his brow furrowing. He carries no clipboard.

He bends over my bed, his wig tilting. "Patient Twenty-Nine. So like her, you are."

"Ahem." A feminine voice from the hall calls, and Dr. Cloud straightens, adjusting the spectacles. Nurse Spare lives on campus, not having her own family.

"Nurse Sally. Might I help you?"

"Yes, doctor. I believe you are wanted on Ward Thirteen." The bird comes to hover at my doorframe.

"Is that so?" he sneers.

"Yes. And the dawn is coming. The shifts will soon change."

"Yes, yes," he mutters, shuffling toward her and turning in the direction of her bony outstretched finger.

They halt outside my door, and I remain statute-still, trying to eavesdrop.

"My love, you must not take such risks."

A growl. An inhuman growl. Shuffling away.

"This girl, she is not like the others. She is not worth it."

And with a voice that could stop a beating heart: "I shall decide who is worth it. You play no part in this."

I wait, fighting the balloon of panic in my chest telling me to run. Run now.

I remain stock-still till the shuffling is no more, my eyes scanning back and forth across my sketches.

Scrambling out of bed, I open the window as Sebastian leaps inside, instantly burrowing into my bed. Mason is nowhere to be seen. He must've shimmied his way down to the ground off the fire escape. I swallow. I hope he did not break anything in the process.

I sit on my bed, trying to make sense of the overheard

conversation, letting the walls, the sketches soothe me. I blink and stand, intuition touching my spine. *Something.*

I whirl around, trying to discern what is wrong. *What is different?*

My gaze flashes back as I recount the section of the wall near the window I have deemed "my childhood."

One of my sketches is missing.

"Jules, we *must* set a date. There is much to be done."

My hand drops from the windowpane, and I tear my eyes away from the corn. "I understand that, dear boy, I just"—I feign a cough into a handkerchief—"do not feel up to it as yet. My father made you aware of my weak constitution before you asked for my hand."

Willis chews his bottom lip. "Yes, I know, my dearest, but it has been some months now, and I will handle most of it, if it comes to it ... "

I often feel the roles are reversed with Willis. He being the one pining for the wedding, I perpetually finding reasons to put it off.

I muster a great hacking cough, over and over, till my eyes convincingly water. He gives my back an awkward pat. His hands are massive—they remind me of a small bear's paws.

I feel a twinge of guilt as he looks genuinely concerned and says, "I'll fetch you some water then."

Dabbing my eyes, I nod.

Truth be known, my constitution was frail as a child, but I soon learned it earned me freedom.

Freedom from my father's constant controlling presence. *"Play your violin as such,"* and, *"I do not like the color in this room. We shall paint it blue. Must you wear that color? Blue is your color."*

Father's personality was so domineering; I was not even permitted to make decisions normally bestowed upon the female persuasion. *He* decorated our entire manor, my apartments included—or at least delegated his ideas to others and paid them to complete his whims. My dresses, my hair, all controlled by him—down to the color on my cheeks.

One would imagine I would be anxious to depart.

Willis certainly would permit me free rein—in fact, he has told me whatever I desire at Lockwood, his estate, would be his very command. Indeed, I will control *him*, the way he is smitten with me. I thought that would please me.

Something.

The anxious feeling lingers on the tip of my tongue like a forgotten tune or lyric.

I walk back to the window to stare again at the corn. *Something holds me here.* As if a piece of my soul is somehow tethered to this manor. I glance back at my bed. *The dreams.* They come most every night now. The birds. The ravens and bluebirds, dancing over the cornfield. When the music comes, I hear it.

Something crashes in the other room. "Sorry. Sorry. I'm alright."

I shake my head, picturing those great paws crushing Father's dear Swarovski crystal.

And I hold no great love for Willis, but a woman must be

practical. To marry for love *and* a desirable match is rarely ever achieved. I must be happy he is not a tyrant and I will be provided for. A small, spoiled part of me is pleased. The superficial side—which adores gowns and parties and attention. I, at least, know myself. Can see my own faults.

My eyes steal across the room.

My mother resides here. At least her memory. I fear if I leave, I shall forget her. There's not one portrait of her on any wall. Father removed them all; as if, if he could no longer see her, then she would cease to exist.

A memory sparks. I hurry over to my nursing uniform and pat the pocket.

Willis returns with a full water goblet, and I hurriedly recline on the pink chaise. *I detest the pink chaise. Of course, chosen by Father.*

I vaguely think of plunging the letter opener into it and ripping out its expensive guts.

"Here you are."

I drink deeply and then smile.

"Better?"

"A trifle." He leans in to kiss me, and I deftly pull him into an embrace so that I may check the time on the mantelpiece. I have endured, erm … *entertained* him a full hour. I can in good conscience send him on his way.

He pulls back, staring at my face. His fingers stray to the beauty mark—a real one, not the kind ladies don for vanity—on my left cheek.

"I love this, you know. It's perfectly adorable. Like you."

I catch his fingers and squeeze them. "Willis, my dear, I am—"

"Weary. Yes, I see it in your eyes."

I finger the locket at my neck, as I do when I am tired. As I have since childhood.

His fingers stray and stop over mine. I drop them, and he lifts the locket, peering over his spectacles. "It's lovely."

"My mother gave it to me."

He nods, not wanting to upset me. "Shall I call again tomorrow? Same time?"

"Yes, that will be lovely." If I have my way, I shall be at the hospital tomorrow. The only thing Willis sees in my eyes is what he wishes to see.

He kisses my hand, bows, and turns to go.

I wait till I hear the front door open and shut, and then slink to the window overlooking the front entrance.

The door is opened for him as he steps into the carriage. His eyes flick up to my room, and I instantly drop to the floor. "Curses."

I crawl on hands and knees to my uniform and pluck out the sketch. The one I took from the patient's room a week prior. I carefully unfold it and cock my head, staring.

I fold it again and carefully open my door. The only sounds are those coming from the kitchen as the servants prepare supper. Father shall not be home from Soothing Hills for at least an hour.

I weave my way out of my apartment and cross the bridge to the servants' quarters. My father, ever idiosyncratic, had an *actual bridge* installed in our house, connecting the front of the estate, where he has his office and our apartments, to the back, where the servants live and work.

Father was all about tidy divisions.

I roll my eyes as I remove my boots to stare down into the vestibule.

In my childhood, I was never permitted to play on it. The structure, situated on the second floor, was a definite head-shattering drop for impulsive, impish little girls. I used to seethe with envy as the servants' children darted back and forth, taunting me, reaching the very edge of my side and sticking out their tongues before bolting back.

I pad across it defiantly, staring down.

Lucy, one of the young maids, enters the vestibule below, and I halt, standing stock-still in the middle. If I do not move, she shall not see me. Only the bottom of the bridge will be visible to her upturned gaze.

Her footsteps halt, and I hold my breath as I know she stares up.

Above me is a central skylight of beveled glass. The sunlight is dim currently, but should it choose to brighten, my shadow shall be cast on the wall.

"Lucy? Hurry up with that bread. Do not dawdle." I hear her scuttle into the kitchen.

I release my breath and hurry over the bridge into the servants' quarters. My heart is hammering loud in my temples. If caught, I shall have a devil of a time explaining myself. And he is not beyond the punishments.

As a child, he would lock me in one of the rooms, devoid of toys or any comforts—till I cried. Confessed and repented.

Maeve would sit outside the door when he left for the asylum, singing to me in French. Lulling me to sleep as I curled against the crack beneath the door.

But now, I see no one. All must be down in the kitchens or stables.

The only entrance to the attic is on the servants' side. I reach up to tug the concealed ceiling square, and it creaks down as I cringe and wait again.

When no soul arrives, I hurry up the stairs.

I've just managed to light the lantern when voices filter up the steps.

I lurch forward and pull the rope ladder up, shutting myself in the musty attic. I press my finger beneath my nose, staving off a sneeze, breathing through my mouth till my eyes water.

Scanning the dark with the lantern, I quickly find my target. I reach the steamer trunk, place the lantern on the floor, and heave it open.

Mother's jewelry. Her dresses spill out onto the dirty floor.

I pull one to my face and inhale. Tears fill my eyes. I was so small when she passed.

I do not see her, really, but *feel* her. Feel her arms about me. Cradling me, crooning in my ear.

I shuffle the dusty dresses aside till I see it—the only portrait of her left in the manor, at the bottom of this dusty trunk.

I slide it out and prop it up, holding the lantern aloft. My fingers fumble as I remove the sketch from my pocket, tearing the corner in my haste.

All the breath has vacated my lungs.

I hold them side by side, and I collapse to my knees.

"Jules, are you up there?"

I hastily wipe the tears from my eyes. "Yes, I'm coming."

CHAPTER NINE

Frost's fingers grip my cheeks, turning my head side to side, black eyes examining my bruises.

"Now, look at the damage you have done." He releases my face with a snort of disgust. "It seems you have fooled Dr. Grayjoy, Twenty-Nine, but I have a question for you. Do not lie."

For all my life, Frost has ruled this asylum with fear and pain and some would even say death. It was as if the board were under the spell of his charm, which he could flare and extinguish at will, like a guttering candle of personality. Of late, his spell is fading. There are rumors of a new physick to take his place. But still no one challenges him, allowing him free reign over every ward—his word is carried out above all others.

"I have a question for you. Do not lie. You know I detest falsity."

At the very words, my legs quiver beneath my skirts—thinking of the dunk tank, the leeches, the crème of tartar. I vomited it for weeks.

I nod.

"Do you still wish to escape?"

"I was not trying to escape, Dr. Frost."

His dark glare scrutinizes me. "I do not believe you. Convince me otherwise."

"You may deem me mad, but I am no imbecile. I understand I have no means by which to care for myself even if I should escape. I would end up a street harlot or in St. James's graveyard. I know I must adhere to the proper discharge procedures."

Your proper games. You monster.

"'Tis too true. And very cognizant of you to be so realistic. There may yet be help for you."

At his mild words, a ray of sunshine spikes in my heart, and I hold my breath. Perhaps my punishment shall not be so very terrible—

"I must, naturally, however, make an example of you. No matter what Grayjoy says. You will always be under my care, Twenty-Nine. No matter what ward I am assigned to. No matter where you are."

The vision of sunlight fades as dark thunderclouds roll in. Fear ices my heart, pumping a cold, violent stream to weaken my legs. I bite my lip to hold back the whimper.

"If I do not, others shall think running through the corridors at night is acceptable behavior. In mere moments, we could have a riot. Your beloved savior Grayjoy has not yet experienced such chaos."

"I do not think anyone else saw me, sir. I am very sorry. I—"

"I am afraid you 'do not think' is not sufficient. Word travels fast here, as you are well aware. I daresay your little escapade has reached the whole way to Ward Thirteen by now."

As if anyone in Thirteen would understand.

I hear my breath, rattling faster and faster, awaiting his decree like the *whoosh* of a guillotine.

Frost rings a bell, and Alexander and another bulky orderly appear as if by some detestable asylum magic. Frost nods, and they flank me, restraining my arms.

"Solitary. One day."

A wail escapes. "No. *Please*, Dr. Frost, please."

He makes a show of removing his white gloves, digit by digit. "Make it two."

I wail again but do not protest further. I hang limp, like a flower wilted, refusing to walk, and my feet drag behind, creating a terrible scratching sound as they haul me down the corridor.

"This is blooming crazy, Alex. Hold 'er here. I'll be right back."

The surroundings fade as my mind begins to recoil from reality. All in my sight dims as I begin the lonely crawl to the corners of my mind. Prepared to huddle, to survive.

A hibernation from life's cruelties.

In a moment, I feel the cold metal of the gurney against my back and the straps as they're yanked tight across my ankles and wrists.

I am gone now. Humming middle C, over and over and over. Its colored blips coming and going like red stars in a sea of blackness.

I long for laudanum. If it were here, I would crush the poppy seeds, swallow them whole. Anything to find the numbness.

We reach Ward Thirteen, where the padded cells line the halls like a soundproof purgatory. For all I know, it will be the scalpel. The ablation. The death of my person, my soul, my mind.

The feel of the rough material resurrects my mind from where it cowers in a dark recess.

The straitjacket.

A guttural growl escapes my throat.

I scream and flail, kicking out at every angle. I feel my foot connect with Alexander's jaw and hear the *snap* as his teeth grind together.

"Shove 'er arms in, *now!*" His voice is livid.

"No. No!"

My senses heighten. *The smell of urine, the scratch of the fabric, the clang of a cage slamming.* Panic swells, filling my brain.

I thrash, gnashing my teeth, and growl. "No, *pleease.* Help me, please!"

Tears cut hot tracks down my cheeks. I am hoisted, the vest restraining my arms in a crisscross, tied behind my back.

"I have an idea. She likes this one, she does."

The other orderly laughs. "What's that?"

They swing me, one grasping my arms, the other my ankles, at the entrance.

"One." *Swing.* "Two." *Swing.* "Three."

Weightlessness. I am airborne for a very long moment and then *crash* to the padded floor, my breath rushing out like a bellows. My head collides face down on the floor, my nose instantly gushing blood.

Because of the jacket, I cannot stay the flow. I am trapped, face down in my own blood.

I find the presence of mind to rock my legs and to roll.

In time to hear the click of the lock.

I lay still, trying to place myself elsewhere. *Anywhere.*

When I was ten ... they *forgot* me here. The panic swells.

I nearly starved to death.

Nurse Ginny eyes me warily. "You are certain Dr. Frost instructed you to be here, on this ward, Jules?"

Her black eyes search the nursing roster of Ward Three, the convalescent ward. Arguably the easiest ward in Soothing Hills. The patients are primarily older gents in wheeled chairs, many easing their way in to senility as their families steal their fortunes—but many sharp as tacks, their wits intact in stark contrast with their bodies' deterioration. It is also the tuberculosis ward—and I am risking my life—but there is no chance of seeing Father here. He leaves this ward to the other physicks.

I nod fervently. "Oh, yes. He said I should be exposed to all the wards. To see where I might best fit."

Her eyebrow rises, so I add, "To be the most help. I know there have been staff cuts."

"More likely no one daft enough to work here, with a bloody killer on the loose," she mumbles.

"What?"

"Nothing."

"The asylum must be cutting costs wherever possible. I mean, look at these uniforms. They're dreadful."

Ginny's only reply is a scathing look, and I bite my lip in embarrassment.

"I am sorry. I never have been good at controlling my tongue."

She scans the airy, open room, the residents packed like elderly silver-headed sardines. "Very well. You best bridle it here. Insubordination is not tolerated. I am never in want of staff, to be sure. I primarily work here and on Ward One. You know ... I feel as if I have seen you before. You are certain we've never met, perhaps outside the asylum? Something about your face is familiar."

"No. I'm quite certain."

I notice the white circle around her left ring finger. She once wore a wedding band. I stare at her. Young and pretty. Vibrant auburn spirals against the pale skin of her neck. She currently wrinkles her nose at a particularly pungent tincture, and the smattering of freckles ripple in time.

She is like a light in this dark place.

Nurse Ginny riffles through no less than six clipboards before she finally decides upon my assignment.

Father is somewhere in the asylum. But I know for certain he is *never* on the convalescent ward. He views it as no challenge. I shall have to avoid running into him, as it is decidedly not my scheduled day. Nor was the day before, or the day before that. I stifle a smile.

Willis shall be calling on me at five. If I am not yet returned, I have Maeve presenting him with an alibi.

I must return to Twenty-Nine's room. I must see if there are other sketches. Sketches of the woman who, at least from the back, looks eerily like my mother. I cannot be certain. I was only six when she passed.

"The laundry. Take the patients' bedding and soiled clothing over. Help out if needed and bring them back when complete."

I nod and follow the direction of her outstretched finger toward a massive, wheeled laundry cart. The stench is overpowering, and my eyes begin to water whilst I am still ten steps away.

I smile. Another deterrent from people examining me too closely. *Perfect.*

I hold my breath and heave the cart to rolling, and the orderlies throw the massive metal bolt to open the doors. They swing wide to permit my exit. I keep my eyes downcast.

I have donned a pair of my lady's maid's old spectacles and wrapped my hair tightly beneath the nursing cap to avoid further detection.

The halls are dead quiet, the only sound the squeaking of the cart's wheels.

In my mind, I shift through the puzzle pieces of this mystery.

The music I hear—though this is not new; it has been present since my childhood. The words buried within the compositions. Maeve's admonitions to never, *ever* breathe a word of it to Father.

I hear them in the corn around my house. Only from what I have deemed *the corn music.*

The *eyes* in Dr. Grayjoy's study. Nearly identical to my own.

And the strange picture, of a woman who is possibly my mother. And the other girl by her side. I am an only child. *Who could she be?*

It makes not a whit of sense. None of it.

I grind my teeth together and murmur, "I *shall* make sense of it."

If there are two subjects at which I excel, it is music and riddles.

GrayJoy

Frost shoves the papers under Gentile's bespectacled nose for the third time.

"*I am telling you*, the procedure was a success."

Frost's eyes have the familiar manic gleam—in such a state, he is nearly impossible to derail, perseverating on whatever topic festers in his mind, intent on convincing his audience.

"I remain unconvinced." Gentile's voice is low. I recognize the tone—it is the same he uses with patients on a knife's edge, ready to slice free.

Frost paces. "*Philistines*. The lot of you. I shall be the one to live in infamy—once my findings are published—neither of you shall have a say. I shall decide which patient is in need of ablation."

Gooseflesh erupts down my neck, and I fight to hold his gaze. He is like an animal. To keep his respect, and his ferocity at bay, one must show no fear.

I bristle. "You do realize, Frost, my degree is from Harvard. And before that, Oxford?"

Gentile's bleary eyes widen, and we exchange a silent conversation. "*Mistake,*" his gaze all but screams.

Frost whirls, teeth bared. "Oh, beg pardon, Dr. High and

Mighty, Lord of the Manor and apparently of Soothing Hills. You were wetting your nappies when I was giving injections. You—"

Gentile placates, "No one is doubting your abilities, Isaiah. We just think you may be embracing procedures too quickly, without even research—"

"Dr. Frost?"

Nurse Sally pokes her head round the door, and Frost stiffens. He cocks his head to stare at her.

"One of your patients is in need of your ministrations."

Frost straightens, tugs his waistcoat, and stalks off.

I wait until I am certain he is out of earshot and then slump before Gentile, letting my hand drag down the length of my face. It drops to my lap, and I stare at my mentor.

"I know," is all he manages.

JULES

Passing through the halls of Soothing Hills is like a journey through the levels of insanity.

It is simply arranged, with the ever-higher numbers corresponding with the levels of madness.

Ward One, for those about to be reintroduced into society. A trial for their stability—to assume their would-be professions, if able, before being let loose into the oft-confusing world.

Ward Three, the convalescents. The mysterious tuberculosis. I have overhead many an argument with nurse and physick alike, from, "It is rarely contagious," to, "One should not even breathe the same air." Often, lifers to the asylum are placed here. Family cast-offs and even an occasional nobility. Tuberculosis does not see class.

On Ward Four, the moderately impaired. Where one moment the patient may seem right, his mind pure as the snow outside, and then with the wrong word—a raving, whirling lunatic. This is my destination, where Patient Twenty-Nine is housed.

My eyes skip down the corridor to the higher numbered wards, where even the *air* seems caustic. As if the tunnel itself holds its breath against the patient's screams.

Thirteen. No hope of return. It is also the place for medical experiments. I have witnessed only a few ... but there are whispers of horrors.

A procedure called ablation—for the violent.

The resulting creatures are docile, but no remnant of their personality remains. They are walking, eating, existing zombies. Nothing more.

I shudder and push the cart faster.

I reach Ward Four and knock. *Please do not be Nurse Sally.*

My heart trips out a staccato rhythm, and I force myself to breathe. *One in, one out.*

The sound of the bolt thrown in the lock.

I blink. The door swings wide to reveal a leering orderly, his name badge proclaiming him *Alexander*. It is the monster from the incident with the older woman and the straitjacket.

"Alright, then." He cocks his head, his eyes narrowing. He catches a whiff of the laundry stench and takes a step back. "You must be new ... "

"Daphne," I say, lowering my voice. I give a little limp as I go. The less accurately he remembers me, the better. "I am a laundress."

He wipes his eyes from the stench, gesturing to the rooms. "Have at it, then. All the loons have presently flown the coop."

Anger flushes my face. "Sorry?"

But he is already sauntering away. "They's all in the airing yard."

My cart is divided with clean linens, and an empty bin for the dirty.

I pull out a laundered, fresh sheet and spread it across Ward Four's laundry. I will still need to be effective, snooping or no. I separate the ward's dirty cast-offs and set quickly, room to room, clearing beds and bins.

Finally, I reach the room. Twenty-Nine.

I step inside, whirling about, my eyes darting here and there, trying to take in every inch of the sketch-littered walls.

It is breathtaking. This mind, no matter how ill, is capable of much beauty.

Winter scenes dominate the room. The asylum—black spires, white snowflakes, and drifts, undoubtedly a view from another window. Couples skating. Couples and children sledding. Sleigh rides pulled by massive white horses adorned with red and white bows slung about their snow-dusted manes.

Visions of what must be the asylum gardens in bloom. Walkways borne of seasons: daffodils in spring; brilliant yellow, orange, and maroon mums in fall; and blood-red poinsettias to cheer the dead of winter.

I spy a section, closest to the cot, where the drawings are more childlike. Children around a woman with an open book.

Tears spring to my eyes. *How long has Twenty-Nine been here?*

"*Meow.*"

My eyes flash to the window, heart in my mouth. A very large tabby cat sits on the sill, head cocked, tail swishing madly. "A cat? Here?"

It leaps, padding across the floor to entwine in my skirts. I bend down to pet its head.

"*Hisssssss.*" Gray ears go flat, back arching. A low, threatening growl escapes its throat.

"Here, kitty-kitty."

It flies to the sill, wriggling out the cracked open window.

"Odd." But what about Soothing Hills is normal?

My eyes return to the childlike drawings.

Twenty-Nine has been here a very, very long time.

I see the set of paintings and hurry over. The woman's form is vague. But I squint, looking beside the woman with the children. Beside her is ... *sheet music.*

I step forward, my heart seeming to vacate my chest, lodging in my throat.

"You best be hurrying, little bird. The crazies will return soon." The leering orderly has returned.

I shove the glasses up my nose and pick up the day dress on the floor. "Twenty-Nine doesn't like people viewing her art?"

He laughs. "Twenty-Nine is where she belongs. In solitary."

CHAPTER TEN

*T*he walls.

I shall never forget the walls of this room. I lie on my back, my stocking-clad feet tracing the padded edges, over and over. The walls have gone, but in their stead, a black, mind-numbing gloom, thick as spiderwebs, spreading, spreading from my brain to my soul.

I may not make it back this time.

My mind flashes images, and I wince.

Ten-year-old me, hands splayed—at first on the walls, then writhing on my belly as the hunger pangs ripped through my guts. To starve is a horrible, painful way to pass.

My mind wandered when I was near death.

Memories seemed dislodged, as if a long-forgotten, long-banished part of my past resurrected for a final good-bye.

I saw my mother plainly for the first time. More than her face, I heard her music. She taught me to hum middle C.

I suddenly remember it was she who discovered the feeling it produced for me. Her ghost-memory floats over me now, humming it over and over, swaddling me in comfort—as she did when I had a fever.

My heart thuds like a kettledrum with realization. *I once had a home outside of Soothing Hills.*

I must have a fever once again. It is the only time I see her clearly.

My tears scald a track from the corner of my eye to my mouth, and I taste the salt. Delirium. I have delirium.

Extended isolation ... picks one apart. Like invisible rooks, their veins full of lonely, *peck-peck-peck*, eating bits of my mind.

It has been my most irrational fear since the first incident.

Every minute, every hour, every second—*tick, tick, ticking*—*pick, pick, picking*. Panic rages as the feeling intensifies, as if an entire unkindness of ravens feasts upon my sanity.

I hear a familiar squeaky sound and roll toward the door. "Twenty?"

The squeaking stops, and I see gnarled hands grasping wheels, angling it toward my cell door. "Twenty-nine? Are you in there, my girl?" She bends to look through the food slot.

I sob but try to control my voice. "Yes, I'm here."

"I knew when you weren't in your room for dinner, something had happened. I used my pass to come and find you."

I squeeze my lips and eyes tight to stifle my sob. Patients are granted passes for good behavior. Twenty not only used one of those coveted pieces of paper, she no doubt wheeled herself through each floor she was permitted, searching for me. My heart swells with gratitude.

"Thank you, but I don't know what you might do. I am here till himself says I am free."

Twenty knows of my fear of isolation. And there is no need to explain *himself.* He was her physick as well.

Her quavering voice takes on a steely edge. "We shall see about that. Hold fast, dear one."

The squeaking resumes, and I am once again … alone.

"Jane?"

I blink. I must've passed out. The last I remember, Twenty had found me.

Now the wretched fever is causing hallucinations. Voices. I giggle uncontrollably.

"Why not? I hear them in music. Crazy, crazy, crazy Jane." I giggle harder.

The sound is mad. It sounds like Ward Thirteen.

"*Jane!*" My imagination becomes more insistent.

I blink hard, trying to force the focus back into my eyes.

"Over by the door."

Solitary confinement has no window, not even in the iron door. A peephole is above so that the physicks may monitor me.

Monitor me doing what? Rolling about on the ground like a serpent?

The only contact with the outside world is through a revolving tray at the door's bottom, where food might be placed and spun into the room.

I roll toward it and *whuump* to a halt, my face staring at the door. A hand reaches through, searching.

"Jane. It's Mason."

I feel the hysteria bubble and rise. Relief, but mixed with fear of the no-longer-tethered horror breaking forth. My breath shudders out in hard, choked sobs, as if my tight throat suppresses the air.

The world wavers in and out like the heat on a summer's day.

"Shh. Shh," he croons, the whispered phrases drenched in his heavy accent. "Twenty sent me. Give me your hand, girl."

"I cannot."

"What? Why?"

"The jacket."

A beat of silence and a string of profanities in Gaelic. His voice is gruff as he growls, "Yes, you are so bloody dangerous, you need the jacket. In solitary. I would like to strangle them with me bare hands."

"*No.* Then you will be here, too. People disappear here. Not just patients."

"Stay put. I will be right back."

It is true. I remember when I was about eight, there was a very sweet nurse who took a shining to me. She began to ask me questions. Lots of questions.

What did I remember? What was my name? How I learned to read so very well.

In a day, she was gone. Vanished. They told me she quit … *but I know better.* I had dreams of her shuffling on Ward Thirteen, then into the corn. Following those ruddy birds.

I lay my head on the ground and must doze off, because his voice is the first thing I recall.

"Jane, roll your back toward me. Wiggle left now ... Perfect."

I feel his hands grip mine, and I gyrate with ... a sawing motion?

"Lie still, I don't want to slip and cut you. Then they will say you are trying to off yourself and keep you here longer."

My hands pop free, and I sob, in relief this time. For some lost moments, I am rocking and weeping, my arms wrapped round my knees as I wait for the pins-and-needle sensation to subside.

"Jane. Jane. Are you alright? Come take me hand girl."

The blackness recedes slowly, like an oppressive mist gradually lifting.

I finally scoot toward the opening and grasp his outstretched hand. It is like a warm life preserver in this cold pit of despair. Forcing me to cling to hope.

"Talk to me, Jane."

I am quiet. I cannot speak, as so often happens when the world inside these walls becomes too great to bear. I am told I was silent for a year.

"Shall I talk to you, then?"

Mason indeed talks. The words flow in his rich, deep Scottish tones, the pitch and pace of his intonations washing over me like a deep, cleansing river.

Telling me of his childhood. Of his rich, titled childhood. Of his headstrong, arrogant father, his wicked brother.

"I knew you weren't common," I whisper, but then fall silent and allow him to continue.

He tells me of his father's death and his subsequent

disinheritance once the estate passed to his brother.

"I am the second son. So my brother holds the fortune, the estate. Everything."

I finally find my voice. "Whyever are you here, Mason? I know naught of the world, to be sure. But there are other, decidedly less awful ways to earn one's coin. I would think you fit for a barrister, or an officer?"

He hesitates. "Do you trust me?" Then, in a rush, "I know that question to be ludicrous. You scarcely know me. But when first I saw you—you were in the airing yard, alone. The one on top of the building. Sketching the trees. And then when I saw you play the other night, heard your music, I ... watched you. You looked at the music one time, and you played it perfectly. I overheard Grayjoy talking, saying it was a test. That you and the other girls had never laid eyes upon that piece before that moment. The other girls played well enough, but their eyes still tracked the music. Not you. It seemed you memorized it. He says you show great musical prowess. A virtuoso."

"You are musical?"

He clears his throat. "After a fashion. I read notes, I carry a tune, I play an instrument. But I am more of a lyricist. Words are my siren."

"Words? Tell me some of your lyrics."

He laughs and is quiet, but I wait, biting my lip, happy for the wall between us so he might not see my anxious expression.

"I am not used to people *wanting* to hear them. My father considered it a lark. Thought I should concern myself with more serious pursuits."

"I love *all* to do with music. Please. Tell me some."

"Nefelibata."

"What? Whatever is the meaning of that word?"

"It means 'a cloud-walker.' One who lives in the clouds, or their imagination, and defies convention. It is the very essence of you, Jane."

Tears fill my eyes. "I am afraid I *am* a nefelibata. But if I ever wish to leave here, I am told I must learn to control these tendencies."

Mason's voice is quiet. "I … don't think so. I have been here six months. I've … observed you. Jane, you are saner than many I have met outside these walls. Nefelibata is a gift. A protection for your mind."

I bite my lip. "It is, I suppose." The ghost of a smile haunts my lips. "I do like this game … tell me another."

The intonation of his voice shines like a lantern, driving back the darkness of the melancholy. If I close my eyes and only listen to it, I can almost pretend I am sitting in a parlor with him, holding a teacup.

His whisper is tentative. "I don't imagine you played many games as a child."

Pain shoots through my nose, and I pinch the bridge. "No. But I used to pretend … when I was alone. I … made my own toys."

"Alright. We shall make up for it now. We'll play games till your heart is filled." He is silent for some moments, thinking. "Numinous."

"What does it mean?" I wrap my arms about my knees and keep my eyes closed, focusing solely on the warm timbre of his voice.

"It means fearful … yet fascinated. Awed … but attracted." His breathing is the only sound filling the void. "For me, it means *you*, Jane."

"Fearful? I frighten you?"

"When first I came, everything at Soothing Hills scared me. I had never been around any illness in my privileged, sheltered life. I knew not what to think of the residents."

"What think you now?"

His voice is grave. "They are merely people. Downtrodden, unfortunate people, who could use a friend." After some moments of quiet, he adds, "The forgotten."

We are silent yet again, the words hanging in the air of my solitary confinement chamber, lingering like the ghosts of residents before me who had passed the endless hours in this dismal place.

Our fingers lace together through the space in the door.

His thumb traces circles on the back of my hand. "I … have secrets, *mo cridhe*. I would not divulge them to you, lest you be put in more danger. You have been to Ward One. That means you are being considered for discharge. Able to leave here."

Silent tears leak again, and I am happy he cannot see my face.

I force the tremble from my voice. "I fervently wish … and *fear* that day. This place is all I have ever known. I would not know how to live, out there. I need to learn. And Ward One is where such teaching takes place."

"*I* will teach you. I will not leave you alone. I give you my word."

My mind and heart seem to spasm and ache—for a future unconsidered. Unobtainable to the likes of me. I never considered myself fainthearted, but the very notion of any such arrangement is stealing my breath away.

To love …

To love such as I believe he is proposing, should I choose to try, will be the most dangerous undertaking of my life.

With love, you give power to others. The power to hurt you.

"I am frightened." My voice breaks on the word.

His grip tightens. "As am I. We shall be frightened together."

Together. My lips wrap around the word like a promise. Never have I had *together*, with any soul.

"That is even more terrifying."

He doesn't speak. I almost hear him holding his breath.

"But … I want that. I want *together*."

"Then you shall have it." The smile is plain in his voice. "Now, you should sleep. We need to get you out of solitary. I could steal the key, but that would do naught but get me dismissed and you, most likely, more solitary. We must play their game, Jane. At least for the present. I will let you know if the time comes to renege, if I feel we cannot win. If I cannot release you properly … then rules will be broken."

I wrap my free arm around myself in the dark and slide closer to the slot—my other gripping his hand, curling it to my chest.

He begins to hum, a beautiful tune.

"You are a tenor. The C one octave below middle C."

The smile-voice again. "That is correct." And he hums again.

My mind slips, riding the notes in my mind. Some red, some blue, but all warm. The curtain of consciousness closes, and I sigh in relief.

JULES

I head to the laundry and proceed to tend to my duties. It is, quite possibly, the longest six hours of my life. Finally, when I return to Ward Three, Ginny grants me leave to depart. I explain I relieved Miss Frost, as she had to leave unexpectedly. Ginny barely spares me a glance as a horde of patients descends upon her medicinal cart.

Ginny slides a sweat-drenched lock from her forehead and tucks it behind her ear. "You are welcome to work this ward anytime. I always can use an able-bodied, no-nonsense woman. Pray, what is your name again?"

I hope the wig I've donned is still intact. I keep my fingers from tracing the nameplate I found in the laundry room. "Alice."

If I am ever to have answers from this place, I must move with anonymity. Not as Dr. Frost's over-monitored daughter.

Nurse Ginny's perceptive eyes flick to the nameplate, then back to my face. "Alright, *Alice*. You best be off. Carriages depart the asylum every hour till eleven. If you miss the last one … it is two long, dark miles to the entry gate. I do not recommend walking it, especially at night. We have had few break-outs, but one can never be too careful of who or what one might run into."

I wonder at her tone, if it be earnest or sarcastic.

Regardless, I give an involuntary shudder. "Yes, I will be sure to catch it."

My stomach clenches as I catch the time on the clock face. One hour.

The asylum is vast. Over nine hundred employees, let alone the residents. Its gargantuan nature will allow me to slip around unnoticed, once Alice becomes accepted for her person and position.

I quicken my pace. To make it to the main entrance on time shall take a quarter hour to be sure.

Then there is the risk of meeting Father. I know the wards he is to work, but he may be anywhere within these walls. I wonder if he would recognize me, disguise and all.

He is often here overnight when his duties call.

I hope and pray he *is* here, because I am entirely, completely past my curfew, and he does not have me on the schedule to work this day. If he returns home and I am not present, he shall be frantic. Might even go so far as to contact the constable.

Maeve will cover for me as she can, but he will only be dissuaded so long.

Earlier, I saw Patient Twenty-Nine's file on Dr. Grayjoy's desk.

My mind flashes to the music in the sketch upon her wall. I was interrupted, unable to have a proper look. The woman resembles my mother in a large way, but the way the woman is angled, so that one sees her side profile, I cannot say for certain.

At this rate, I am *not* going to make it to the office and back to catch the final carriage.

I force my shoulders back and inhale deeply, trying to fill my lungs with much-needed courage. The old man, he told me about the entrance to the tunnels. I will bet my life there is one on every ward.

Shuffle-shuffle step. *Shuffle-shuffle* step.

Someone approaches. I hear them, just around the corner. Ready to turn the corner.

Hide. You must hide, you fool. But there is nowhere.

I am near the ward kitchen. I smell the baking bread. I whirl, flying toward it. I enter and, out the window, see I am near the cornfield.

Shuffle-shuffle-shuffle-shuffle.

He or she is running.

A cold sweat breaks down my back, and I enter the kitchen proper and drop to all fours, scuttling across the floor, weaving out of the way of the staff voices. They are in a nearby room— the clink of bowls and cups tells me they're loading the carts for washing.

My heart thuds so hard and fast, I fight the swoon. Blackness around the edges of my sight. I search furiously, looking all about the kitchen.

"Think, think, Jules."

And I see my salvation. A dumbwaiter.

I scramble to my feet in time to hear the creak of the door opening behind me. I hurry inside and jam down the door. *I slid it down before he saw.* Please *let me have slid it down before he saw.*

It *is* a he; I smell his cologne. It's pungent and somehow sickly.

I sit still as the stone- gargoyle sentinels that keep watch on the asylum roof, pressing my hand over my mouth to control my breathing. My heart beats so hard I only hear its sloshing in my ears.

Breathing. Ragged breathing.

Right outside the dumbwaiter.

I bite down hard on my lower lip, stoppering the low moan before it leaks out. Blackness threatens, and I shake my head. *Do not swoon. Do not swoon.*

Too-long fingernails touch the metal door, scratching the length of it.

I am done for.

Music. *Oh, my word,* orchestral music, from the corn.

The fingernails pull away, distracted.

And I hear it. My heart skips two beats, and my breath breaks through my hands, my chest heaving.

Words. The words embedded in the music say—"Run. Run, *Jules.*"

I lurch forward and yank the rope, and the dumbwaiter plummets downward. It strikes the bottom of the shaft, jarring my teeth together. I flail sideways and fling open the sliding metal door, roll out and heave it shut, but not before I hear the door at the top of the shaft creak open.

I *run.*

I forget Grayjoy, I forget Twenty-Nine, and I run directly for the entrance.

To escape the monster that roams the halls of Soothing Hills Sanatorium.

CHAPTER ELEVEN

I see him. The shuffling monster, silhouetted in one of the top-most windows.

The birds. The birds sit outside my window, peck-peck-pecking. *One opens its pointy black beak, and my name harmonizes with its caw.*

I sit straight up, eyes darting, chest heaving. I press my hand against my sweat-soaked shift. I whimper over and over, my eyes darting to the window.

Nothing.

Slowly, too slowly, reality seeps back into my mind. I close my eyes, trying to remember.

My canopy bed. I am home. It was a dream—but it was not.

"Easy, Jules, you half-wit," I breathe, worrying I am now talking to myself. As if Soothing Hills is somehow leaving an indelible imprint on my soul.

It was a *memory*. I *did* see him as I alighted into the very last carriage, and then shrank back tight against the seat, away from the window, staying that way till we rattled down the lane.

I stare out my window at the yellow glaze upon the horizon. It is nearly dawn.

"*Ma colombe.*" Maeve enters my room, shutting the door behind her with a quiet click. Anxiety twists my gut. Something must be awry—she is up early, even for her.

She swiftly crosses my room to sit on the edge of my bed. Her dark eyes are pinched with anger. "Where *were* you? If your father would have been home, and I'd lied for you—he would dismiss me. You know that to be true. *Ma colombe*, your days here are numbered, you must behave until then—"

A foreign rage overtakes me. I am ever good. Ever proper. Forever doing as I am told.

"I am tired of being his puppet."

My tongue traces the bite marks in my lower lip.

Her eyes narrow. "What options have you? Speaking of your options, Willis showed up last night and was quite put upon that you were not here when you promised you would be. Willis will have a breaking point as well and eventually mention these absences to your father."

My hands go clammy with fear that I shall be banished from the asylum. There are mysteries there I must solve. I feel as if I shall never be whole until I do.

Another memory hits. The corn knows my name.

"What is it, Jules? Your face is bone-white."

I chew my lip, wincing at the pain, and mutter, "It is nothing.

I have overextended myself." I smooth my nightgown. "I shall behave, Maeve. Send word to Willis that I shall see him on this very eve—and I swear on my honor I shall."

Her soft hand strokes my hair, my dark curls a contrast against her alabaster skin. "That is my good girl."

Something in her tone bades me look at her. "What?"

Maeve blanches, her expression pinched. "I … have found something. I am unsure if it is wise to give it to you."

"Whatever are you talking about?"

"The other day, when you were in the attic … I went up later to see what you were up to. I found the trunk, your mama's dresses." Her black eyes fill. "You know I loved your mama. She was my very best friend. The classes between us"—she waves her hand theatrically—"made no difference. We were like zis." She crosses her long, delicate fingers.

I smile. "Yes, I know."

She reaches into her pocket and then holds her closed fist before me.

My mouth goes dry. "What is it?"

Her long fingers open.

"A locket?" My hands fly to trace my own. It is identical. Silver. Heart-shaped.

"Why would she buy two lockets? Did you ever see her wear it?"

Maeve's face drains whiter still. "No. I never saw her wear it." She abruptly stands, walking across the room. "I have much to do. Keep it safe."

I sit, staring at the heart, trying to fathom why my mother bought identical lockets. And wondering why I need to keep it safe.

"Get her up."

Frost. My heart pounds as fear shudders through my veins, shaking me awake.

I blink repeatedly, the solitary walls blurring into focus. Sometime during the night, after I had fallen asleep, Mason must have departed. I roll onto my back and scoot backward toward the wall.

"I said, get her up, Grayjoy."

The young physick strides forward and stoops beside me, pulling my torso away from the wall. His hands reach behind my back and stop, registering my freed hands.

Our eyes meet, and I hold my breath.

"Dr. Frost, I need your signature." Alexander stands at the door, clipboard in hand.

I plead with my eyes, staring up into Grayjoy's handsome face.

His lips press tight together, and he hauls me to stand, fingers flying, releasing me from the jacket.

Frost whirls, his eyebrow cocked. "*Did I say* to release her from the restraint?"

Grayjoy folds the jacket in two, effectively hiding the cut straps.

"I did not like the color of her hands. I read in a journal the other day that with certain patients, blood flow might be compromised. The patients whose fingertips are consistently cold to the touch and tinged purple. That is Twenty-Nine."

He is right. The man's wits are lightning-quick.

Frost's eyebrows pull down. "Hmm."

He walks forward, and I instinctively take a step backward toward Grayjoy.

He examines my cheeks again, his hot fingers turning my cheek to and fro.

"The bruises should be healed by next week. I decided to believe you. That your roommate had assistance. Perhaps she was planning to escape—and her accomplice turned on her."

I curtsy. "Thank you, sir."

"When you are well, we shall try the Ward One Trio once again. It will be just in time for the next fundraiser." He heads for the door, murmuring, "Of course, after those bruises heal."

"Capital, Dr. Frost. I feel Jane displays excellent potential for success."

He uses my name. Not my number. I see from Frost's expression this is not lost on him.

As we turn to go, Frost halts me, grabbing my elbow to lean in close. "I have a favor in exchange for Ward One, Twenty-Nine. I shall come to speak to you in confidence when the time is right."

Chills lick my neck. Something in the tone of his voice …

The need to leave, a survival instinct, rears its head within my chest.

I must find a way out, Ward One or no. The time has come.

"When I stopped by the other eve, you were out. I'll admit, I was sorely disappointed." Willis's pinched face looks truly despondent, and I sigh.

"I am sorry. But I am here now. What shall we do tonight?"

Willis crosses his long legs, which reminds me of a man-sized cricket.

"Why don't you play for me? I do love to watch your fingers trailing across the pianoforte."

I smile. This request I am always happy to indulge. I sit and flinch as he stands behind me, leaning over. Tentatively, he places his fingers over mine on the keyboard.

"Let me remain for just a refrain. I do wish I had any musical ability. But, alas, tone-deaf as they come."

I begin to play Mozart, a piano concerto in D, and his fingers tag along.

He releases me, realizing he slows my pace, and comes to sit beside me on the piano bench.

I feel a twinge of guilt as I glance at his smiling face. He is a good man. A sweet man. And I do not love him. He deserves to be loved.

"How is the nursing work progressing?" Father enters the room, beaming, as he always does when I play.

I see the set of his mouth, the light in his eyes. He is *Good Papa* this day. I will have no troubles from him. In fact, if I have anything unpleasant to discuss, I must seize upon his countenance.

I cease to play. The music brings Mother back into the house. When she lived, the house was filled with music, light, and parties. And Father was almost always Good Papa.

Not that I did not hear the screaming matches—they tried to conceal them, but I am too astute. He changed when she died, his horrid half rising to take command over his better self.

"The nursing is an education, Father. One in direct contrast to my Latin, music, and history studies. It is an education of the world, of what lies outside class and privilege, and I am better for seeing it."

"Here, here." Willis does a little stage clap, and I blush.

Father's eyes are indiscernible. "Yes. I can see how you could benefit from it. Tell me, when will you have arrangements ready to play for our ensemble once again? There is another gathering in a fortnight, and the physicks requested an encore."

I smile. "I shall be glad to prepare for it."

I suffer through dining with Willis and Father, every few seconds glancing at the grandfather clock, whose hands seem stuck with the treacle tart on the table, by the rate they crawl around its face.

Finally, I am at the vestibule, bidding Willis goodnight.

He leans in to kiss me. I turn my lips at the last moment, and it plants upon my cheek. He pulls back, his eyes shining with frustration. I throw my arms about him and give him a tight, brotherly hug. "I shall see you soon."

He tips his hat and is gone in a flash.

I shut the door behind me and lean against it, closing my eyes.

I sense a presence in the vestibule. *Please not Father, I cannot bear one of his lectures on how to better myself.*

"Jules." It is Maeve.

I open my eyes, and her expression is pinched. "I have something to tell you, but *c'est notre secret, ma belle.*"

I lower my voice. "What secret?"

She glances up the stairs, then pulls me into the parlor to sit on the chaise.

"I wanted to wait till you were old enough, so do not be cross wiss me." Her French accent increases twofold as it does in times of stress.

My boot taps in dread and anticipation.

"I know where you may find more of your mama's personal effects. They ... are hidden away."

CHAPTER TWELVE

"Jane, Jane, where are you?"

"Huh?"

I turn away from the window, where the dogs frolic in the courtyard. Biting, chasing and sliding in the new snowfall.

The past few days have flown by—I have not seen Mason since our deep discussion in solitary. Truth be told, I am afraid I was too bold and frightened him away with my honesty.

Nurse Ginny sits across from me.

"Where is your mind today? Jane, it is no secret you play well." She cocks her red head. "That is a gross understatement. I will wager you are a virtuoso."

My face flushes as I think of paper upon paper of symphonies, hidden in my room beneath my floorboards. But we are here to make me useful, so that I may someday depart these walls.

I hear her voice. "Perhaps a governess? I think … "

But no position in the world can compare to music. It is what has kept me alive and as close to sane as I might manage.

Frost detests hearing about composition. Indeed, when he was my personal physick, too many times to count, he would rage on: "The *gift*, as you call it, is quite impossible Jane. These *supposed* words imbedded in the music. They are a hallucination. Your fractured mind cannot discern reality from fantasy—and thus, this frailty impedes you. Keeps you alienated from polite society."

When I was young and hopeful, I tried in vain to convince him.

For a short period of time, he entertained the thought, having scores and scores of music played for me. Musicians parading in and out of the wing at his whim.

I tried to explain it is only *certain* music in which I hear the messages. Precious, precious few times in my life.

"It is a disassociation. An *ab-nor-mality*, nothing more. Your mind *creates* the messages, the voice, the color of the notes, Jane. *Not* the music."

I grind my teeth at the thought and square my shoulders. *I am not mad.*

Sheltered? *Yes.*

Abused? *Much.*

A mind that has seen too much torture? Irredeemable? *Perhaps.*

But I *hear* the words in the music, as sure as I feel the breath of life in my chest. As if an ethereal hand stamps them there, not my own inner voice, with a red-hot poker—leaving every note of the symphony with its brand. A rainbow of notes.

Other music appears in multi-color, each according to the note. Middle C being red. Always in red. And the corn music. It too, is forever red. Other, falsely pious men were quick to whisper, *Witchcraft.*

In the Bible, God wrote a message on the wall with an invisible finger.

If that were possible, why is this not?

"Jane. Jane, are you listening to me?"

I shake my head and force my focus back to Ginny. "I will learn whatever occupation you deem fit," I say.

"I think we should pursue the music, of course. But I want you to learn more common jobs, as well. In case … " She trails off, as if unsure whether to proceed.

"In case I slip and am expelled from an orchestra for my abnormalities. This may sound odd, but I accept my issues. I learn from them and am willing to work around them, however necessary, to try a new life."

Her smile is bright, the pure soul beneath shining through. She is the perfect match to help the patients find their ways. "That is profound, and shows excellent insight into your condition."

Her expression clouds. "Jane … " She leans in conspiratorially. I do very much like this young woman. "Dr. Frost and Dr. Grayjoy are often at odds as to your treatment remedies and … punishments. I am going to follow Grayjoy's treatment plan. But please, keep that to yourself, should you have any sessions with Frost."

I twist my fingers before my lips and toss the invisible key behind me.

I slide open the loose cluster of faux stones in the wall of my room, allowing Sebastian to slide inside. His long tail lingers, and I carefully tuck it in.

Long ago, I placed a bed for him there—well-washed cloths, stolen from the laundry carts, a piece at a time. I have fed him from my meager trays, cared for him as best I could. I have never tried to crawl into the tight space myself ... a burning fear of confinement from years of solitary and straitjackets.

My heart swells as I watch him curl into a contented gray-striped ball, purring. I slide the board back into place, leaving a slight crack should he wish to slip out. I stand, wrapping my arms about me, to stare out the window.

The snowflakes are beautiful, crisp, and bright, as they swirl and fall before the face of the old clock tower.

I smile, and my fingers cover my lips. *Afraid.* I am afraid of this happiness.

For perhaps the first time ever, I have ... hope. It fills me and is repeated with every beat of my heart. Even the mystery of the deaths seems dampened this eve.

Someone, nay, *two* someones, believe in me.

I have never experienced such. The joy is tempered by fear—but I refuse to give it free rein.

Tonight, I will relish this joy—memorize it, and thrust it out as a shield against the melancholy, when it comes. *And it will.* I am not so foolish to think it has abandoned me at the first sign of light in my life. The melancholy will scatter like spiders in the light, waiting in the shadows for my joy to dim. To return.

My teeth chatter, and I wrap my arms tighter. Then I relent and reach for the heavy, tattered shawl flung on the back of my rocking chair. It is so very cold on the ward. Both physicks have already visited and moved on to other wards on their rounds. A young nurse is on duty this night—not the normal, controlling, skeletal Nurse Spare. Sally Spare.

Did her parents not see the cruelty in this name?

She and Frost are thick as thieves. I see the way she looks at him, the unveiled desire. She probably thinks me incapable of such realizations.

"Pfft." I've know it since I was old enough to dress myself.

I wander into the cold hallway to pass Mr. Entemeyer, walking, as he does each and every night. His hand brushes the wall as he ambles *back and forth, back and forth.* The sweet old gent is not dangerous, merely confused—and should not be on our all-female ward.

He will continue his endless walk till they force him to bed. Which shall be—

"Oy. Entemeyer. It's lights out. Back to yer hallway."

I breathe a sigh of relief. The orderly is not Alexander. I have the makings of a perfect night before me. I feel the hint of a smile curl up my lips. *I may even compose.*

The music plays in my mind, traveling down my nerve endings, twitching my fingers— begging to be put to paper. A swirling tornado of colors, notes, and music, storming through my brain.

It will lie in wait, haunting my dreams, becoming the overture of my days, till I can dispel it.

I crawl into my bed, sliding on my threadbare socks, and add the extra layer of dressing gown. I long to call Sebastian from his closet, to feel his steady purr against my chest, but I do not dare, lest someone enter unannounced.

My eyes cast to the bed, to the new, warm coverlet—Mason's second gift. Since its placement upon my bed, my sleep is almost dreamless. As if his concern and protection have driven the wretched birds away.

Tap-tap-tap.

He may have driven them from my mind, but not my window.

A massive raven sits on my sill, coal-black wings dusted by the white powdery snow.

I walk softly toward it. "What do you want?"

It opens its mouth—and I crumple to my knees, barely registering the pain as my flesh tears on the cobbles.

Music. Layered music, like an orchestra, flows forth from his open beak.

The colored strobe of notes rising and falling like variegated waves of the sea. Words. Suddenly a singular voice cuts in. Altering the notes.

All in red.

"She is here. Find her. Find me. Find us. All is not lost, my darling. Come to the corn."

I shake my head, cradling it in my hands. It cannot be. It cannot be. Never have I heard the red music outside of the corn.

I crawl beneath the covers, pulling my legs to my chest, my hands over my ears, praying it leaves.

I lie still for what feels hours, all my joints screaming from the cold, till finally Sebastian curls about my face, biting my scalp with a little too much insistency.

I sit up and flinch with dread as I slowly turn to regard the window.

It is gone. The bird is gone. The windows are frosted over, skewing my view of the clock face.

I crawl back to the bed, sliding into the layers and breathe deeply. Not for the first time, I think, *Am I mad?*

I almost taste the bitter of laudanum and the sherry used to sweeten it. I breathe deeply. I must be strong. I must live life in the present, endure all of its facets, be they pleasure or pain.

I grasp the coverlet and inhale its pleasant scent. I exhale with its comfort. The bottom of the cot remains scratchy and lumpy, but the coverlet is the best I have ever known.

I fidget, waiting for the lantern and gaslights to disappear in the rooms. Only one light per hallway, except at the nurses' station. And honestly, many employees covet this floor—the nature of the patients being so docile and compliant that staff secretly take turns napping during the night shift.

My eyes wander and hold, staring at the bare space on the wall, above the other bunk where the plea for help was scrawled. A chill creeps up my neck, and I fight the urge to close the door. With it comes the nagging claustrophobia.

I worked so very hard to have the privilege of the unlocked door.

My door is cut in half, as is the case with all "trusted" residents. The bottom may lock to deter entry to the dazed wanderers, and a mosquito net draped across the top—allowing more cognizant patients a measure of privacy and safety—is only a measure.

It would merely *slow* a determined patient, not stop him.

I creep out of bed and silently close the bottom of my door and slide the deadbolt.

A very, very large privilege, indeed. To be locked in. A level of trust awarded to only four other patients I have met. Only the nurses and two physicks possess a key. It is a trust only won by the few the staff are convinced are not suicidal. We are permitted one hour of solitude per day.

I bite my lip and unbolt the door, slipping out, down the hall. The only sounds are loud snores. I find myself at Patient Twenty's room.

I stick my head over the top, pushing the netting aside. She too has earned the right to the split-entry door.

"Twenty? Are you there?"

"I'm here, deary."

I slide inside and walk over to her bed in the gloom, but it is still made. I cock my head.

The moonlight is so bright; it streams in through her window, illuminating the entire room, turning every chair and mirror to mother-of-pearl.

I turn to see her silhouette still in the wheeled chair, still by the window.

I hurry over. "Why are you not in bed?"

Her cloudy eyes meet mine. "Apparently, I was forgotten in the shift change."

I bite my lip but force my voice to be strong. "Well, we must get you to bed, then."

I have seen Twenty's bottom, with the sores that sprout because of her inability to reposition herself. I do my best to help her, but I know which nurses might be relied upon—so it is odd she was overlooked.

"Was Tilda not in to do rounds this eve?"

She shifts back and forth in her chair, grinding her teeth at the pain.

"No. 'Twas Alexander."

"Of course it was," I mutter and angle her wheelchair toward the bed, lock the brakes, and wrap my arms about her waist. "We shall stand together, alright? Will do you good to have a few moments on those legs. Ready? One, two … *three*."

I haul Twenty up, her legs accepting the weight as I shift her toward the bed in a pivot. But tonight, tonight, she tilts, her knees giving way.

"Twenty-nine! I am going down!"

"No, you are not." I compensate, quickly shifting her weight backwards so her bottom hits the bed—and I fall forward, landing on top of her. We end in a heaping sprawl of arms and legs upon her bed.

"Are you alright?" I worry.

Her chest hitches, and I raise my head in alarm.

But it is not tears. She is giggling like a little girl. "Get your scrawny person off me before you break my behind rather than help it to bed."

My head drops back, and I guffaw. We laugh, till tears leak from the sides of our eyes, at the ridiculousness that is both our lives.

I manage to scramble off her and readjust her body so she is side-lying, to permit her ulcers some relief.

When I finally turn to leave, she says softly, "Jane."

I bite my lip and turn back. We are not to use our given names. Punishments are severe. "Yes, Kate?"

"Do not be afraid. Whatever kindness is given you, child, take it. Take it and run with it. It is worth the risk."

Tears fill my eyes. "Thank you. Sleep well."

I fly back into bed, pulling the coverlet over my head.

Not a half hour later, I wake in a sheen of cold sweat, listening. Something awakened me.

Knock, knock, knock. Very soft rapping at my door.

I slide out of the covers and pad, shivering, to the door. I see Mason's form, hovering behind the mosquito netting. I bite my fingernail. I should not let him in.

I cannot imagine the punishment for such a crime. "I shouldn't."

I think of Kate's words.

"Both nurse and orderly are currently napping—quite possibly with the aid of a tip of the laudanum. We shall not be missed—we'll return hours before the light. And besides, I took your room key from their ring." He spins it round his finger, his lips upturned on one side.

I rip down the netting and throw open the bolt. "You did *what?*"

He holds up the key and sets to shutting both top and bottom door behind him. "If they try, for some reason, to get in your room, it will take them ages to find the duplicate. They are housed in the main office, an hour by foot."

I realize he is carrying a small steamer trunk. "What is that?"

His smile glitters like the sun on the newly fallen snow. "A very big surprise. Do open it."

Fear floods my mouth in a taste so metallic, I would swear I swallowed a penny. I open the steamer trunk.

A pure white muff, a beautiful blue dress with shining black buttons and lacing, a pair of boots, and … a corset. My cheeks produce a violent blush.

Mason's face is also flushed. "Allow me to explain."

He lifts it out, and beneath it is a white pair of ice skates.

I lick my lips as my eyes dart to the sketches upon my walls. He follows my gaze and smiles widely.

"If you are to learn to skate, you must wear a corset. It would draw much attention otherwise, *putan*."

"Why do you call me that?"

"Isn't it obvious? You're cute as a button. Much as I hate to use an overused phrase. I can honestly say I've never felt it applicable till you."

I lift the clothes to my face and inhale deeply, peering through the lace to stare at him.

I resist the urge to drop my gaze and ask, "Why me?"

He presses his lips together, his eyes suddenly flicking about the room.

"I … have never met a soul so pure, Jane. Ever since I first laid eyes upon you, you have filled my every thought. I tried *not* to think on you … my own situation is very complicated. But the more I speak with you, the more I want to know your thoughts… on everything. I find what should be my primary goal paling in comparison to where you are, if you are safe."

His wandering gaze finally halts, scrutinizing. "Am I … Am I too forward?"

A sudden rush of fear—that he might halt his attentions—

pushes the words from my lips. I leap, the words tumbling from my lips in a rush. "No. I have never known a kindness, let alone this ... *shower* of it. In your eyes I see ... a *mercy* that I have never known in my life. I feel safe with you. Prior to meeting you, had one asked me to describe that word, I would not have done it justice. But now I can." My heart is beating so hard and fast, I grip the bed for support.

His eyes are intense. My head swirls as if I am on Frost's contraption, but I swallow and plunge on. "Safe is the feeling of your hand in mine. I honestly feel I am somehow living another's life and shall soon awaken to find it all a dream."

He removes my hand from the bedrail to squeeze it. "I assure you, I am quite real, as are you. Now, if we are going, we must hurry."

My hands cover my mouth. "We are going *tonight*?"

He nods, gesturing toward the window. "Yes, the temperature is perfect. I cannot risk you contracting frostbite for a turn on a lake, now can I?"

"This is what you meant? When you asked me to take a turn with you?"

"Yes, now don't dawdle. I shall turn my back while you change."

My face burns hot, and I shake my head with mortification, but he has already turned.

When I have finished, Mason extends his hand. "If we are to do this without discovery, we must away."

I take it.

CHAPTER THIRTEEN

"I cannot *wait* to hear you play, Miss Frost." An overly eager, small man with a waxed moustache bends to kiss my hand.

His whiskers tickle my skin, his searching lips reminding me of a walrus.

Willis manages a look of borderline irritation—the closest someone of such an affable personality can manage. "Yes, Jules's music is quite wonderful. Do excuse us, would you?"

He wraps my hand about his elbow and pulls me from the man.

I give him a grateful smile. So sweet. I am truly sorry I do not love him.

"Are you ready, darling?" Father has arrived, positively dashing in his tuxedo.

His jet-black hair and piercing blue eyes make women

everywhere swoon. Indeed, as he cut through the crowd, no less than ten sets of feminine eyes followed his trail to me.

Until he spoke. Brash, unadulterated truth always falls from his lips, like a burr that tangles on delicate feminine personalities. Once a woman knew him, she avoided him.

He showed no interest in remarriage once mother died, and that was so very long ago. I was still in the nursery.

"Jules?" His voice is impatient. "Stop daydreaming. Follow me."

He turns without sparing me a backwards glance. Willis shrugs. He is no match for Father. No match for *me*, for that matter.

Father eyes me up and down and says, "The idea is brilliant. A costumed recital. You look perfect, Jules."

I catch sight of Nurse Ginny and swallow. She is nearly unrecognizable in a beautiful black gown embossed with scarlet brocade.

I pat his hand. "I shall see you after the recital. Father says that nurse is a friend. Perhaps you should go talk to her. The one dressed like a fairy."

I bolt, hoping my disguise is truly that. I try to imagine what Nurse Turtle shall wear.

I follow Father up the stairs, holding fast to the elaborate mahogany banister. This shall be my first concert *within* the asylum. My mouth is as dry as the dirt in the many potted plants strewn throughout the physicks' apartments. I glance nervously about, fearing my deceptions shall betray me.

"Alice!"

I flinch and trip on the train of my dress. Both hands shoot to the banister as I manage to right myself before falling. Father's head whirls around, his gaze narrowing at my atypical clumsiness.

I turn my head, trying to keep my face calm as a young man bounds past me, taking the stairs two at a time.

"Alice!"

A pretty, blond thing halts at the top, smiling widely for him. He wraps her arm in his. "I thought I'd never find you."

"Whatever is the matter, child?" Father's voice is near-livid. He teeters on the edge of violence tonight. He is very close to *Mad Papa*.

I shrug. "I merely wish to make an impression upon your colleagues."

He turns back, climbing the steps once again. "Do not be foolish. You are the best musician I know." Then, as if he thinks I cannot hear him, he mumbles, "Save one."

We reach the top of the stairs, and I halt, astounded at the wing.

Floor three is solely for housing the asylum physicks and their families. I stand, dumbstruck, at the top of the staircase.

A woman's shoulder strikes mine, jarring me out of my shock, and I step forward, unstoppering the flow of well-dressed society, which bottle-necks behind me on the stairs. A myriad of animal faces stream past like a freakish nightmare.

The contrast between this floor and the ward floors is inconceivable.

Expensive Turkish rugs cover the floors and potted ferns line the hallway. Ornate mahogany furniture complements the tall, dark-wood pocket doors with stained-glass vestibule tops. And light. So much light here.

In the dusk, I just manage to see the spire of the old clock tower from the window. It chimes, deep and low like an old man's voice.

Seven o'clock.

I right the mask on my face, fighting the urge to scratch.

It was Father's idea, that all of the musicians wear a costume of sorts. My own is crystal, and heavy. My gown, off-white with downy feathers about the bustle.

"A swan," Father had said. "It suits you."

"Over here, Jules." His voice startles me, and I hurry after him through the crowd.

A small stage is erected at the end of the hallway, and several of the girls are already present, examining and tuning their instruments.

I hum middle C under my breath. It calms me.

"I shall return, Jules. A few minor details need seeing to. I will be stealing Willis as well."

"Take your time, Father."

I take advantage of the rare freedom and steal champagne from a passing waiter as I make my way down the hall.

The physicks live here. *In* the asylum—the only thing separating them from patients on either side is a wooden double door at the end of the hallways.

Several children giggle and run past.

My eyebrows rise. *They have their children here as well.*

I shudder, wondering at their sheltered upbringing, which seems too entirely like my own. I stare after them. A brother and sister poke one another with vehemence while walking behind their unsuspecting parents.

"At least they have one another."

Many of the doors of the apartments are flung wide, and I realize each is set up as an open house. I pass one, glancing inside, and see a table set with a myriad of wines of every shade and color in brilliant crystal goblets.

I walk faster, hoping I have time to see them all before I have to play.

I enter the last, and I stumble as the hammer of déjà vu strikes.

Paintings. Everywhere, paintings adorn every inch of this doctor's room.

I take a step back, and my boot catches, twisting my ankle. My leg gives way, and I twist, plummeting toward the floor when a viselike grip latches at my elbow, instantly righting me.

"Miss, are you alright—"

Our eyes meet and his widen. As if in fear.

An ice-blue gaze regards me, nearly obscured by a shock of raven-black hair. Full lips turn up in a strange, perplexed smile. He even cocks his head, as if trying to discern a puzzle.

"I am so sorry, sir. I was … I was overcome by these many paintings. Tell me, were they done by the patients?"

He gently sets me to rights, releasing my elbow, which now stings from the force of his grasp. I absently rub it; I shall most certainly bruise.

He breaks our staring contest and walks; no … this man *saunters,* around the pictures, his fingers gently tracing them. "Yes, they are all from the residents. Magnificent, are they not?" He only dons a mask, like Father. Too proud to play the game, I suspect.

His stare flicks back and locks with mine once again. A stare so intense I resist the urge to shrink under it. One eyebrow cocks as if trying to discern my thoughts. He takes in my dress, my arranged hair.

"You are a musician?"

I nod, vaguely indicating to my violin case, which lies forgotten on the floor.

I have seen him on the wards, but from afar. Never have I seen a man so ruggedly handsome. His hair is longer than is fashionable, wavy and thick. *Piercing* is the only word for those eyes.

"Is this your first time playing in public?"

I must look the complete dolt, staring at him. "Oh no. I have been playing since I could walk." My hand waves away the notion. My eyes shift to the pictures near the large fieldstone fireplace, and I walk over, warming myself before the grate.

There's a picture of a plump tabby cat on a snowy windowsill. Outside the pane, the outline of the clock tower is visible.

I point. "Whose picture is that?"

He walks behind me, and I shiver at the smell of him. Musky, manly, but very, very pleasant. *Am I bewitched?*

"I am afraid I cannot reveal which patient drew which picture. That would be a betrayal of confidences. They are, however, for sale. If you care to purchase one, the bulk of the proceeds go to the patient, to help them buy niceties, and a small portion to the asylum, for their care."

I stare up at him, blinking madly.

He stares, as if he wishes to whisper a secret. His eyes stray over my eyes and then halt at my hair. *Linger* on my hair.

"Is that your natural color?"

"Excuse me?"

His face instantly colors. "I am so sorry. How incredibly bold of me. It is just ... " He takes a deep, steeling breath. "Never mind. Anyway, do you wish to buy the cat print? I see you are taken with it."

The trance is broken. The familiarity, or whatever it was, has vacated the room.

My eyes wander over the walls, and I walk back and forth, feeling the swish of the ivory against my legs and the tickle of the costume's feathers. Several pictures are of hands. Hands with ink stains, and a quill poised over music.

"I shall take the cat and every picture here with the sheet music in it."

His eyebrows rise, and his forehead wrinkles. He is my senior, perhaps a score and ten. It matters not; he is wholly intoxicating.

I drag my eyes away.

"They are not dear, but neither inexpensive. Are you sure you might afford that many on a musician's earnings?"

"Jules!"

Father's voice is cold and sharp as the ice frosting the windowpanes. He slides into the chambers, his eyes narrowing as he instantly assesses the situation. "I have been searching everywhere for you. It is nearly time to begin."

The man goes rigid at the sound of Father's voice. They are more than acquainted; I have no doubt as I observe the now stiff set of Grayjoy's shoulders.

I walk toward Father but notice a painting leaning against a desk, half hidden on the floor. It seems to be a pair of eyes, with a singular word beneath them.

Colourata.

I swish past him and out the door. Father nods. "Grayjoy."

"Frost."

I call back over my shoulder, "I want every one of them."

I hear his reply as I exit his quarters. "You shall have them, Miss Jules Frost."

I shiver as he uses my name, but I square my shoulders and hurry toward the stage.

I can scarcely breathe.

Mason looks exhilarated, not afraid. The freezing cold bites his cheeks, and they are flushed red.

After a terrifying canter through the catacombs below the asylum, we followed the tunnel to its very end. It seemed a mile long. All the while my heart ticked back and forth like a metronome—vacillating betwixt trying to appreciate each moment with Mason and a mind-numbing fear of discovery. In which he is dismissed and I am back in solitary.

For a year.

Where we surfaced at the barn, I quickly changed, stashing my patient uniform beneath the hay, my teeth chattering with the cold.

I emerge, and for a moment, he is still. "You are breathtaking."

Smoothing the dress self-consciously, I bite my lip.

He notices. "It is alright. I will let no harm befall you, Jane."

I smooth the blue gown again, staring down at the flowing layers, wiggling my toes in the laced-up, fine boots. I feel, again, like someone else. The urge to flee is strong.

He offers me his arm, and I take it, and we leave the barn.

We stand directly outside the asylum's first set of gates. My first time ever outside it, to the far south. In the distance, a sleigh approaches, with lanterns attached to either side, swinging gently with the gliding movement.

I swallow. "When I am with you … I am not afraid."

Mason smiles widely, his blue eyes crinkling. "Jane. What an utterly perfect name. And it is perfect for you."

He puts his hands on my shoulders. "Remember, you are my cousin, in from England, should we be stopped and questioned."

I nod. I have read enough of England in my library books that I believe I might pass any inquiry as to landmarks or basic history.

The sleigh halts with a jingle, and off it steps a man so old, I fear he may disintegrate and blow away with a sudden gust of wind.

"Mason. Here she is. Be sure to have her back by dawn's light."

Mason takes my hand, leading me toward the front seat. He tips his hat. "I will, Mr. Krain, you needn't worry."

The man pulls out a key to the southern gate and, in moments, is limping toward the barn.

My mind explodes with music. Music of escape. *I am going outside the gates. I am going outside the gates.* The note-colors are so blindingly bright I am momentarily distracted.

I slide onto the cold seat and shiver. Mason slides in beside me, the leather reins wrapped about his gloved hands.

Shimmering white globs of snowflakes fall all about us like a glittery wonderland. As if we are inside a snow globe.

My teeth chatter with the cold, and Mason smiles.

"Have a cup, now."

He nods behind me, where I spy two mugs and a teapot. I spin to carefully lift it, and as I tip it, a deep, rich, brown liquid pours out as the smell of chocolate fills my nostrils.

Tears sting my eyes again as I turn to sit, sipping it daintily with my white-gloved hands. What care he has taken to arrange this outing!

All for me. It seems impossible, as if I have fallen into the pages of the library's books.

He reaches to grab the other cup, and a small leather book tumbles from his pocket to our feet.

"Oh."

I bend and pick it up, smiling wickedly. "Whatever is this?"

"Nothing," he says, but he lurches to snatch it away.

I hold it aloft, away from him, and laugh quietly. "That is quite a bit of reaching for *nothing*."

I crack it open and stare. *Names. Rows and rows of names* stare up from the worn pages.

He smiles and looks forward. "I told you. Words. They are my weakness. I am a bit ... obsessive about them."

I look through, reading the collection of T's before me, all penned in his perfect penmanship.

Scottish Descent

Tara: goddess of the sea

Taveon: twin

Thane: follower

I smile widely, but he is still looking forward. "What is the meaning of your name?"

He laughs softly, melodic and deep. "Stone cutter. *Superbly* interesting."

I slide closer to him, my face heating with my forwardness. "*I* think it is interesting. In fact, I think you are the *most* interesting person I have ever met."

One dark eyebrow rises. "Considering where you come from, I would say that is saying something."

We both laugh, too hard.

But too soon it dies, as if the mere mention of Soothing Hills kills any and all mirth in the world. The snowfall is heavy, muting all sound, covering the entire countryside in a hushed undertone. I blink as heavy flakes gather on my lashes. The sound of the sleigh through snow lulls my senses, and we are quiet for some time.

As if feeling my dread, he says, "Do you know the meaning of your name, Jane?"

I shake my head and shrug. "Cursed?"

He turns to meet my eye, and his smile is sad. "Gift from God. As I said, it suits you."

His eyes narrow, studying my expression. "What is it?"

I shrug again, staring forward. "Every minute I spend in your presence seems stolen from someone else's life. Like one of the novels from the library."

He smiles widely. "That makes me very happy. Now drink that before it goes cold."

I stare down at my now cold chocolate.

Hot chocolate is a specialty, and very dear, served only twice a year at Soothing Hills. On the eve prior to the new year and on the anniversary of the asylum's opening.

My finger's stroke the leather cover of the book like a worry stone.

"Keep the book."

"I couldn't. You said you've had it since you were a lad."

"I will ask for it back one day. For now, it is officially on loan."

The black horse shakes his mane, sending a shower of snow to either side, and I smile.

"Please tell me more about your life. About … "

"Outside?"

As if on cue, the sleigh slides past the final set of wrought-iron gates. This exit, used primarily for deliveries, is not even visible from the Asylum-proper. I glance back to see Mr. Krain securing them.

My heart flies, seeming to bounce against my insides like a bird trying to flee its cage.

I nod, "Yes, outside," feeling another blush suffuse my cheeks. At least I have the excuse of the cold.

The sleigh rails glide through the snow, as if we are phantoms, hovering above the drifts. The countryside is quite dark except for our lanterns, and far off in the distance, a bonfire awaits.

"What do you wish to see, once you leave Soothing Hills?"

I sigh. It all seems impossible, to even picture it, but I force the words out.

"I wish … to see an opera. To eat in a real restaurant and … "

Mason turns, eyes tightening. "Go on, then. No secrets."

"No secrets," I murmur. Another impossible concept. "I wish … to ride a carousel."

Mason's arm slides about my shoulders, and he gives me a squeeze. "You are quite possibly the sweetest creature on the planet, *mo cridhe*."

My cheeks heat again. I know not what that means in Gaelic, but I recognize the prefix. He called me his … his … *something*. I find I cannot summon the courage to ask.

"Whoa."

We draw close, the bonfire's orange flames a sharp contrast in the white snow.

Who is he, really?

Doubt flickers in my heart. He has gone to too much trouble and, I will daresay, expense. Asylum workers would not grant such favors for free. If cut off from his fortune, he is obviously not destitute.

The sleigh halts, and Mason slides out, covering the horse's back with a thick wool blanket. He hobbles the horse before tethering him loosely to a nearby tree.

He walks back, his eyes tight and indiscernible, to hold out his hand. He does a quick, formal bow. "Miss … "

"I don't know, remember?"

He nods and waves his hand as if pushing away the unpleasant thoughts. "Miss *Geamhradh*." He bows deeply.

Smiling I hesitate. "And what is the meaning of that word?"

"Miss Winter."

I must look perplexed, because he adds, "Your hair. It is the color of snowflakes."

I blush violently, the heat scorching from ear to chest.

"Might I have this dance?"

I slide toward him and laugh too loud. "This shall be more of a *fall*. But I am certainly all yours."

After a few minutes' struggle, my skates are on. He glides out onto the ice, showing off, his scarf flying out behind him like a pair of wings.

He skates about the whole circle, fluid and graceful, and even manages a little spin, sending a shower of shaved ice into the air.

I clap and smile. In my imagination, it was neither so cold, nor so awkward. A strange fear presses. I have not been out of doors, save the Asylum Gardens—I am like a domestic cat, thrust into the wide open spaces.

"Come, Jane."

I take his outstretched hand as he skates backwards, towing me out to the center. My ankles wobble as I fight to keep them stiff.

He nods encouragingly. "That's it. Control your movements."

After a quarter hour, and several painful spills, I have mastered staying on my feet. The drifts surrounding the lake seem surreal, as does the tiny fire, which blazes on the shore. Mason stops every few minutes to stoke it, fearful we will freeze.

Our eyes meet, and he skates quickly toward me, spinning so that he turns behind me, his chest bumping my back. I give a nervous laugh.

He pulls me close, and my heart beats so fast I feel light-headed. He turns me so that my back is flush against his chest.

Below my corset, both of his gloved hands grip my waist. His hot breath and low voice are in my ear. "Slowly now."

I push off, feeling his hands guide my hips, right, left. I keep my hands out, trying to stay my balance, but they gradually fall, layering over his.

The falling snow reflects the lantern light, making certain flakes appear alive—as if tiny white fairies dart and whisk to the ice below.

Mason picks up our speed, and I try to keep pace, concentrating on my feet. *Push, push, glide, glide.*

The rocking synchrony of our hips distracts me. Desire dowsing me.

I almost stumble, and my hands fly to cover his—his grip tightening on my hips.

I am breathing hard. Not just from the speed, which feels like flying. Snow wetting our faces as we whizz around the lake, our legs move in harmony. Music explodes again. Yearning notes, pulling at strings, for thoughts and wants I never thought possible. Never dared entertain.

Of the dance between man and woman, I only know what I have read and seen in the novels buried in the hidden library.

But as he guides my hips with his hands, my imagination erupts in images.

I lose my concentration. My skate tangles in his, and they intertwine, sending us sprawling to the ice with a heavy *whuuump.*

"Good heavens! Are you hurt?" Mason's eyes are wild. My body is flush against his, sprawled flat on the freezing ice.

I may faint.

I clear my throat. "No. I am fine. Well, perhaps I shall bruise, but I will most certainly live."

Our faces are inches apart. "Jane." His voice is a hoarse whisper.

I lean forward, and our lips connect in a warm, stroking dance. I feel the vibration of it to my core, and my breath shudders out.

He moans softly and roughly grips my cheek with his hand, his tongue finding the inside of my mouth.

At first, I resist, not knowing what to expect—but my body weakens, as if my bones dissolve, till all that remains is the blessed union that is our mouths.

"Jane, I—"

Craaaack.

His eyes go wide with fear, and I feel his frantic heart against my chest. "Do not move."

"What is happening?"

He gently slides me off, and begins to slide on his belly, across the ice. "Do as I do, quickly now."

Craaaack! And I see it.

A jagged line, traversing the ice, headed directly for the spot where we fell. I hoist my skirt to give my knees purchase, and we scramble frantically for the shore.

Mason reaches it first, immediately turning to thrust out his hand for me to grasp.

I feel it before I hear it. My legs depress, tilting below my waist. Then, the cold. *Like no other cold.* Piercing my skin with crippling pain. "Ahh!"

Mason's hands are under my arms, hauling me toward him. "Hang onto me!"

I wrap my arms about his waist, and he grips a low-hanging tree limb to keep from sliding into the deadly water. "Crawl up me."

"What?"

"Like a bloody ladder. Do it, Jane!"

I move my hands to his shoulders, jam my boot onto his

belt buckle, like a ladder's rung, and launch myself to the snowy ground.

In moments, he is beside me, lifting me into his arms. "We must hurry. We haven't much time in these temperatures." He utters a curse. "I was a fool."

Worry eats at my brain. Worry that he refers to our adventure, not to his taking a chance with me. *Me, the idiot, the imbecile, the lunatic, the ...*

That is the last I hear before the shivering commences. Rattling my teeth so hard and fast I swear

I hear each bone of my skeleton following suit.

Chapter Fourteen

"I should have the lot of you dismissed. Of all the irresponsible, reckless, not to mention illegal—"

The voice is familiar, but so far off. It is muted, bringing to mind a submersion in the dunk tank, and my body responds with a violent shudder.

A warm hand is on my shoulder, the fingers somehow calming. My breathing slows.

"*Do not touch her*." Dr. Grayjoy.

The hand grips tighter. "I *shall* touch her, and there isn't a blasted thing you can do about it," Mason retorts.

"Oh, there is much I can do," Grayjoy replies. "The question is, what is best for *Jane*—not you."

My legs feel so very cold. Cold. *The lake*. The events rush back as quickly as the icy pond waters that covered my legs.

They will dismiss Mason for our recklessness.

That thought ices the blood in my veins, damaging me far more than any frozen pond ever could.

I try to reach up my hand, my eyes fighting to flutter open. "Do not quarrel, please. I am f-f-fine." My teeth still rattle with the cold.

"You are most certainly not fine," Grayjoy retorts. There is a new, foreign tone to his voice. *Protective?* I cannot say for certain.

I open my eyes to see them standing on either side of me—two sets of clenched fists and furrowed brows.

It is odd to hear him be so bold. I know he detests Frost, disagrees with his treatment of me, but I also know being a physick is most important to him. Were he to push Frost beyond his limits, he would lose his position. And that position is first. All other causes, no matter how important, come behind that fact.

Mason gathers my hand in his and gives it a little shake. "Jane. I am so very glad you are alright. When you swooned … "

"You brought her *to me*," Grayjoy sneers. "Release her hand. It is highly improper."

I bite my lip, and slowly, he does, placing it gently upon the sheet, my fingers instantly growing cold.

"Please, Dr. Grayjoy, do not dismiss him. He was merely trying to help."

Grayjoy's eyebrows disappear into his hair. "*Help?* Is that what they are calling it nowadays?"

My mouth drops. I have known the good doctor for going on four years and have *never, ever* seen him lose his composure. Not under Frost's scrutiny, not even in the midst a wailing, head-banging patient. But our rebellion … this affects him, somehow.

Mason's expression is black. "Do not be ridiculous. Jane is chaste as the falling snow."

"That remains to be seen."

My face colors when I realize it is my maidenhead they discuss. "Dr. Grayjoy. I *assure* you nothing whatever of that sort has happened."

Mason's expression shifts as his eyes tighten. "I fear for Jane. These murders, every single one her roommate. You do not find this odd? And what about the rumors?"

"Rumors?"

"Come now. Rumors abound through the hospital grapevine… about a monster, roaming the corridors and the catacombs below?"

Grayjoy huffs, but as we both remain silent, his eyes narrow. "A monster? Speak plainly, man."

Mason's eyes shoot nervously to me and back. "A staff nurse told me it chased her. It was on *Jane's floor*. The nurse saw it and fled. She had the dickens of a time giving it the slip."

My heartbeat escalates. I feel a prickle of anger that he did not tell me.

As if hearing my thoughts, Mason turns to me. "I was going to tell you, Jane. I was just waiting for the right moment. Your whole life is vexation; I did not wish to add to it."

Grayjoy stands, his hand vigorously rubbing his five o'clock shadow. "Fine. If any other reports of this *monster* arise, I insist you contact me immediately. Mason, keep this incident between us—no other staff members. But so help me, you step one more toe out of line, and you are gone. And no amount of Jane's pleadings will alter it. Do I make myself clear?"

Mason nods.

A worry shivers up my spine. *I wonder why he wants us quiet. To involve no one?*

"Now, I shall take Jane back home," Grayjoy says, tugging on the waistcoat beneath his lab coat.

Mason's face colors. "It is not a *home*. It is her room. I am perfectly—"

"*You*, sir, are an orderly. *I*, the physick. Go *to your home*, Mr. Worth. I suspect you are soon expected to start your shift?"

Mason shoots me a final look of resignation. "I shall see you on the morrow."

I nod, fighting the urge to grab his hand; he keeps the monsters in my mind at bay. I swallow and nod, squaring my shoulders.

Grayjoy watches Mason go, then stalks across the room, only to return with a wheeled wooden chair. "In, Jane. We have much to discuss."

He eases me gently into the chair, but not before I catch sight of a painting. Chills explode from my head to my feet.

Eyes. *My eyes*. With a single word beneath them.

Colourata.

PART TWO

CHAPTER FIFTEEN

GRAYJOY

"I must speak with you about Patient Twenty-Nine." I stand, shuffling my feet like a ruddy schoolboy.

How does Frost make me lose every shred of self-confidence?

I stare at him. Despite the perfect waistcoat and the pristine, polished boots, there is a recklessness about him. The care-not expression. His impulsive decisions, which, infuriatingly, more often than not end in a work of sheer genius.

His dark eyes nearly glow with a manic energy. He is like a spring coiled, awaiting the precise word to explode.

I clear my throat, and the piercing gaze fixes upon me. "I have reviewed her chart in preparation to take over her case, and her records are exasperatingly thin. For a patient who has been here her entire life, how is that possible? The chart should be massive." I waggle the barely-there pile of papers at him.

One side of Frost's lip curls—a sure sign of his growing irritation. I ascertained the top marks in school at deciphering people's countenances, an essential skill for a good alienist—knowing when they are happy or sad, even if the words falling from their lips say precisely the opposite.

Frost is oblivious to anyone's thoughts, feelings, or mind, other than himself.

His voice is low. "There is precious little to say about Twenty-Nine, because she is a simple person."

Anger bubbles in my chest, and I force in a deep, steeling breath before speaking.

"She is *far* from simple. And from what I have seen of her musical prowess, the young woman is a virtuoso. She could do much on the outside, Frost. She seems ready to move to Ward One *this instant*, if you ask my professional opinion—"

"*I did not* ask your opinion, Doctor." Frost's eyes blaze with cold rage. He paces before me like a tiger, trapped behind bars. Societal bars.

Truth be told, most days the man seems one step away from a patient himself.

"When I want your opinion, Grayjoy, I shall give it to you."

I grind my jaws together to kill the retort rattling behind my teeth. I force myself to sit, clenching my fists tighter and tighter, till my joints ache. Never have I allowed myself to be spoken to in such a fashion. I clear my throat and try again.

"Twenty-Nine's hair. I have never seen white hair on any person so young, except an albino, yet her eyes are green-blue, not pink."

Now Frost's hands grip—open-*closed*, open-*closed*—as he clearly struggles to keep them from throttling me. No other physick questions him. They are all cowards who bow to his ridiculous whims. But the board of directors is forcing him to relinquish several cases to me. They finally fear he is ... overworked.

And Frost does not take orders well, or more precisely, *at all*.

A long, tapered finger waggles in my face. "You, young Grayjoy, should be worrying about Twenty-Nine's wild behavior and flight risk, not her bloody hair color."

I cock my head. "She has not tried to flee since she was twelve."

"Balderdash. She tries every other week. She was trying when you insisted she not be punished. The staff have become soft and entirely too attached to her and refuse to report it, for fear of retribution. *You* are too soft on her."

I think of her face, suddenly as alabaster as her hair, as she twirled *round* and *round* on The Adjuster. The sick nickname Frost christened the whirling contraption, and swallow. I think of the cut straitjacket.

I switch tactics. "What would *you* recommend for Twenty-Nine?"

Frost tugs at his necktie, staring in the window at his reflection. Something shifts in it. "She is too innocent. Too trusting. Also too abnormal for society to accept ... "

I cover my mouth with my hand. "Too abnormal? How so?"

I flip through her chart to the very oldest entries. Wild temper tantrums as a child. Banging her head off the floor and walls till she passed out. I swallow.

"In the past few years, she's had nary a word of defiance, let alone an action."

"It is her eyes. I see the rebellion in them."

"You *see the rebellion?*"

I now concur with my superiors that Frost may well be on his way to a forced, early retirement. It may be the custom of some to admit women whose husband's have decided to trade them in for a newer model, or to lock away an overly active female imagination, but it is decidedly not *my* way.

"Have you heard of Marie Antoinette Syndrome?"

Frost's face hardens, as stony as the gargoyles that flank the asylum's entrance. He straightens his well-cut suit, giving the waistcoat a tug for emphasis. "Balderdash. I have never seen one in all my days as a physick—"

"The first documented case is from the Jewish Talmud."

"What has this to do with Twenty-Nine?"

"Has Jane's hair always been stark white?"

Frost whirls, flinging his cup. It shatters against the wall, raining down in a million tiny shards of pottery.

My heartbeat goes wild, my mind slipping into crisis mode, quickly assessing my location. Close to a door, within calling distance of a nurses' station. My eyes flick about, searching for a weapon if necessary. We are evenly matched. It would be a struggle to take him down.

Frost takes a deep breath. The anger seeps from his face with an exhale as he stoops to gather the fragments of the broken cup. "I am sorry, Jonathon."

The use of my given name is not lost on me. He is trying to placate me, so I will excuse his lack of decorum. His lack of self-restraint is legendary.

He stands, slowly depositing the fragments into a bin. "I do not believe in the use of the patients' given names. It breaks down the barrier between doctor and patient. It—"

"Makes them human?"

Frost's face convulses, his eyebrow twitching madly over his left eye. I have never challenged him, but the need to protect Jane forces the words from my mouth, deuce the consequences.

"Affects our decision making, as she clearly has already tainted your own."

I scribble a note on the chart, turning toward the door. "Fine. Thank you for the consultation about Twenty-Nine. I shall see you at the staff meeting tomorrow."

I spin on my heel and throw open the double door, storming into the hall and down the corridor. The man is hiding something. And I shall unearth it.

It is so very cold this eve. Despite Mason's gift, my teeth chatter, and I slide the pillow over my head to block the draft seeping in from my window.

Beneath the covers, Sebastian snuggles closer against my leg. I am taking a risk with him in my bed—but the night is so cold, I fear for us both.

I think of the picture of my eyes in Grayjoy's office. *Colourata.*

The word seems foreign, but doesn't. As if I have heard it before but cannot remember where. They were most definitely my eyes. The artist capturing the flecks of gold in the blue of my irises—even my white lashes.

Shuffle-shuffle-shuffle.

Oh, no. *Not now.*

My teeth chatter more violently—the cold and fear clattering them together like a bony xylophone, the sound echoing through the stillness of my room.

I clasp my hands over them. I dare not try to shoo the cat. I pray the cold will drive him to keep still and quiet.

I feel his claws touch my leg. He senses Cloud's presence.

I reach down to stroke his head, fighting the fear and dread pulsing through my veins.

The shuffling halts outside my door.

"Do not go in there, Cloud. You are not in the right mind."

"An' who would be you, to tell me of my mind?" A bitter laugh.

Two voices. One is Frost's, I am almost certain.

"I … I wish you to be gone." Definitely Frost. He sounds … It takes a few moments for my mind to reconcile the word to the man. Because never, ever in my life would I have placed these two concepts in the same sentence.

Frost sounds scared.

"I do not believe you."

"Twenty-Nine is—"

"You mean Jane?"

Frost's voice trembles with rage. "Do not speak her name. You are not fit to utter it."

"Ivy. Jules. B—"

"Do not speak it. I will kill you."

A strangling, rasping cough issues forth, and my entire body trembles.

Frost is going to kill Cloud. Frost is going to kill Cloud.

Cloud's voice: "I took her. And I shall take her again. Till I have mastery over the entire field."

"No. No, you won't." He is crying. Oh, my good heaven above, Frost is crying. "I will not *let* you."

"You know what must be done. With all who look too closely. You *let* me take Ivy. She has been there such a very long time. But for me, that is ... convenient."

"You are a devil!" Frost roars. "She was ... "

"Your wife?" A laugh, so hard and cold, my heart freezes in my chest.

Frost's wife's name was Ivy. *She is dead? Did Cloud kill her?*

Something clatters against my door. I believe it to be a head.

There is struggling as a pandemonium breaks out in the hallway, and I finally sit up, chest heaving, trying not to whimper.

"Oy, you there!"

I have never been glad to hear Alexander's voice—but tonight, were it Mason on duty ...

I scramble out of bed and crack my door in time to see his massive frame lumber past, one meaty paw tapping the billy club against the other.

The exit door is swinging closed. Frost and Cloud are gone.

Alexander turns round to leer at me. "You best go back to bed, nosey-posey. Lest you'd like some company?"

I slam the door and slide down, collapsing at the floor. I stay there the rest of the night, listening, and freezing, trying to make sense of what I have heard.

Could Cloud or Frost be the monster?

CHAPTER SIXTEEN

The carriage rumbles to a stop at the asylum's front entrance, and I swallow the ball of fear lodged in my throat as the footman swings the door wide.

"Miss Frost." He nods and extends an assisting hand.

I smooth my dress and grasp his hand, alighting down the stairs. Staring up at the overbearing stone walls, I feel ridiculous. I have grown accustomed to coming to Soothing Hills in a nursing uniform. But today ...

Sheepishly, I stare down at my dress, which is nothing short of spectacular—navy blue, with a crisscross across my décolletage, it fastens at the nape of my neck and has an extremely cinched waist.

"Jules, *are* you *trying* to attract attention?" was Maeve's retort, her eyebrow arched, upon seeing me as I left the house. "You shall succeed. You are breathtaking, my dove. Should I ask toward what lucky man this attention-seeking is directed? Because I am quite certain it is not Willis."

Whom indeed.

I sashay through the entrance, strategically entering the door furthest from the ward on which I work. Should any staff see me, adorned in my finest, I would instantly lose all credibility.

The greeter stops me, checking his clipboard. The man looks ancient but is dressed as if the fact was lost on him. He's donned the latest Paris fashions. A feather in his lapel matches the one in his hand.

"Miss … "

I curtsy. "Miss Frost. I am here to pick up the paintings I purchased the other evening from a Dr. Grayjoy?"

The old man smiles, adjusting his half-moon spectacles. His yellowing eyes scan across the page till he says, "Yes, here we are. Of course, the benefit auction. You are expected, Miss Frost." He makes a check mark with a flourish, then, using the feather as a pointer, says, "Up that hall and to the left, you shall find the good doctor's office."

I stop dead, my heart beating in my mouth. *The picture of the eyes.*

"Are you quite well, Miss Frost?"

I smile, insipid. "Oh, yes. Excuse me." And I scurry up the stairwell like the rat I am.

The physician ward is quite striking, I note as I wander down the hallway. There are twelve mahogany doors—at the top, their transoms thick and seemingly unbreakable against patient attack. I stop dead, chills lifting the hair on my arms as I stare at the door before me.

"Isolation room."

The word, spoken aloud, seems to shatter the silence and I look quickly up and down the hallway. But I am alone.

A peephole is fashioned for observation, and a revolving lazy Susan is at the bottom as a means of feeding the wayward patient without ever opening the door. This is an observation room, so that the physicians on this ward might observe and offer all their opinions on the offending patient.

My hand trembles as I touch the knob and slowly swing the door open.

My heartbeat doubles as I thrust my head inside and fight an irrational claustrophobia. Biting my lip, I fear that the door shall swing closed of its own accord, trapping me inside.

In the hard, stone floor, there is a drain for the patients to relieve themselves.

Chains. Two sets, in four corners of the room. *Two high, two low.*

Manacles—for hands and feet, so that the subdued patient would resemble a destitute starfish when secured.

If they should fall asleep, I picture a patient slumped, manacles cutting deep into the suspended wrists from the hanging body's weight.

Tears fill my eyes, and I blink them away, shutting the door.

I hastily wipe them with the back of my hand and, with a shuddery inhale, turn in the direction of Grayjoy's office.

Each of my steps echoes like a gunshot in this still, cold area of the asylum.

After a year of my life seems to pass, I arrive at his office and pause outside, collecting my reserve. I knock and wait several minutes, nervously glancing up and down the corridor. After some long moments, when it is apparent no one is coming, I turn the knob, and the office door swings open wide.

I step inside, intending to wait for the elusive, handsome, jaw-dropping doctor.

The smell of books, leather, and musk fills my nostrils. The room is a personification of the man: polished, grand, but above all, *interesting*. The space is hard, but touches of womanly endeavors soften it. Paintings litter the walls here as well, seemingly of the same hand that sketched the one I purchased from the auction.

My breath catches. A sketch near the floor is of sheet music, with a slender feminine hand poised overtop. I cock my head.

Something is familiar in the tilt of that hand. The way the fingers drape.

As if I should know it but the recognition dangles just out of my reach. I stoop down to read it. Inching closer, my eyes skim it as my hands instantly pluck the notes on my imaginary violin.

The music *roars* to life in my mind, each note pulsing and blaring with red. The red. Middle C's red. Frightening me with its intensity.

Never has an arrangement presented itself in all red.

My conscience whispers, *Except the corn music. It is forever red.*

My hand cups my mouth, my pulse beating in my neck.

Words. Messages in the music.

"*My doves. My two turtledoves. Fear the corn, my lovelies. Find my lost red sparrow. Never follow him. He is not whom he seems. Do not forsake—*"

The door opens, and I go rigid, standing so quickly black and white stars pop and blink in my vision. My breath quickens as I clutch at the desk to remain upright.

"Miss Frost?"

I whirl around, the world nearly swooning as I plaster what I hope is an innocent smile on my face.

Dr. Grayjoy's face pales, all the blood draining away.

I take a step toward him, befuddled by his response. "Are you alright? Oh, good word, shall I summon another physick?"

His mouth twitches in astonishment, his eyes drinking me in from hair to boot. He clears his throat, swiping at the rebelling curls occluding his eyes. His hands form fists, but not before I catch sight of the tremble in his hands. "I am so sorry, Miss Frost. Do forgive me, I have been ill."

I place my hand on his arm, and he stares at it. "Are you quite well, now, sir? I am sorry if you do not recognize me—when last we met, I wore a mask. I assure you, I *am* Miss Frost."

When his stare continues, I add, "I bought the paintings? I was a swan?"

He nods, but a light sheen of sweat dots his brow. "Yes, of course."

I reluctantly let my hand drop. "I am sorry to have startled you. Perhaps I should've waited in the hall? But one never knows what may lurk around corners at Soothing Hills … "

"No, no, I would've preferred you wait inside." He slowly walks behind his desk to retrieve two paintings, wrapped in brown paper and tied with a string. "These are much too large for you to manage on your own. I shall escort you back to your carriage."

I smile widely. His eyes are adhered to my face. I flush.

I feel a *draw*. A reluctance to leave the picture as the musical refrain blares in my head, over and over.

My heartbeat trips against my rib cage. *Who wrote that piece? But more importantly—whose voice speaks through it?*

We walk into the hall, and my words tumble forth, as they do when I am vexed. "So, I truly love these. So much so, I would like to purchase the one in your room, with the sheet music?"

"The music, you say. That is one of my favorites."

He gives me not yes, nor no. If it is no, I shall resort to common skullduggery to obtain it.

He returns the smile, seeming to be recovered from his ailment. "When shall I have the company of your presence once again?"

"Tomorrow? I ... " I drop my voice conspiratorially. Suddenly, my mouth seems to be in charge of my brain, the words slipping out. "Might I tell you a secret?"

He stops, staring at me, but his eyes are light. There is even a hint of a smile playing on his lips. "Oh, please do, Miss Frost. I must confess it has been an age since I heard a secret outside of Soothing Hills."

"Jules. Please call me Jules." Bold, I know. To ask this just after our introduction.

I nearly swoon. He is so very, very handsome. Dark blue eyes, one slightly larger than the other. Rather than unbalanced, it somehow manages to make his face more interesting.

The sweat has returned, dotting his brow. "Very well, *Jules*. What is your secret?"

"I work *here*, as a nurse in training."

His eyes widen, and I cannot tell if it is with interest or

blatant shock. His eyes scour my dress, as if trying to turn it to a nursing uniform by sheer will.

"You do? Which floor?"

"I float. Just go wherever I am needed." I flush at the lie. I am to remain with Nurse Turtle-bird at all times. Be confined to her ward alone.

He begins to walk again, his fingers wrapping around my elbow to steer me. "Is that so? Your father has given his consent for this?"

I give a false laugh. "Oh, he is wholly unpleased, but willing to make concessions at times."

We reach the entrance, and I sigh with frustration. I wish to be near this man. There is something … magnetic … about him. It is more than his looks—indeed he seems to scarcely be aware of the effect he has upon the feminine sex.

Even to follow him on his patients rounds would give me so much more joy than the evening of whist that awaits me.

"I hope you enjoy the paintings." He nods, turns to go.

"Dr. Grayjoy?"

He spins back, eyes clouded. "You may call me Jonathon."

My heart beats wildly. Very unconventional.

I smile so widely it hurts. "Jonathon, might I stop and see you if I am near your floor?"

His eyebrow rises at this overt rebellion of polite society. "To avoid a scandal, perhaps I should find you? I … would be glad to do so."

My face burns with the blush. "Wonderful. I shall see you tomorrow then."

I scarcely remember entering the carriage, and as I return

to my senses, I stare out the window as it rumbles towards the wrought-iron gates, past the corn. My infatuation has driven out the musical refrain, but I roll the words over in my mind, over and over like the surf.

"Two turtledoves, one red sparrow," I whisper.

JANE

The day is clear, bright and cold as I walk outside into the faltering gardens, but the sun shines brightly, glittering off the melting remnants of snow. I wander down to the dog pen, drop to one knee, and wait.

Within moments, Tiger and Wolfgang hurry over, half crouching, half happy, tails tucked partially between their legs.

I reach into my pocket and hold out a scrap for each, and they wolf them down in a blink and then are trotting back to their pack. Their life is nearly as poor as mine. They are not always friendly to others, but to me, they are like domestics.

I turn to go, heading toward the topiary maze. Inhaling the stinging air, I sigh. I have not seen Mason in several days.

Again, the worry, despite our kiss. Worry that perhaps Grayjoy has frightened him away from me.

The rambling stone walls line the paths as I make my way toward the hedge maze at the center. Another of my favorite places. Second only to the secret library.

In the heart of the maze, no eyes peer, watching, evaluating, scribbling, and overanalyzing your every move. Entrance here is only granted to the least volatile.

One may cry there, if one has the need. Or smile. Or spin in circles or—

"I don't understand why it can't be *now*, Mason. I have waited long enough."

I halt, frozen to the ground. Voices come from inside the hedgerow.

I should not listen, it is wrong, but ... Mason is inside with a woman whose voice I do not recognize.

"It isn't time. The plan must be enacted perfectly, or it shall fail. You know that. If we act too soon, what good shall it do you?"

"What *good*? Are you the one digesting crème of tartar? Or allowing people to thrust syringes in your bloody legs?" the feminine voice rages.

"No, I am not." His voice is sad. Very sad.

My cheeks heat with color. He cares deeply for this woman; I hear it in his tone.

Anger. Betrayal.

My chest aches as if the surrounding thorny bushes have grown out of my heart, spreading to envelope and prick each organ. I swallow, fearful a writhing stem may poke its way out of my mouth.

Tears flow, and the anger flares, hard and fast and heated. I do not cry.

I begin to pace, knowing my mind to be unraveling. Knowing, but powerless to stop it.

"I do not cry. I do not cry. I do not cry."

Tears stream in an unrelenting flow, and I turn and stumble, not bothering to be quiet—my only thought to flee. To make it back to the confines of my wretched room. The only home I shall ever know.

"Ow!"

My knee collides with a stone bench, and I lurch forward toward the maze's mouth.

"Jane!" he calls, his voice full of dread.

I spin and walk backwards. "*You.*" I jut my finger at his face. "You are a devil. *Come with me*, Jane. *I am yours*, Jane. Did you mean a bloody word of it?"

The woman hurries up behind him. "Miss? Miss, do wait!"

But I turn and bolt toward the gardens, heading back to the Asylum.

Outside the wrought-iron fencing that surrounds the gardens lays the cornfield.

"*Caw. Caw.*"

I hear them. The corn music begins. It seems to be coming from their *mouths*.

My breathing breaks into panting. *I am hallucinating.* I must be.

Perhaps I do belong here after all.

Bluebirds join the fray. They dip in and out, swooping between the beating black wings in a soaring ballet.

I reach for the handle and hear the first words riding the song.

"*Don't take too long.*" I plug my ears and push inside. Away from him. Away from the blasted music.

Chapter Seventeen

Grayjoy

"Nurse Chloe?" I stand in the ward's nurses' station, behind the iron bars.

Chloe halts in mid-stride, dropping into a hurried curtsy. "Yes, Dr. Grayjoy?"

"Come near, won't you?"

She struggles to keep the scowl from her face, her eyes flicking first to the corridor toward a moan issuing from a nearby room, then to the watch pinned to her uniform front. I am impressed she keeps her toe from tapping.

"It won't take but a minute," I assure her.

She wipes her hands on her uniform as I swing open the barred door.

"You have known Twenty-Nine for a very long time."

Her face goes rigid, almost protective—like a mother toward an invasive schoolmarm.

"Yes, sir. I expect I know her better than most."

I step past her to gaze into the corridor, checking up and down for eavesdroppers. The asylum is fraught with them and rumors and all the vile conspiracies that go with a closed-off, tightly knit community.

I meet her stare. "Where is the rest of Twenty-Nine's chart?"

"Why, whatever do you mean?" she says, but her face is white as the snow gathering round the eaves.

"How many years have you been employed by the asylum, Chloe?"

She swallows, her hand nervously fingering the uniform's trim. "Ten, sir."

I hate to use this tactic, but I am desperate.

"And would you like to stay employed?" I ask, knowing the answer. Her husband has passed, and she has a small boy at home.

"Of *course*, Dr. Grayjoy."

"I assume you have been sworn to secrecy. Again, with the threat of dismissal. You are between the rock and the proverbial hard place."

Her face morphs from ash to fire in a blink. She presses her lips tighter. Tears form in her eyes.

"I shall ask questions, and you merely answer yes or no." I place my hand on her shoulder, trying to comfort her. "Therefore you have not betrayed a confidence—blameless. I am not the enemy. But I *need* this information."

She nods, still not speaking.

I hold up Jane's chart. "Was Twenty-Nine's chart always this size?"

Sweat has broken across her brow. "No."

My eyes flick across the charts strewn across the desk. Each has a sketch of the resident on the front, done by one of the patients for identification purposes. Most of the pictures are yellowed and worn, depending on the patient's year of entry.

I stare at Twenty-Nine's, which looks astonishingly new for a girl admitted at the tender age of four.

I hold it up for Chloe to see. "Did Twenty-Nine always look this way?"

Chloe blinks, and a tear escapes. She angrily swipes it with the back of her hand, her nostrils flaring as she exhales. "No. No, she did not, Dr. Grayjoy."

Fear and excitement rush through my veins. I nod encouragingly. "Do you know where the remainder of the chart is? Does it still exist?"

The tears are a constant stream now. Her lips quiver as her resolve finally gives way.

"Here, sit down, dear girl. I shall not dismiss you." I pull out the chair for her to sit and collect herself. "I shall shield you from his wrath, I promise you."

Fear knits her eyebrows together. "I ... I's hid the chart. He told me to destroy it ... but I knew that wasn't right. It's ... "

Another nurse's heels click by the bars. I nod to her. "That all sounds well and good, Chloe," I say, a trifle too loudly. "But these tonics must be administered precisely per my instructions."

The other nurse turns forward, quickening her pace.

I place a handkerchief in Chloe's hand and lower my voice to a whisper. "Where?"

She hedges.

"How about if I guess … so if anyone should ever ask, you would not be lying?"

She sniffles. "Alright."

She stands and walks to a shelf at the back, beside the teapots. She stands on tiptoes to slide a dilapidated book into her hands, then points, as if it is a clue.

My finger taps against my lips. "A library? There is no library in Soothing Hills."

Her blush deepens yet again, and I fear an apoplexy. "There was. Long ago."

I had no idea. "Yes, thank you. That will suffice."

She inhales deeply and smoothes her uniform. As she slides past me, I grasp her hand and force open her palm to deposit some coins.

"I don't want it," she protests.

"Do not be ridiculous. It is for young Jeremy. I overheard you saying he needed new boots. It is a gift, nothing more. With no expectations, I assure you."

Her eyes fill with tears once again. "You are a good sort, Dr. Grayjoy."

She curtsies and hustles back onto the floor. In the direction of the moaning, which has continued without letup.

A library. I must find it.

I walk into Ward One so nervous I swear my heart has crawled into my mouth. I feel the steady, rhythmical beat of my pulse through my neck as it pumps out a steady stream of my fear.

"Hello, Jane!" Ginny says with delight, clasping her tiny hands together.

She is one of the few people I actually believe is truly excited to see me. That is a very new sensation, so I smile.

"Hello, Nurse Ginny."

"Just Ginny." She hands me my violin. I lovingly trace its grooves. It has a distinctive scratch on the front, but to me, that doesn't mar its appearance a bit.

It's merely careworn. Like me.

The other girls, Claire and Susan, wait patiently for me. My eyes drop to take in Claire's fingers—they are a constant tremble from too much laudanum. It happened to me. Frost's doing, once again.

It was the only time he was ever kind to me, because I believe he thought me incapacitated. *And I was.* And I refused it. It took away my pain, but also my music.

I remember waking one morn to the sun shining and the smell of summer wildflowers wafting through my window. Nurse Sally Spare had been absent—a complete rarity—the shriveled woman was never ill. It was as if the ravages of disease found her body so nearly corpse-like already, they deemed her an unfit host.

I missed my dose of laudanum that day, and my world swam painfully back into focus.

I had missed an entire season. No recollection. When I tried to summon the music to my head, to comfort me ... or even to hum middle C ... nothing.

That terrified me, more than anything I had ever seen or felt.

Dr. Grayjoy had only just arrived, and I told him it was killing me. Refused to take it.

And thus began a year of weeping, difficulty catching my breath at the slightest exertion, and my skin ... my skin was alive, as if a million tiny cockroaches crawled over every inch. At times it bled, as I dug my frantic nails into my flesh. Anything to stop the sensation. 'Twas the longest year of my life—

I swallow, blinking back tears of empathy for Claire's plight. I hope her fingers do not worsen and take away her music. I force my eyes away from them, praying she did not catch my stare.

For two blessed hours, we play, first the master's, then our own compositions. All the while, Ginny sits at the back of the salon, eyes closed, swaying dreamily for the better part of the pieces.

Another aide appears with a silver tray topped with real china teacups filled to the brim with thick chocolate. The smell permeates the salon, and my stomach gives an unladylike roar.

Ginny laughs loudly, handing me a cup.

"Might I have a word with Jane?" At the sound of his voice, I nearly choke.

My blood seems to freeze inside my heart as it stutters several times before resuming its beats. I place the teacup down so my shaking hand does not spill it.

Mason.

Ginny's eyebrows rise, and she cocks her head as they seem to exchange a silent conversation.

Finally, she nods, adding below her breath, "You best hurry, Mason. No telling what he will do if he sees you."

The *he* needs no explanation.

While behind the other girls, she gives a significant look at them as she says, "I know you are supposed to, but be quick about it. You know the rules about schedules."

Tattletales abound. Mostly due to the fact that Frost, Spare, and Alexander are famous for rewarding snitches with cigarettes, chocolate, liquor—any contraband to compensate for secrets.

Mason's fingers encircle my elbow and guide me to the vestibule, which leads to the veranda. We are still within sight of Ginny's anxious gaze. Her eyes flick up and down as she continues with a pretense of conversation with the other girls.

"You have been avoiding me. Which is saying something, as I have been assigned to your floor twice."

I have. In the past fortnight, when Mason was assigned the night shift, I stole away to the library, confident he would not report me. True to form, no lashings resulted.

My heart ... could not take the rejection.

I shrug, feeling my face heat.

"Jane. That woman. It was not what you thought."

"It seems nothing I believe to be true can ever be trusted."

"What are you talking about?"

"Nothing. I shall be glad to return the clothes." I lower my voice. "And the skates."

My stomach flips with the thought. It was the very best night of my life. At least he cannot take the memory.

Frost could, however. I shiver, picturing how a trip to Ward Thirteen would erase any meager happinesses I manage to wring from my life.

"Don't be ridiculous. Those were a gift. *It is not what it seemed.* She ... " He shifts nervously, his voice lowering to a whisper, eyes flicking all around. "She is my sister."

I cock my head. "You're *what*?"

"Yes. She was admitted here under false pretenses. Her husband ... decided he preferred a younger woman. So, he had her committed. Trumped up a myriad of symptoms so they would incarcerate her. It happens quite often, I am afraid."

The heat leaves my face, snaking into my décolletage. "It was Frost, wasn't it? Frost admitted her."

He nods. "I believe he may be taking bribes, forging symptoms just so the board will cooperate."

I hold completely still, except for the traitorous tremble in my lips.

"Jane, every word, every sentiment was true. Please, I *cannot* stop thinking of you. I am to be fabricating her escape, devising a plan. But my mind keeps returning to you. Please, help the both of us and just say you forgive me. And that things can ... *progress* as they were."

I feel a burn behind my eyes. Tears. Asking to be let free again. I blink.

"One outing cannot be where this ends. I ... I will not have it. Please, Jane, put me out of my misery."

A massive fear grasps my heart and squeezes—but I ignore it and swallow.

"Of course."

"Mason." The fear in Ginny's voice rings down the hall. I hear the panic in it.

Frost. He is come.

"Go, Jane." Mason turns, heading for the exit. "I will see you soon."

I nod and walk quickly for my seat, having just enough time to arrange my skirts as the door opens.

His eyes instantly find me. "Ginny. Let us see what the girls have accomplished thus far."

But I manage a smile, even under Frost's pinning gaze. Mason still cares for me. There is hope, after all.

Frost cocks his head at my expression, one eyebrow rising in silent question.

JULES

"And where, pray tell, have *you* been?"

I stop short in the entryway; my heart turns to glass, shattering in my chest.

Father.

I was out. Unsupervised. Unescorted.

"I … I went down to asylum to collect the paintings I purchased."

I stare down at them, covered in brown wrapping paper. I will my hands still, but they tremble and the resultant rattling echoes off the vestibule walls like an indoor, fear-induced thunderstorm.

Father's eyebrows knit. I cannot yet discern his demeanor, and I hold my breath.

"I see." His voice. I hear the horror; my knees go to water.

His eyes are bottomless.

I walk slowly for the stairs.

The hard lines of his face, the storm in his eyes … He is dangerous.

He is Mad Papa.

I try to slide past, but he grips my arm so tightly I issue a little cry.

I halt beside him on the stairs, refusing to meet his eye. Like an animal, if I do not challenge him, fight him, the confrontations will lessen.

"I suggest you spend more time on your music, and less at that infernal hospital. It is no place for a young woman of your stature, of your—"

The front doorbells rings, and I start, nearly crying out with relief.

Our butler, Mansfield, shuffles past, ignoring us, to open it.

"Mr. Willis Graceling, sir."

Willis. Oh, thank the heavens, Willis.

Willis's slightly plump face is ruddy with the cold as he taps his boots, shaking off the snow. I gently extricate myself from Father's grasp and step to the landing, smoothing my hair back into place.

"Willis. How *are* you? It is so very good to see you." I hear the falseness of my tone, but Willis smiles. He believes, hears only what he wishes.

Father tips his hat. "Good day, Graceling. I'm off."

He sweeps onto the porch, black traveling cape swirling behind as he alights into the waiting carriage.

I breathe a sigh of relief, only to inhale in anxiety once again. Time to face the music.

"Shall we go sit? I will ring for tea."

After a few moments, we're arranged in the parlor, and the maid places the pot and teacups on the table. "Might I bring you anything else?"

"No, thank you, Anna."

I bend to pour the tea into his cup, and his warm hand envelopes mine. I halt and take it in my own, forcing myself to stare into his light blue eyes.

"I think … we need to talk, Jules."

"About the wedding, of course. So many decisions. I know you preferred pink for the girls but really—"

"I … know you do not return my affection in the same fashion, but I had hoped it would grow as we spent time together. And honestly, we have rarely seen one another the past fortnight."

If Willis breaks the engagement, I shall never return to the asylum. Father is only kept at bay knowing my charge will soon be turned over to another. But I *must* find out about that painting. I push the images of strapping Grayjoy out of my mind as guilt sears my cheeks.

"I am so very sorry, Willis. I tend to get over involved. In everything. I will clear my schedule today. Can you … spend the day with me?"

His face lights up and my guilt *surges*. I feel ill. I am going to deeply wound this man. And he does not deserve it. He deserves someone much, much better than I.

"That would be capital."

CHAPTER EIGHTEEN

The knock on my door is quiet, but I startle anyway.

"Jane?" It is Ginny. "Might I come in?"

She pokes her head inside, and I smile. "Of course."

It is one of the reasons I love Ginny; she acts as if I have the right to refuse her entry, when we both know full well I do not.

My smile falters when I see her face. Something wicked my way comes.

"They have found you another roommate."

I sigh and take a last look at the pictures. Chances are good my roommate will be uncontrollable, and to save my sketches, they will have to be removed, unless I want them trampled, torn ... or eaten.

"Should I begin taking them down, then?"

Ginny looks sheepish. "I think that would be wise."

I clench my fists. I cherish the solitary periods between roommates. "How bad is it?"

She won't meet my eye. "Should I help you then?" She reaches to start unfastening one.

I touch her hand to halt her and shake my head. "No, I am fine. I will do it. It's bad, isn't it?"

She finally turns to look at me, her eyes pinched on the sides so she nearly looks in pain. "Yes, it is intolerable. I shall petition Dr. Grayjoy to have you moved to Ward One, posthaste."

My laugh is harsh. "As if Frost shall agree to that notion."

I begin to carefully collect the drawings. My eyes steal over the sheet music, and it begins to trill in my head. *Two turtledoves.*

"I was not going to tell, because it isn't official, but I believe you are sorely in need of good news."

I stop, my heart surging with fear. "What ... What is happening?"

"Frost has been permanently pulled from your case."

My mouth pops open, but I quickly shut it. "Why? How?"

"I know not the particulars, only that if Grayjoy is now in charge, we most certainly agree you belong on Ward One—and we shall both fight the board for your transfer."

It is as if a prayer has finally been answered.

I look around the room, a massive lump clogging my throat as I feel the prickle and burn in my eyes.

I may actually depart this ward.

Expectation postponed makes the heart sick. This scripture struck a chord with me. When one has prayed, long and hard, to a creator you feel certain has forgotten you—or worse, may not know you exist—to have your heart's desires finally answered ...

I swallow, again and again, as I continue to remove my sketches, one after the other. I pretend I am not moving to another room, but preparing for my wedding. To leave this place on Mason's arm.

It is a more mature fantasy than the ones of my youth—when I would pray deep into the night for a family. A long-lost relative to come and collect me.

Each day my dream slipped further away, my heart shrank—shriveled, really—till I thought it a dormant black seed in my chest.

"Twenty-Nine, are you alright, my dear?"

Ginny lays her hand on my arm to halt my fervent packing. I, indeed, have begun packing, despite no idea when I shall move to Ward One. "There is naught to fear. It is normal for one such as you to have misgivings about leaving. It's called the *institutional mind*, and happens to most everyone. It—"

"I am not afraid." Rage heats my cheeks. "Whatever lies outside these walls, whatever perils, whatever poverty. I shall be free."

My chest heaves, and Ginny looks mortified to have further upset me.

I stride to the window and press my hands against the cold pane. "I shall flourish or perish by my own hand. My own wits. So please, do not insult me that I am afraid. I am many, many things, but a coward is not one of them."

"No. Of course not." She sounds horrified.

She spins me to face her and holds my shoulders tight. "*Jane.* You are the bravest person I have ever met. Do you understand me?"

She continues to utter my name, breaking a rule for me. To encourage me.

My eyes prickle, and my shoulders give way, the anger draining. I nod.

But in my chest, a tiny sprout of hope begins pushing its way out of the shriveled remains that are my heart.

GRAYJOY

"I go down where? This is the way to the library?"

Chloe refused to show me, so I figured I would go to Jane. I believe the girl knows the asylum better than anyone.

Jane's face is a mix of fear and excitement as she tugs hard on my arm. "Here." And pulls me into a bloody broom closet.

I hold the lantern up, squinting in the darkness, but all that meets my eye is a myriad of bottles, liniments, and bandages. It is the nurses' closet.

Jane places her hand over mine to swing the lantern toward the back and indicates I follow. I acknowledge the bolt of electricity, the attraction. It was there from the first moment I laid eyes on her, but I knew it to be wrong, that she was not whole. Guilt flares in my chest as I admit to myself ... if I would've taken her for my wife, she would've been free of here, free of Frost. But my fear of condemnation from my family, from my colleagues, stayed my hand. As well as my own consuming pride—that she might not fit into my highly academic, highly sought-after life.

But this Mason, he seems to care not for this fact, the fact that stayed my hand these four years. He wants Jane anyway.

Insists he will find a way to get her released.

I swallow and taste the bitter truth. That despite my training, my years of building a reputation, this orderly apparently is more courageous and noble than I.

I swallow again. *You are a coward.*

"Hurry, Dr. Grayjoy. Do watch your step."

But now, it is as if Providence has finally smiled on me with ... Jules.

She ... is Jane. Too eerily Jane. They look very similar. Not twins, but much too close to be discounted. The eyes are identical.

I need to know how that is possible.

How the life of a physician's daughter and the life a life-long patient of this asylum intersect. Because intersect they must.

Which is why I now risk my appointment, digging into secrets that may well have been better off buried.

Jane stoops, sliding aside a rug and, "Viola!" she says, her feline eyes dancing in the lantern light.

A square-shaped trapdoor lies in the floorboards.

"Tunnels, sir. After you reach the bottom of the ladder, go straight, six sconces. There is then a Y. Here, bear right." She stops, discerning my face, assuring herself I am listening.

I nod. "Yes, Jane. Go on. We haven't much time till the shift change." When I shall be expected to return to the doctors' wing. Frost had a seemingly uncanny sense of when I would depart and return. I am now discerning that may very well be by design. I suspect he follows me.

"The tunnel will look like it is caved in, but it is not. Merely make your way round the rubble, and you will see it."

I slide myself into the opening, and she clutches my arm,

her fingers twining into my sleeve in fear. "Please be careful, he is often down there. Many a night have I played cat and mouse with him in the dark."

"Frost?"

She shakes her head. "No. Dr. Cloud."

GRAYJOY

I descend carefully, rung by rung, my mind debating what I reckon to be Jane's supposed illness versus ... a frightening possible truth.

Frost's case notes insist Jane has hallucinations—that she sees and hears voices and music that do not exist. This has been the cornerstone argument of keeping her a Soothing Hills resident since her admission.

Dr. Cloud.

There is no Dr. Cloud on the hospital roster.

Granted, the Soothing Hills staff is massive, 900 employees. Naturally there are staff I have never met. When first I met Jane, I used to think Dr. Cloud a personification, her fear of men come to life in her psyche. A compilation of whatever trauma had befallen her in childhood, presumably from a male.

But then, other patients under my care mentioned him. This doctor who only kept rounds at midnight.

I have questioned every physician, even the physick-superior, to no avail.

My questions were met with cocked eyebrows, which seemed to call my own sanity into question. I decided to continue my search for him in private—till I had concrete evidence to present to the board.

"Are we, perhaps, catching our group psychosis, Dr. Grayjoy?" Their stares seemed to imply.

I never again brought up the subject of Cloud.

I slide my way into the tunnel's blackness, the feeble light of my lantern barely keeping the darkness at bay.

Group hysteria? I have read of the concept, of course, but have never seen it on display.

I inhale deeply, and my lungs seize in a coughing fit. The dank smell of the tunnel permeates my nostrils, and I cover my mouth with my arm. I hoist the lantern above my head to spy a creeping black mold spiraling and swirling on the ceilings and walls. I pull out my handkerchief, plastering it over my nose.

I shall have to warn Jane. These molds can be quite dangerous.

In the distance, so it is barely more than a pinprick, a lantern hangs. At one time, these tunnels were a main source of transportation for the staff, but they closed a decade prior, after the disappearance of Patient Twelve. They are supposedly off-limits, with various cave-ins and disrepairs, but apparently *someone* is using them.

Someone—

I stop, dead still, and lift the lantern to extinguish it.

The shuffle of stones.

I bite my lip, hard, trying to remember the shape of the tunnels before me. It is dark as death. The *Y* Jane spoke of was visible from where I stood, before the light extinguished.

Step, shuffle. Step, shuffle. Step, shuffle.

Footsteps hobble forward, like the beat of a faltering heart. Growing louder and louder as they make their way toward me. Off beat, but rhythmical just the same.

The hairs on the back of my neck rise in intuition, and I finger the tiny pistol in my belt. A sweat breaks around my hairline at a sound, a sound that in any other place would be familiar, normal.

Sniff, sniff.

This man, this creature, is tracking me. Smells me in the dark.

I carefully slide off my overcoat, which I am certain is a virtual olfactory mish-mash of my life. My own cologne, ladies I have escorted, the woodsmoke of my fireplace office, medicines spilt and long forgotten. I lay it on the ground and slowly slide away from it, clinging to the wall like a spider.

Shuffle, step. Shuffle, step. It halts. Directly across from me in the dark.

The tunnel is large, but I know him to be very close. My heart beats so fast a wave of blackness ripples through my thoughts. I bite through my lip to clear my mind. Glorious, orienting pain drives back the mist of my mind, refocusing me.

I slowly pull the pistol, but do not cock it.

If this creature can smell me, its senses are highly overdeveloped for a human. The quiet click of the trigger would resemble a gunshot in the dead quiet of this tunnel that may soon prove to be my tomb.

Dr. Cloud. *This* is Dr. Cloud. I know it to my core. He *does* exist. Jane is not hallucinating. My mind whispers, *Is this the monster of Soothing Hills?*

Step-shuffle-step-shuffle-step-shuffle. The sounds move away, hurrying toward the smell of my jacket. This is my solitary chance.

I slide as quietly as I am able till my fingers feel the wall give way. The *Y*.

I turn right, hurrying down the corridor as quickly as I can. I reach the rubble and ease my way around it, as Jane suggested. The smell of the cave-in—dirt, plaster, mold—*should* conceal my scent. I ease my way around it and halt, fighting to keep my breathing even.

An inhuman growl.

My hands tighten on the pistol, jamming it out before me into the pitch-black.

Shuffle-shuffle-shuffle-shuffle. Off-kilter running. Like a hunchback.

I picture the ambulation pattern in my head.

He is retreating, furious I have thwarted him. I wait several minutes, till I am certain he is gone, before relighting the lantern.

I see it, down the corridor. The abandoned library. As I hurry forward, I do not know which frightens me more—that Dr. Cloud is real, or the fact that Jane is most likely not insane.

And has been imprisoned here ... her entire life.

The library is frigid, and I furiously rub my arms in a feeble attempt at warming them.

I have been searching nearly a half hour to no avail. Novels, non-fiction on everything from nature to politics to psychology, but no missing Jane chart.

The room is so odd. It is nearly clean. The wood floors remain, the bookcases intact. Even two wingback chairs, with just the beginnings of mold snaking up their legs, have stood the test of time.

I walk over to one and see ... a blanket?

I pick it up, rubbing the material through my fingers, and smell it. My stomach instantly tightens. It smells of Jane. Clean, with a tinge of flowery underlay.

"*Meow.*"

I startle, my head jerking backward to smack off the heavy mahogany bookcase, instantly smarting. I rub the spot and curse.

I whirl to spy a very large cat, tail swishing madly, yellow eyes staring, in the corner. It takes off, flying into the tunnels. I roll my eyes, feeling ridiculous. I've barely caught my breath when another tumult erupts.

A great ripple of noise, like sheets whipping in the wind. Overhead.

I drop to my knees, instinctively covering my head.
Bats?

I hold up the lantern, and my blood runs cold. *Ravens.*

A bloody unkindness of ravens sits on the reinforcement rafters above. Some upside down. I blink, rubbing my eyes. Their wings flutter, a whipping pell-mell of artificial wind battering my eardrums. But not a one squawks.

A single white page flutters down, and I lunge to catch it.

I flatten it, my eyes flying across the page to read at the top: *Patient Twenty-Nine.*

My heart skips several beats.

The unkindness takes flight as one, zooming out of the library, banking left, to barrel out the tunnel, and in a breath, they are gone.

As if they wanted me to find this page.

I am wholly aware of the irrationality of this thought as I proceed to walk to the wingback chair. I am a man of science. This is preposterous.

You just saw a creature who sniffed you out like a ruddy bloodhound and now a hive-minded flock of ravens that so much as handed you a page from Jane's chart like a bloody carrier pigeon.

I drag the wingback chair over to the rafter on which they were perched. I lift the lantern, and my breath sucks in.

Atop the rafter sits a very thick pile of parchment, a large rock holding it in place. The missing part of Jane's chart.

With considerable effort, I move the stone aside and slip the papers into my arms before stepping off the chair. I quickly sit and open page one.

Before I realize it, fifty pages sit nearby, and I shake myself. I have utterly lost track of the time. I shall be missed for certain. I rifle through the file, trying to find any last bits that may help me.

My eyes catch sight of a familiar word, written in another physick's hand. Dr. Gentile, one who has since partially retired from asylum life.

Upon entering the nursery today, I could not believe my eyes. Had I not done the child's intake myself, written down her history with mine own hand, I should've thought another physick to be mad from drink. Upon entering a week prior, the child's description reads as such: "three-year-old girl, blue-green eyes, catlike, dark brown hair."

As I called to her this morn, and she burst forth to greet me with her winning smile, her hair ... is utterly white. Not a strand of brown remains.

Marie Antoinette syndrome, *it is called. The phenomenon was said to occur in the disease's namesake on the night prior to her beheading. I thought it poppycock.*

But here she is, in the flesh. I cannot fathom what horror has befallen this sweet child, to precipitate such a change.

I concur with young Frost, however. She does, indeed, hear sounds others do not. I observed her standing by the window, staring out into the corn, humming, twirling, repeating words, as if they were being whispered into her tiny ear. A slack, incomprehensible expression on her pretty face

"Fear not the corn," she said. Most peculiar and precocious.

She should at the very least be kept for observation. But as I know her to be orphaned, I fear her fate may be such as to become a permanent resident.

The next page contains a sketch of a strikingly beautiful child. With brown hair. The same almond-shaped eyes that I have seen once per week for the past four years stare back from the page.

I collapse to the ground, closing my eyes, swallowing hard, again and again.

The same almond-shaped eyes that I, myself, painted. My embarrassing, forbidden obsession with Patient Twenty-Nine—that if I could not have her, I should paint her, to gaze upon her in my private chambers.

My personal resolve to rehabilitate her—to free her from the asylum.

The reality crashes down on me like the cave-in. She *had* dark brown hair. I try to imagine it, and my mouth goes dry.

The picture conjured is nearly identical to one *Jules Frost*.

I fidget as I fold the patients' bedclothes. Nurse Sally Spare approaches, and I jump, smacking my hand on the table, and promptly suck at my knuckle to quiet the stinging.

"Whatever is the matter with you, Jules dear? You are nervous as a pig on Christmas."

I smile. "I am sorry. I am feeling under the weather."

Ward Seven's door opens, and my heartbeat doubles as Dr. Grayjoy sweeps in. His handsome, rugged face manages to maintain its kind expression as no less than three patients pounce, all hurtling questions and requests in tandem.

I stare at him, my hands halting their automatic folding.

He is a large man and could be imposing if he chose to be, but no patient cowers from him—as they do Father. I stare, evaluating him.

I decide it is his eyes. They sparkle and crinkle about the edges—they are naught but welcoming and nearly scream, *Talk to me, tell me your troubles.*

And the patients are all too willing to oblige.

Dr. Grayjoy holds up his hands. "Ladies and gentlemen, I request you wait for this doctor to make his rounds in an orderly fashion, knowing I shall meet with each and every one of you, not leaving the ward till I have heard your complaint and, or, story."

My stomach drops to my knees, and they weaken. Grayjoy's eyes flick over the patients' heads to meet mine. And hold.

Something is different in the way he regards me, as if seeing me for the first time. My mind cautions restraint, but the thought breaks through—that perhaps he is seeing me, as I see him. As one I would shed name and title and dress for.

He is ten years my senior, but I have never felt such attraction. It is not his appearance, per se. Although it is far from lacking.

Dark, wavy hair, a well-groomed beard of the same shade. Deep, large, blue eyes, one slightly larger than the other. And he a muscular man—with more the physique one would see on a longshoreman than a man with his eye behind a microscope.

In my short time here, I have witnessed Dr. Grayjoy subdue unruly patients without the assistance of an orderly. Once they are restrained, he whispers to them—croons, really. The women, and even the men, eventually quiet under his murmured words. I suspect it was one of the key reasons this man was hired—that and his obvious empathy, which does seem to be in very short supply in these largely esoteric men, these alienists, who seem to view these wretched residents as experiments or with a singularly clinical eye.

They are people. *Every last one, someone's child. Someone's mother.*

I stare at the pillow case I am folding and blink back the sting of tears as a warm, large hand encircles my wrist.

"Nurse Frost?"

I turn my head, looking up into the depths of that deep-blue gaze. "Yes, Dr. Grayjoy?"

He murmurs low, so that only I may hear, "Jonathon."

I smile and nod, but do not repeat his name, should someone overhear us.

Indeed, Nurse Ginny, who is never an eavesdropper, seems astounded at the sight of us, her hand poised in midair, halted in her task of separating tinctures.

Dr. Grayjoy follows my stare and clears his throat, which prompts her eyes to drop back to her task at hand. He flips open a chart, pointing to words that do not match the ones coming forth from his mouth. "I wish to meet with you." He points with his writing utensil, as if showing me important facts. "Today, if possible."

"Where?"

He slides the quill, inserting it into the top of the chart. My eyes follow obediently.

"I would like ... to take you to dinner."

My mind roils. *How is that possible?* How can I manage that without being seen by someone who would undoubtedly tell Father ... or Willis?

My heart throbs with equal measures of guilt and desire.

"I ... I have to work."

He chews the end of his pen, contemplating. "Meet me on the lower level at six of the clock. A picnic? Here."

Not precisely what I had imagined—me in my work uniform, vaguely smelling of crème of tartar—but I shall not miss this chance.

I nod.

He drops the chart, his voice rising to a normal decibel once again. "Well, done, Nurse Frost. I expect that remedy shall work directly."

CHAPTER NINETEEN

GRAYJOY

I stand in the hospital hothouse, pacing like an expectant father, awaiting Jules's arrival.

The asylum has begun growing its own poppies in hopes of hiring apothecaries to produce their own special stock of laudanum.

The room is sweltering—the only warm place in the entire asylum, I suspect. The glass windows, fogged from the heat, overlook the cornfield on the asylum's north face. I swipe a peephole in the condensation with the heel of my fist to peer through. Not a very pleasant sight, the once green stalks dying and withering beneath the daily threat of snow.

I rub my hands together and swallow the lump of anticipation. I feel ridiculous.

It is then the squawking begins, and I turn my head. It feels as if time has slowed, an eternity for my head to swivel over my shoulder to spy the corn. My eyes widen as I swipe at a raised plant bed for support. *Again those infernal ravens.* A black, undulating blanket crossing the corn tops. Screeching and biting one another.

A strange, eerie dread creeps up the back of my throat.

I have never been a man to believe in the hereafter, but of late, a plethora of extraordinary circumstances seem to be swallowing me, like some living, gaping maw of incredulity. I rub my eyes in disbelief, but when they clear, the scene is unchanged. They seem to stare at me. A sweat breaks on my brow, which has naught to do with the hothouse.

Every beady black eye is glued to my pacing, no matter their location in the sky. Like one of those trick paintings whose eyes track the subject, no matter their location.

I once knew a falconer who refused to work with ravens. He swore they *knew* him. Could differentiate between he and his partner. Were too intelligent, too decisive.

"Any bird that smart, I'd rather eat than train. I jus' don' trust 'em," the falconer would say.

"This is ludicrous," I murmur, the scientist in me recoiling.

I turn away from the windows, feeling their glares sear my back. Ever since Jules's entrance into my life, the laws of the physical universe no longer seem to apply. Unseating my confidence. They have always been my gravity, my way of making sense of the world.

I try to refocus on the task at hand.

I unfurl, then snap open a festive, blue gingham blanket,

spreading it beside the windows. I had my manservant fetch a silver teapot and cups, a small dinner of watercress sandwiches, a block of cheese, fresh crusty bread, and wine. I chose to ignore the incredulous look on his face.

It was, indeed, out of character for me. I am typically turning away women's advances—not restructuring my bloody workday to woo them.

I hold the wine, turning it round in my hand to inspect the label. *Will she think me too bold?*

I sigh. "Too bold? You are inviting a woman you hardly know, unchaperoned, to sup with you in a hothouse. That is not bold, that *is insanity.*"

A throat clears. My face sears with heat. My back is to her. I straighten, rolling my eyes before I steel myself and turn.

"Do you always talk to yourself, Dr.—Jonathon?"

I feel my face flush deeper. "I do, I must admit."

She looks *stunning.* An incredible feat for one who has walked off the wards.

Jules has shed the nurse's cap, allowing her long, dark waves of hair to fan around her shoulders. My eyes sweep over her natural curls—some ringlets, some waves, as if it cannot decide how to exist.

Her eyes, those cat-like, mesmerizing eyes, stare intently. I dare not risk a glance at the rest of her.

My eyes flick back and forth across her locks, thinking of Jane's snow-white counterparts. I banish the thought.

"Please, make yourself comfortable." I spread a hand, indicating she should sit. She walks forward and then slowly eases herself onto the blanket.

She has shed her uniform for a dress of deep, rich blue that highlights the beauty of her dark hair. I surmise she, too, sent word to a servant to fetch it to her before her shift's end. I feel a little thrill course up my spine at the fact that she is trying to impress me. I press my lips together, smothering the desire to take her in my arms.

I place myself beside her, my heart hammering whilst a glut of emotions rush through my head.

Guilt. For perhaps wanting her because she is the facsimile of Jane, whom I cannot have.

Desire. Because she, herself, is stride-stoppingly beautiful.

Curiosity. To know what she is truly like.

Twins. They may very well be twins. Fraternal, not identical. I would need to see them side by side to be certain.

Frost's child. Is Jane, somehow, Frost's illegitimate child?

"You wanted to talk to me?" she implores, looking up through dark lashes.

I hold up the wine. "A drink first?"

She shrugs. "I am off duty now."

My eyebrows knit, staring into the twilight. "I shall take you home. I do not wish you to muss such a magnificent dress in a hansom."

Her smile falters, just a fraction, but I see. "Thank you."

"Tell me about yourself," I request.

At first, she is slightly shy, choosing her words carefully. But after two additional glasses, her thoughts flow as freely as the heat wafting from the fires. Bits of our conversation play in my head. I struggle to pay attention, my eyes roving over her full lips and, heaven help me, full hips.

She smiles widely—her eyes bright from the drink. "I had the best tutors but have never been able to speak with anyone outside of my household ... till this year. Till I have been able to work here. It has been a dream realized."

My eyebrow rises. "Working *here?* A dream realized? I must say your sense of dream may be distorted," I jest.

She shrugs, her eyes dimming. "Life is relative. Luxury to one may seem nirvana to another—who has wealth but no freedom. They may be willing to risk all to control their own life's path." She stares at me, cat-eyes narrowing. "Does that seem ludicrous?"

"No. I understand perfectly. Very well said."

"So that was growing up with Father." Her eyes cloud suddenly as she puts her hand over her mouth. It's nearly comical. "I am not showing discretion, you being his colleague and all. But something about you makes me say too much."

My heart sinks as all joy drains from her face. The change is astounding.

She ages before me, her eyes reflecting a gravity no woman her age should possess. I swallow hard.

Now, she is nearly indistinguishable from Jane.

Her mouth turns down as shudder of fear flits across her features.

I reach over, tightly grasping her hand. "No need to worry. I am an excellent secret-keeper. I *am* a doctor."

Her expression doesn't budge, so I add, "It is even on my calling card, right after my credentials." I make a move to rummage through my pockets.

Finally, she laughs. "Stop teasing."

I hold her gaze steady, willing my eyes to convey my sincerity.

She nods, eyes leaving mine to stare down at her lap. "Too true." When she looks up, tears shine. "I ... I must confess something. But, I must speak first. Please do not interrupt; I fear I shall not force my words out."

I nod, dread tightening my stomach. I fight to keep my expression blank.

"I ... intentionally bought those paintings. I wanted to be able to see you again. Since I began nursing at Soothing Hills, I ... have watched you. The manner in which you address your patients, allay their fears, truly seem to *care* about them. It's like no one else in this morbid place." Her voice drops an octave. "My father included."

I nod and boldly place her hand upon my cheek—desire screaming in my head and heart. I press my lips together to keep silent.

Her words bubble forth, like water over stones. "I know this is wrong, inappropriate, improper, and I am well aware a lady should wait on a gentleman's declaration, but ... I find you fascinating. I wish to *know* you." Her face flushes as red as the spiraling bougainvilleas above her head.

"I have a confession as well."

What am I doing? This was not in the plan.

My mouth forms words and confessions without my permission.

"You remind me of someone I knew. Someone I ... loved from afar. Albeit, an unrequited love. But I have watched *you* as well, Jules. You are quick-witted. And so very talented. And your beauty is a mere trifle to your person. I have not seen the likes of you anywhere. Of course I wish to know you as well. Why else would I propose so ludicrous a meeting place?"

She drops her head shyly. "Thank you."

"We shall have to proceed carefully, but proceed we shall. Does that please you?"

Her eyes sparkle. "Oh, yes. Very much."

"I would love you to play for me."

"Really?"

"Most certainly."

Her face lifts, her bottom lip trembling. "There is something else. *Promise* me if I tell you—you shall wait till I am finished."

"Of course."

Her hand claws mine. "No, *promise* me."

I stare. Her eyes are terrified. "I vow to listen till you are finished." I return her squeeze, putting both my hands around hers. They are utterly smothered, lost in mine.

"I ... am engaged. To another."

I feel the heat rising up my collar. I fight to keep my hands on hers, but my fingers twitch.

You want *her. Like you have never wanted anyone before. So she is taken. Fight for her. Take her.*

Visions of her and I entwined flit through my mind, and I shove them away. For a fleeting moment, I consider eloping. To take this girl and run with nothing. Begin again on our own.

I think of my dear mother, and my sister. Of how that would break them.

I come back to my right mind to register tears streaming down her face.

Her eyes plead with me. "I do not *love* him. I have not ever loved anyone my father has forced on me. He controls everything in my life."

She extracts a hand to grasp her hair, her entire person quivering like the leaves above her. "My hair, my makeup. When I rise, when I practice, when I sleep. I have wanted to escape, would do *anything* necessary to escape his rule. Even marry a man *I do not love* and bear his children, just to be free of him. But then … I met you."

My head swirls at this revelation. I blink, trying to focus on her words.

"I began to rethink every decision. To hope, nay, *to live* inside this insane possibility that perhaps you might want *me* as well. And … " Her hand clutches her chest, which is heaving. "And you do. At least you did."

My mind makes the decision. "I do."

To not have her, possess her, is unthinkable. Insufferable. I shall do whatever is necessary to make this our reality.

Her chest heaves as sobs rack it. "You do? You still do?"

I nod. "Am I pleased at this confession? Of course not. But how could someone as beautiful and singular as you not be attached? Truth be told, I suppose I am lucky you are not already wed."

"My father. I do not really know him. I never know how he shall be. After working here, I realize he shares many of his patients' traits. One moment he is loving, the next, a spitting, raving *lunatic*, one word away from pummeling me."

I swallow. "Has he struck you?"

She shakes her head. "He is too clever for that. He *has* locked me in a closet. Broken my violin before my eyes. Burnt my dolls as a child. Too many incidents to recount."

I nod. Precisely as I suspected. "Does anyone know of this?"

"My governess, who is now my lady's maid. She has been with me since I was very small. When my mother died."

A black mass takes flight from the corn, pulling my eyes to the darkening sky.

Her eyes drift to them and widen, then quickly resume their normal almond shape. But there was something in that look. Recognition, perhaps?

I pull out my pocket watch. "Jules. It is getting very late. You will be missed if he is heading home. I will not put you in danger."

She nods, fear pulling her dark brows together. "What shall we do now? How shall I see you again?"

I pull her to me, cradling her face against my chest. Her heartbeat is a wild, fluttering bird against my forearm.

I bend to kiss her, and force my breath to remain steady. Her lips are smooth as a worry stone against my own. I press harder, desire shredding my control.

Her mouth opens, surprising me. Fueling my fire. Her darting tongue shoves me towards a precipice I dare not tumble over.

I break the kiss, both our chests heaving.

"We shall find a way. It may take time, but allow me to think. We shall tell your fiancé when the time is right."

The night is so very cold. I pull the coverlets about my head, leaving only a gathered circle from which to peer out, always keeping the window's streaming moonlight within my sights.

Sebastian purrs against my leg, and I curl my body around him in a *C* shape as we mutually drink in one another's heat.

I sigh, and my exhale puffs out into my room, misty and curled like smoke from a dragon's nostrils.

Normally the gloom would ride the cold, burrow into my heart, settling there for the entirety of winter.

But now ... now I have hope.

It is a mere fraction of an idea that I may make it out of Soothing Hills, but it is all I need to keep the melancholy at bay. This shall be my last night alone in my room. My roommate is set to arrive on the morrow.

I hear the door creak open and stiffen, my hand instantly going to Sebastian to quiet or shoo him—depending on the visitor.

I hear the chair propped beneath my door handle, and my blood runs cold as the ice frosting my windowpane.

It might well be Cloud.

I hold my breath for what seems a life, then feel a warmth as someone slides behind me in bed. Tears well as I breathe in the familiar smell. His hands wrap around me, pulling me close, my back to his front.

"*Mo cridhe,*" he whispers.

My heart swells so full and large I worry it will burst in my chest as it always does when he croons to me in his mother's tongue.

I know the phrase to mean *my heart*.

"It is so very dangerous," I whisper.

"It is too cold. Too cold for all of them—but I cannot lie with all, keep them all warm, so I shall have to be content with you and that mangy furball."

I smile and burrow backwards, allowing him to pull me tighter into his embrace. Sebastian resumes his purring, his feline chest rising and falling in the slow rhythm of sleep.

"Sleep, *mo cridhe*. I am here. You are safe. I shall watch over you."

I nod quietly, glad he cannot see the grateful tear which escapes the corner of my eye to trail to my mouth.

I fall quickly asleep, astounded that, at last, the dread of my life is lifting.

And for the first time, I do not dream of birds.

CHAPTER TWENTY

Mason strides into my room and boldly takes my hand, despite it being broad daylight.

My face must show my fear, for he says, "All shall be well, love," and gives my hand a little shake.

My new roommate, Anna-Leigh, sits in the rocking chair across the room, neatly placed below the barely perceptible words of the madman scribbled on the wall.

She is quite beautiful—in an unkempt wildling sort of fashion. She rocks. That is all she is capable of. Unable to feed herself, unable to speak, barely able to walk on her own.

My eyes tear up. I do feel sorry for her. "She does not belong on this ward."

Mason's blue-green eyes are tight, and his lips press into a fine straight line, but I see the compassion. "No, she does not."

Our ward is for harmless women. However, women who are able to speak, to take care of themselves—women working toward Ward One.

This girl belongs on Two or Three, where the patients require a heavy amount of nursing.

"He is doing it to punish me." My voice cracks on the last word. I begin to pace. "It is because I am no longer under his control. He is showing me he can still affect my life. By placing her here with me."

I stare at Mason. "So that you may no longer visit me at night."

My chest feels as if an invisible hand presses down, smothering me. I clutch at it, collapsing to sit on my bed.

Mason squeezes my hand and pulls me toward the door. "Come with me."

I glance up at him and then out at the sun and cock my head in question. It is like we are creatures of the night—only able to show our love and spend time together with the setting of the sun. Never have we walked together in daylight—other than running for our lives through a cornfield.

"I don't understand."

He pulls me out into the hallway, and I stop short.

Ginny stands, one door down, beaming. She pours a patient's elixir onto a spoon and winks at me. "Be careful, darling."

I turn back to stare at Mason, dumbfounded. "I pulled some strings to get Ginny here today."

Indeed, he had. Ginny was almost never on this ward.

Before I have had a chance to process this revelation, I feel his warm hand gather mine and pull. "We still cannot afford to dawdle. Somewhere, Nurse Spare lurks." He leads me over to the nursing closet and opens the door. "I am certain she is quite out of sorts to be removed from her natural habitat."

We step inside the closet, and he closes the door, lighting a lantern.

"We are using the tunnels?"

He smiles, his eyes crinkling. "How else might one travel undetected in this place? It is my turn to show *you*, something."

Curiosity rises. I am certain there are secrets of Soothing Hills I do not know. Many tunnels I have not entered—they are just too far from my room to chance being caught. I've had to content myself with travel within my mind and be grateful I found my library to feed my imagination.

We drop into the tunnels, hurrying along. But not a soul is in sight. Most likely all are enjoying the reprieve from cold on perhaps the last autumn day before winter comes to stay.

We reach an oversized wooden door with a large metal lock in its center.

"Hold this, *mo cridhe*." Mason hands me the lantern, his eyes dancing in its light.

I smile, despite the oppressive gloom of the tunnel.

He fumbles in his pocket, extracting a very large key.

"Whatever is that?"

"Skeleton key." His grin is huge. Like a naughty little boy, proud to be working mischief. My eyebrow rises in question. "It can open any door here."

"What? Wherever did you find it?"

He jams it in the door, and it makes a resounding click. He stands up straight, almost laughing. "I stole it from Frost. From his own desk."

My mouth pops open, but I do not have time to fear, because he is hurtling me through a long hallway. At its end is a pinprick of light.

We reach it, and he holds up a hand to still me, peering carefully out of what looks to be a small window.

"It was another hidden observation glass. Hold still now, I want to be sure no one is afoot."

We are staring out into the maze.

For several long minutes we wait in silence. His thumb gently caresses the back of my hand in the near dark.

When it is apparent no one is coming, he says, "I chose this day, this time, for a reason. Do you know why?"

I bite my lip and think. After a moment, I say, "It is examination day. Twice a year massive rounds are made in preparation for the board."

"That is right, button. And Ginny has already forged yours. No one will be out here."

With that, he scrambles through the open window and waits.

"Come on!" He laughs and takes off running into the hedges.

My heart pounds in my chest, and I giggle, trying to suppress my fear.

We are out in the light. We are out in the light, my mind repeats over and over.

I cannot find him for several moments, but I know where to go.

To the heart of the maze.

I hurry there and round the corner, chest heaving, to see him sitting on the stone bench, face upturned to the sun. I stop to stare. He is breathtaking.

His mouth is pulled into a closed-lip smile, his eyes closed as he drinks in the sunlight. There are tiny striations in his blue eyes, making them appear deep and layered.

"Come here, *alainn*," He extends his hand.

I step forward, as if in a dream. "What does that mean?"

His smile is so intense, I blush.

"Beautiful."

He pulls me to sit on his lap, and we are quiet for a moment, worshipping the sun. Together.

"My mother is Scottish. I speak the language well … for an Englishman. She was the love in our house. I am told my looks favor her. I was forever underfoot as a wee laddie, my father spending most of his time with me elder brother."

Our hands are joined in my lap. I suddenly feel a coolness slip about my finger. I stare down to see a tiny silver band on my right ring finger.

I pull back to stare at him.

"That is a promise ring. I give it to you here, in the light. Which means no more hiding, no more darkness—only honesty. It means you will be my wife one day—if you will have me. And that I will drive away the darkness of this place from your mind and heart. By leaving it."

Blackness presses in and out as if an ethereal blanket seeks to snuff my consciousness.

"Jane? Good heaven, are you alright, lass?"

I laugh, loud and raucous, drunk with happiness. "Yes."

Tears stream from my eyes to drip off my nose and onto his white shirt. "Yes, I am perfect. And yes, I accept."

I hug him so tightly, I feel his chest rise and fall against mine. I slide off the ring to stare at it. Inside, there is an engraving. "It says *misneach*."

"What does that mean?"

"Courage." He nods gravely. "That is what we will both need to see this through."

As we start back through the maze, he adds, "And if I picked one word to describe you, Jane, that would be it."

A FEW DAYS LATER
JULES

I hurry down the corridor, glancing back for the tenth time to assure I am not being followed by Nurse Spare. I could scarcely wait for my shift to end.

This time, however, I am prepared. I brought a dress and changed forthwith. Granted, it's only a day dress, as nothing elaborate would fit inconspicuously in a bag, but one that Maeve assured me was truly flattering.

"Take most care, *ma chere*," she had whispered. Maeve was worried but knew that once my mind was set, there was no turning back.

It is odd I have come to think of any room in this asylum

as *our* place. I wonder how many other trysts, between patients, between staff members, why, even the forbidden—between doctors and patients—have occurred between these walls?

My mind leafs through all our meetings. Our murmurs, our pledges, our kisses. How quickly our relationship has progressed.

I have now not only been introduced to desire, but we are well acquainted.

It has been Jonathon's resolve and regard for my virtue, not my own, which has kept my reputation and chastity intact. If he said the word, I fear I would shed good name and petticoat if it meant a life with him. No matter the time or place.

I smile. There is no *vanilla* in Jonathon Grayjoy. Nor curry.

Indeed, he is the most spectacular combination of a man, with layers of interests—like a well-made dish in which one notices new tastes one layer after the next.

The heat blasts me in the face as I crack open the hothouse door. I am struck with the myriad of botanical smells which I have come to associate with Jonathon.

I hurry, snaking around the winding stone paths. Small trees overhang the stone walkways that weave around pools with lily pads and floating flowers. Plants grown for medicinals as well as decoration inhabit this hot haven. Red poppies line most every inch of the place.

Jonathon stands staring out the window, his broad back to me.

I hurry forward, and he turns to catch me as I launch myself. He holds me aloft, his tongue finding mine as I tilt my head to better reach him. *How I wish.* Wish this was over. Wish I were his. Wish this part of my life to be a distant memory.

As if hearing my thoughts, he pulls back, lowering me to the ground.

He has once again brought supper. "Mr. Blackstone is beginning to think me a true outdoorsman with the number of meals I am eating outside of our house."

I smile. "I can think of many indoor sports that might hold your attention."

His lips curl in a half smirk. "You are indeed a minx. Talk like that could land you in here. Promiscuity is indeed grounds for admission."

We sit and begin to eat. As usual, his staff has outdone itself—cold duck, wine, and crusty rolls. The heat lulls my senses, and I fight to keep my eyes open against the comfort of the hothouse.

After we've finished, he begins, "I have made arrangements with my barrister. The dowry I have arranged would far exceed what your father would be getting from Willis."

I nod, feeling my eyes fill with guilty tears. Not guilty enough, however. I *am* so selfish that I will hurt Willis to have a life with Jonathon.

I attempt to force the tremble from my voice. "Willis is a good man."

Jonathon gives a grim nod. "Indeed, he is. I have enquired about him, his character. I … know many eligible ladies. When we break it to him, once he has recovered from the shock, I shall do my utmost to play Cupid."

My body stiffens. A sound. *What was that?* It cannot be.

I have been so consumed with Jonathon, with my potential life with him, that the mystery of Twenty-Nine and her paintings was nearly driven from my lovesick mind.

Jonathon is still talking, but it is as if I have been struck deaf. Time seems to slow, as if the air about us thickens, the seconds trickling slowly past. I see his mouth move but hear no words issue forth. He notices my expression and squeezes, and then shakes, my hand. I see the fear in his eyes, but I am helpless to it.

The music. The *corn* music.

Stronger and louder than the soft calls from my childhood. It blares in red in my mind—a megaphone of sound and color. A cello plays the center stage.

I rise, as if sleepwalking, to stare out the hothouse window at the dying stalks.

Recognition flares. Father's voice, many times from childhood, "Mr. Barrow, detour round the Field Church Road, if you would."

Because it passed a cornfield.

My mind flashes through other routes, other towns. *Yes, yes, I am correct.* Always the same directions—avoid them.

Is that *why he resisted my coming to the hospital?* Because of the massive cornfield situated nearly against the main building?

Still, the melodic, mournful call of a singular cello. My mother's instrument.

The tones rise, up and down, with the rhythm of my breathing. I see the bow saw against the humming strings, the elegant, long fingers guiding its path.

I drop to my knees, my eyes overflowing with tears, and my heart seizes with want, with sorrow, with longing. "Mama."

It is as if her very essence is embedded in the notes. Not just a reminder—truly her soul, somehow.

As if it is trapped in that very music.

"How is that possible?" I whisper.

Jonathon's hand is on my shoulder, his words far away, as if beneath water.

Words. Words interweave within the music. As if a three-fold chord twirls forth from the cello. I begin to hum. I find I can follow the sound precisely.

My voice, one strand; *the words, the music*, are two twirling, entwining entities. Their notes alive and powerful.

It is as if my mother's voice speaks low in my ear. "My turtledove. You must find her. You may not approach without her."

My voice cracks. "Mama. Please. Where are you?"

I break into a cold sweat as my mind is swept backward in a deluge of memories.

Maeve standing over me as a child, glowering. "You must not ever speak of it again. I believe you, *ma colombe*, but your father ... " She hoists me into her arms, away from the window, away from the corn. "He will not like it. He will punish you severely. You wish to stay with Maeve, do you not?"

Tears flowed as my three-year-old self nods in agreement.

"Zen you only tell me. Not him. Ever. Yes?"

Maeve knew. What does she know now?

More words. As if an ethereal hand grasps my chin to right my attention.

Harmonic words hover and linger about the notes, till the two are indiscernible. *"You need her. Together, you are one. Together, you shall save us."*

My mind flashes, and I see her, as if some ethereal lightning strikes my brain—I glimpse her for but a moment. Cowering, clutching something to her chest against the wind.

Still quite young. In a white gown. I realize it is an infant against her chest and rain plasters her dark hair to her face.

Her face lifts, and our eyes meet. And hold. A terrifying jolt of current courses through my soul.

She mouths the words: *Find us.*

And it halts. She is gone in a roar of deafening silence.

My hands fly to press against the cold windowpane. "*Wait. Don't go.*" I pound it with a closed fist. "Don't leave me. Please. I don't understand."

A lingering tone remains; a single humming like a bell recently rung.

A single note.

Middle C.

She has left me with middle C. Warmth flows over my body, a palpable comfort, as if someone dearly loved embraces me.

It is the feel of childhood. Of a mother and stability. From so very long ago.

I weep into my hands, every muscle violently quaking. My surroundings slowly fade back into my consciousness as I realize Jonathon's arms are wrapped about me. The note is fading, and I now may finally discern his words.

He is the one who is shaking—his face as white as the lily behind him.

"The ravens … They took flight as one, and you collapsed to one knee."

I look up to meet his eyes, pinched and terrified.

"What just happened? *What did you hear*, Jules?"

His face glides upward as my eyes roll back in my head. And darkness comes.

I rub the glass furiously once again, but immediately it fogs.

Something is very wrong. I stare down at the dog pens, blinking, and whisk Sebastian into my arms, burying my face in his fur.

Down below, one of the dogs walks in aimless circles. Another bites his ear, and he docilely allows it, lying down on the ground to give the aggressor a better grip.

I remember overhearing Frost, screaming at Gentile, "Philistines! These canine ablations have been a tremendous success overseas. You are both fools if you do not embrace them here. It shall propel our asylum to fame and much-needed fortune."

Fear tightens my chest. Frost has been conspicuously absent, but now I see him, and Grayjoy, and Gentile, and a few other men I do not recognize, by the pens.

Frost is gesturing to the dogs. My blood ices, and I drop the cat and whirl. I pelt down the hall as my mind places the pieces together.

Frost, one week prior, at the nurses' station. Chastising Kate.

And instead of taking it, instead of lowering her head and allowing him to browbeat her, she fought back. Fought back like that very same dog I saw lunge at Frost two days prior.

He looked murderous.

I begin to cry in earnest. "Kate, Kate, Kate." I whisper her name like a talisman that I am—

Alexander wheels her out of her room, four doors down.

"Wait, please!"

Nothing. Her head does not even twitch in recognition.

I run faster, but Alexander is picking up the pace, pushing her toward the ward's exit.

"You wait, you ruddy"—a string of expletives escapes, and he rounds on me, letting go of her chair so fast it continues to roll without him.

I dodge away from his arms, sliding between his legs, and scrabble toward Kate. "Please. Please. No. *No.*"

Nothing.

My heart breaks. Like it has detonated in my chest and is no longer capable of beating. I collapse to the floor, holding my head.

Alexander arrives. "What is wrong with you now?"

Between short gasps, my chest hitching, I manage, "She's ablated. You took her to Ward Thirteen."

He nods. "Yes. The procedure was yesterday. She is going there permanently, right now."

He grips her face, but she doesn't flinch. Doesn't blink.

She is gone.

All that remains is a shell.

I hear nothing else. I grasp my hair in my hands and pull, and then stumble my way back to my room. And find that bottle. The tiny blue bottle with my liquid salvation inside. I upend it and shudder.

Jonathon paces before the hearth, his arms laced behind him. He furiously worries his bottom lip as if discerning a riddle. We are now in his private study, the door locked.

Despite the luxurious blanket, despite the warm cocoa between my palms, gooseflesh tears across my limbs, dimpling my flesh from scalp to toe. I realize the rippling surface on the cocoa is coming from my own hands; I am shaking.

"You hear *voices* in the music?" His face has drained to stark white; a corpse would have better color.

I nod, and his expression blackens. He rounds on me, squaring his shoulders. I shrink against the intensity of his gaze. "You must *trust* me. Do you trust me implicitly, Jules?"

I nod.

I do. Like no other. Except perhaps Maeve. But with every strange, new revelation, I am doubting even my most trusted companion.

"You must not tell your father of these voices. Residents have been imprisoned for less."

A rush of fear pumps from my heart, weakening my arms, causing the cocoa in my hands to slosh down over my fingers.

"You believe I am ill. I am not ill. This is reality. I hear the words as surely as I hear your voice now. I am not imagining it."

He bites his lip again. "I ... do not know what to believe. But until we sort it out, I must protect you."

I swallow. "You have sent for Maeve, then?"

He flips out his pocket watch, and I notice the shake in his own fingers as he fumbles for it. A hand I have seen wield a scalpel with unflinching precision amidst screams of madness. A hand that did not waver when a surprise blow narrowly missed his jaw.

"She should arrive any moment."

I stand to stare at the cornfield. No sounds emit, except the occasional squawk of the ever-present blanket of ravens perched on the stalk head. The cornfield looks as any other field would. The birds do not.

I shiver, staring at them. All seem to stare back.

Jonathon notices and is instantly behind me, rubbing my arms. He follows my stare, and I hear the hard click in his throat as he swallows. "They are queer, to be sure."

I give a quiet, derisive snort. "I am queer. They …" The words die on my lips.

"What, darling?" Jonathon prompts.

I feel my face color and try not to be pleased with his use of this endearment. "I was going to say wicked. But they are not wicked. I have dreamt of birds for as long as I can remember. They are frightening, yes. But not wicked."

Jonathon's thick eyebrows rise, his unwavering gaze pinned to the flock. "If you say so." His voice indicates he is anything *but* convinced.

I flinch at the soft rapping on the door. Jonathon's eyes whisk from me to the door and back in a blink.

"Hide," he whispers, finger jutting out to indicate a tall cluster of potted trees.

I lift my skirts and dart over, sliding behind the copse of pots to ease myself down into a crouch. I leave one eye room to spy and hold my breath as Jonathon hurries forward, smoothing his waistcoat. He stops at the door and takes a deep inhale before opening it.

I bite my lip as Maeve sweeps into the room. "Vhere is she? Is she alright?"

Jonathon's calm is placating and I bristle. He's using the very same tone he uses to subdue unruly patients.

"I assure you, Miss Beaucage, she is fine. She—"

They suddenly both whirl in tandem, staring at something hidden from my gaze, something approaching in the hallway. Maeve takes a single step backward. Her hand flies to her heart, clutching her shirt, her eyes wide, round circles. She stumbles, but Jonathon swiftly catches her, holding up her weight.

"What are you doing here?" Jonathon's voice is unnaturally high.

I stand, my quivering legs ready to bolt from my hiding place. *Is it Father?* I nearly vomit with fear.

"*Ma colombe?* What 'ave you done to your hair?" Maeve's voice is tight, as if her throat has closed, her breath strangling out every word.

I cock my head at her use of my endearment.

A soft, melodious voice replies, "I am afraid I do not understand." Then, to Grayjoy, "He ablated her. My ... She was my friend. And—"

"The canines, yes. Frost has been campaigning for the ablations with the board for months, insisting many patients are in need of the procedure. You are in danger, Jane. You know too much. I will need to keep someone watching you at all times, till we sort this out."

A girl steps into view. No ... *I* step into view.

My world and perception seem to roll, my mind cartwheeling and righting in a matter of seconds, leaving me heaving and breathless.

My legs give way, my knees striking the hard floor as pain resounds the whole way to my hips.

The girl. My mind reels, lifting up and crashing down like the asylum's dowsing machine.

Not me exactly, but a close replica. *Not my hair.* I lift a curl of my dark brown hair, staring at it as if for the first time. Her hair is *white*. A stark, stark white. Braided on either side and rolled into a tangled bun at her nape. A piece has escaped the twist, and it is longer than mine, reaching the top of her hipbones.

A strangled cry issues from Maeve's already open mouth, her eyes blinking furiously.

"*Ma ... Ma* T-turtledove."

Her eyes roll to reveal the whites as she swoons, but Jonathon swoops in, easing her into a nearby chair.

I break free from behind the trees to bolt toward them, my heart pounding madly in my chest.

As the girl turns, time slows, as if the air has liquefied, pulling against my skin and mind, making each step an effort. I see her profile, the pinched expression in her eyes as she flinches, holding up her arms in automatic self-defense.

Her eyes finally drift up to meet mine—we both freeze.

I unconsciously hum middle C, and at precisely the same time, another voice joins mine, in a perfect harmony.

The girl takes a step closer. The girl in patient attire. The girl is a ruddy patient here.

My mind thunders as the explanations rumble forth, and the

words break free without permission. "You are Patient Twenty-Nine."

Jonathon stands, his gaze darting back and forth between us. Maeve's chest heaves as a wail of utter despair slips out.

"*Ma colombe, ma* turtledoves. *Two* turtledoves." She stands, looking mad, her hands flailing as she paces back and forth between us. Her eyes dart back and forth—seeing nothing here, something long gone.

"I could not stop 'im. I zought you were dead. Good merciful heaven. *You are not dead.*"

Her ashen face drains even further.

"He lied. He lied. He lied."

Her unfixed eyes stare at me, her entire body shaking. She claws her face, murmuring to herself, "You *knew* he lied. You convinced yourself. You did not fight. You did *not try to find her.* But it was better to have one than none. Heaven forgive me."

Jonathon grasps her shoulders, halting her frenetic pacing. "Who lied, Maeve?"

But her words have cracked open hazy, uncertain memories. Memories I had convinced myself were false, had come from a childhood filled with reading.

Maeve and I in the closet, I am small. Her long fingers wrap around my neck to cover my mouth. "Shh, shh, my chere. Please be quiet, ma colombe. It is hide-and-seek. They must not find us."

Harsh voices outside the closet. But I'm not scared, so long as I am with Mama or Maeve, all is well in the world. I snuggle tighter into her chest, waiting, and begin to suck my thumb.

"I have removed her from the house." Papa, on our new device, Mr. Bell's telephone. "Yes, it is most unfortunate." A quiver in his tone.

"I have not told my wife, I shall directly. I was trying to spare her as much pain as possible. I shall tell her it was an accident. A terrible accident."

He hangs up the phone and whispers, "And she was."

Maeve's chest rose harder and faster with Papa's every word. She'd squeezed me tighter, her body shaking, just like it shakes now.

She stands, squeezes my hand, and leads me to Twenty-Nine, who places her hand in mine and takes Maeve's other, so we form a ring, as if we might play ring-around-the-roses. Another memory flashes: childish giggles, two voices, twenty years smoothed from Maeve's upturned face. Mama's face, too.

Twenty-Nine's face quivers. "It is true. I did not imagine it. I had a family. I see you clearly now."

I speak for the first time. "No, you *have* a family."

Maeve's voice is low but certain. "Jules. This is Jane. Your sister."

CHAPTER TWENTY-ONE

JANE

"Please, tell me again"—I collapse at Jules's feet, grasping her hands tightly—"what you remember?"

The past few hours have flown—we instantly began sharing every memory, trying to splice together where the fabric of our childhoods began to fray—leaving me at the asylum and she alone. Opulent ... but nearly as alone as I. I keep hold of her hand, afraid to let it go.

Jules smiles indulgently. "She would sing to me every night before bed. Read to me. Hum—"

I begin humming middle C.

Jules nods, her eyes widening. Gooseflesh ripples my scalp, and I shiver, noticing the identical bumps tearing up her arms.

"What do you feel when you hum it, Jules?"

"Warm blankets."

She nods. "As do I. Do you have any recollection of me?"

I cock my head, thinking hard. "I did have glimpses of another place. But after a time, I convinced myself that I had conjured them—read too many books, trying to place my mind in a safer yesterday."

Her eyes fill with tears, and she presses her trembling lips tight. She has told me of all that Frost has done to her.

Burning her cello. Chopping up her dolls while she watched. Placing a violin out in the rain, just out of reach, as she sat at a window, staring at it.

And as she grew, so did the punishments. *Locking her in a closet for a day.*

At this image, a skeletal hand plunges through my chest to squeeze my heart as I think of solitary.

"You had your own kind of solitary."

Her body shakes, and Dr. Grayjoy slides behind her, rubbing her shoulders as she closes her eyes, breathing deeply through her mouth.

As I watch her trembling hands, I think, perhaps for the first time, that maybe I am the lucky one. Though alone, Frost had limited contact with me. With Jules, she was the focus of all his manic energy, obsessions, and controlling personality.

Grayjoy stares. "Do you need a drink, Jules?"

She smiles, tipping her head back to look at him. "Yes, please."

The way they look at one another leaves little doubt of their feelings. She hums beneath her breath, and I hear, *Let him try to control me now.*

"Do you mean your father?"

Her feline eyes snap back to me, suddenly hard and cold. "What?"

Grayjoy drops the decanter, and it explodes, sending shards skating across the floor. He hurries over, ignoring the slivers as he steps over them. "Jules did not say anything, Jane. She was humming."

I swallow, looking back and forth between the two of them, fear suddenly growing in my chest, expanding like a child's balloon.

"Do it again, Jules. That was one of your own compositions, was it not?" Dr. Grayjoy prompts.

She nods, eyes never leaving mine. She clears her throat.

Humming—D, E, C, chords and refrains. *He shall never take you away now. Let him try.*

My hands fly to cover my mouth, and I shake my head. It is as if Jules's voice speaks directly in my ear as the music plays. As if it is the lyrics to the symphony.

"What do you hear?" Grayjoy demands.

I shake my head, tears falling now. I picture the dunk tank and wrap my arms around my body for warmth.

"You do it now, Jane," he demands.

I chance a glance at him. He doesn't look angry, or concerned, even. He looks terrified.

I hum, long and low. My favorite original composition.

Jules slides from the wingback chair, her bottom striking the floor so hard and loud, I wince at the sound.

"You said, 'I have a sister. I shall never be alone again.'"

I open my mouth, but no words come forth. Those were the

precise words I was thinking as I hummed the music.

Grayjoy begins to pace, absently running his hands through his hair till it is sticking up on end. "Colourata."

"What?" we ask in unison.

Jules slides back to take my hand.

"The ability is called *Colourata*. A musical language. I have read of one other patient who has such an … ability."

MASON

I take a deep breath and make my way into the tunnels, not quite ready to face my night shift. Since my decision is made, that I *must* have Jane, that I must find a way to remove her from this place, whether legal or foul, my life has complicated four-fold.

My sister anxiously awaits any plan, so that I might help her escape as well. Her own plight: A horrible ex-husband, who committed her to Soothing Hills on a concocted charge so that he might trade one wife in for a younger, lovelier model, incarcerated her under a false name, Mrs. Smith.

Indeed, I have unfortunately heard this scenario whispered more than once since starting. These women, used to a life of luxury and comfort, quickly succumb to the struggles of asylum life—conveniently making them appear exactly as their admission papers proclaimed. *Insane.*

Not my sister. She is just as feisty, just as determined to exact revenge as the day they admitted her, kicking and screaming, and cursing her husband's name.

In my short time here, I have seen many a resident far saner than myself. Improper incarcerations abound.

From spousal desertion, to epilepsy, to dropsy. Purely physical maladies—or an unhappy marriage—are equally sufficient reasons for permanent placement. The physicks who practice *these* admissions are less than scrupulous. And Frost is at the front of the pack, wielding his pen like the almighty sword, striking down people's lives with his scribble of a signature.

I sigh, shoving my hands deep in my pockets, and walk quietly through the tunnels, heading for the library. Rage flushes my face—rage at my life, my situation. Although a second son, I had expected a bright future—till my father passed.

And now. Love. I never expected love, if I am honest. I expected to marry, to produce an heir, to continue our bloodline.

I think of Jane.

Her full lips, her striking white-blond hair, her person. Life inside Soothing Hills produced a woman unaware of society's expectations. Her spirit and mind developed into someone so unique, so pure—someone I would die for.

Who I would do most anything to free. So we might be together.

"*Misneach*," I murmur, and square my shoulders against the silence.

Grayjoy told me of the library, of Jane's missing chart. He is being watched, so he requested I go in his stead. Any answers to her past will most likely lie buried here, under forgotten piles of documents and years of layers of dust.

As I turn into the hallway, I make my way around the rubble and focus on the task at hand. The dark seems *darker* here—as if the air has liquefied to ink and is somehow infused in the air of this corridor.

I hold the lantern aloft and stifle a cough into the crook of my arm.

The library is quite large, with books from floor to raftered ceiling. I squint, trying my best to hold in another sneeze. I see leftover patient activities, scattered to and fro on the shelves: an old paintbrush, a chalkboard, and numbers we use to reorient the patients to the date.

A fluttery movement.

I start and stumble backwards. A single raven perches on a rafter beam, staring at me. I cock my head. *A bird. Down here?*

The memory of the unkindness of ravens, seeming to shelter us in the cornfield, resurrects in my head, along with the rising of the hairs on my arms. I swallow, turning away from its disconcerting gaze, fully aware of the lunacy of the thought.

I walk toward the shelves, not having the slightest clue where to begin.

After a quarter hour of searching, I slump into the dirty armchair, my face in my hands. The bird has changed locations. It now perches on what looks to be a natural stone ledge high above the bookshelves.

I squint, and the bird cocks its head, left and then right. My breath catches. Is it standing *on* something?

I sigh, walking to the shelves. I give a hard tug, but they are mercifully bolted to the wall behind. I slide my hand and feet onto the shelves, gritting my teeth as they creak and groan.

One, two, three. I climb, higher and higher, till I can finally grasp a rafter with one hand, fingers splayed on the other, reaching for the mysterious something. *Too far.*

I stretch, but it is too high, and I am far too large to fit in the space between the ceiling and the top of bookshelf.

"*Caw.*"

My nostrils flare as fear pumps steadily from my heart, trying to weaken my grip. This is so very unnatural.

The bird flaps, talons grasping the book to drop it on my head.

"Blast!"

It bounces off my crown and topples to the ground.

I hop down, gathering it tentatively into my hands, dusting off the cover. The initials, *IJF,* are engraved in a beautiful silver script on the front. The bird flutters back up, waiting.

Oh, merciful heaven, it is waiting.

I crack open the book and realize at once it is a diary. A precise but beautiful hand has filled page after page. She has numbered them.

I lose track of time, reading this woman's thoughts. Her words paint pictures upon my mind—the birth of her children, their odd circumstances. Fraternal twins, but born two days apart. I have never heard of such.

I stare up at the bird. "What am I to ken from reading this?"

I feel insane. *I am speaking to a raven.* I feel a sudden rush of camaraderie for poor Poe and a twinge I may be developing his madness. The bird takes flight from its perch to land on the top shelf. My heart beats loud in my ears, drowning out the morbid flapping of his wings. It clutches something in its talons. Dread forms a ball in my throat, leaking its bitter taste up into my mouth.

The object falls by my feet with a tinny clatter. Numbers. It has dropped numbers.

I swallow and recognize the metal numbers used on the wards to reorient the patients to the day and time.

My stomach clenches. *Seventy-five. Does it mean* page *seventy-five?*

"*Caw-caw,*" it chastises, flying back up to the perch.

I blink again and again, trying to maintain control—to reckon this bizarre new reality that has become my life. I flip the pages to seventy-five.

I remember his passion that night. His need. Every touch seemed to linger and burn, like no other night together. Jules's conception was magical. Tender, thoughtful. We lay together afterwards, holding one another for a long while.

Late in the night he woke me, wanting, again. Then ... something happened.

His hand strokes my thigh, pulling me closer. I am still exhausted from the hour prior, but wish to make him happy. I reach for him in the dark, my hands tangling into his hair.

My nose wrinkles. An odd odor. Nothing like his usual musky, woodsy scent I have breathed every day for a decade.

Fear pounds my heart—that this is not my husband, but a stranger who has slipped into my room, my bed ... myself. While I slept in the dark.

"Darling?"

A near growl. Every hair on my body lifts in fear.

I reach up with my trembling hands in the dark to feel the face. The strong nose, long lashes, curly hair. It is he.

"What is wrong?"

His face twitches beneath my hands. Still he does not speak. In moments it is over.

I bite my lip, holding back the tears. In a moment, he slips from me, from the bed, staggering out the door.

I wipe my hand across my brow. My waistcoat is drenched through with sweat.

I look up to see two more numbers placed perfectly in the dirt before me. I was so overcome, so swept away in the woman's words, I did not notice the bloody crow's descent.

I swallow and turn to the page.

I blink, squinting harder in the dim lantern light.

This writing is familiar. Perfectly formed, professional blocks. As if each letter is a soldier, screaming out the intent with each syllabic sound.

Frost. Good heaven above, *it is Frost's hand.*

This journal shall serve as the last will and testament to my wife, Ivy Jane Frost. She explicitly states the children are to be left under my care upon her demise.

My eyes skip down the page, and my breath sucks in. The handwriting has disintegrated to nearly illegible, but I still see remnants of the distinctive block printing. I lift the paper to my nose and sniff. A faint smell of old spirits still clings to the page, a testament to long-dried spots of spilled ale.

She … is not mine. The second child conceived by him. *Born two days later than my own precious Jules. She looks perfect. But I know ... deep inside her beats not my heart, nor the heart of her mother. But him. The heart of a monster.*

The pain of this reality is far too great to bear.

She, the little girl, has confessed her abnormalities to me. I must dispose of her. But I cannot bring myself to do it. Her mother ... has confessed the same. I believe Ivy may suspect my plans.

I love her. Love them both. Love them all.

And hate myself for it. I know now what must be done. I shall perform the procedure.

The library turns, nay, upends, as vertigo spins my head. "Jane," I whisper, my hands shaking as I ball them into fists.

"You monster, you are talking about *my Jane.*"

My mind conjures a tiny, innocent Jane, large blue eyes bulging in terror. I stare around at the library as if seeing it for the first time in all its freezing, lonely, lunatic glory. I picture her pink mouth screaming in terror as he brought her here. "Left her here."

And the mother. *What happened to the mother?*

Rage reddens my sight, flushing my face as I grind my teeth. *He performed the ablation. So she could not protest. Could not condemn him, reveal his secrets. Then what? Is she still alive, wandering aimlessly like the rest of Ward Thirteen?*

I stand, my hands clasping and unclasping. I am vaguely aware the bird is swooping and screaming.

"You monster. You left her here. A wee girl."

Flashes of recognition reverberate through my brain.

I recall Grayjoy's words: "It is a very rare condition. But

indeed, I have seen it twice."

"Split personality. You believe your other half *conceived* Jane, had his way with your wife, because she was born two days later."

Disgust, and a pain so sharp I feel it slice my guts, doubles me in half.

"*Misneach, mo cridhe*," I whisper to the dark. To Jane.

Shuffle-shuffle-step. My blood goes cold in my veins. *Footsteps?*

I hold statue-still, fighting for control of my now frantic breathing.

It is Dr. Cloud. I am certain. *Dr. Frost's alter ego.*

The bird squawks; I duck as it dive-bombs me from the rafter, flapping its way out of the library, soaring into the tunnel proper.

A moving moan echoes through the chamber as the creature ducks out of the bird's flight path.

Shuffle-shuffle-shuffle. Directly outside the catacomb leading to the library.

He is come. My heart pounds hard as a cold sweat dampens my brow.

I am trapped. It is the only way out.

People have died in this tunnel. I grit my teeth—I will not be next. Jane comes to this library. *Alone.*

I shudder—if I die, there will be no barrier between *it* and her. No one to warn her.

I shall *not* die. Not without a fight.

I stare up and make my decision, extinguishing the lantern.

Shuffle-shuffle *step-step-step.* He is loping forward, down the tunnel. I hear his breathing just on the other side of the pile of rubble.

I wrap my hands around the rough beam and swing, *back*

and forth, back and forth, till my legs wrap around the rafter. I haul myself up, straddling it, battling to master my breath, keep my breathing quiet, lest I alert him.

Stones crunch directly below. I *feel* him in the dark. He travels without a lantern, as if he does not need the light to negotiate.

He is a creature of the night.

My senses heighten: the rough-hewn wood scratches against my palms, the air is warm, dense in the high rafters. The smell. *Sulfur.*

He has arrived.

Sniff. Sniff.

I pull my shirt to cover my mouth, to conceal my breath.

Mercifully, his cane taps in front of him, then up the side of the bookcase. *A hollow sound?*

My blood freezes at the sound of a door swinging wide. The footsteps shuffle forward, growing fainter and fainter. The click of a latch refastening.

I swing down and fumble to light the lantern, cursing the shake in my fingers. With a flare of yellow, it mercifully illuminates the library around me. I run to the bookshelves, pulling and tugging every few inches, trying to discover the door. *Nothing.* The room is still and silent as a tomb.

Focus, calm yourself. I hold still, close my eyes, and breathe deeply. After a brief moment, I smell it. The acrid odor of Frost's alter ego. Feeling ridiculous, I begin to sniff up and down the books. My eyes tear, and I blink rapidly as the sulfuric trail flares my nostrils.

I pull out the books, flinging them pell-mell to the ground, searching.

My heartbeat doubles when I see it.

A peephole. Hidden behind a book. So that he might spy on whoever happened upon this place. *Spy on Jane.*

I nearly wretch with dread and jam my fingers through the blasted circle—irrationally trying to damage his ever-present eye in her life.

Rage consumes me, and I swipe the entire shelf of books to the ground. Then I hear the *click.* The whole section of bookcase pops open, and I stand for a second, breathing hard, staring at it in disbelief.

I ease it open with a *creeeak* and peer inside as a thought ices my veins, deadening my heart.

I know precisely where this passage leads.

CHAPTER TWENTY-TWO

JANE

I sit before the hearth, my eyes darting back and forth between the two of them.

I hear the tinkle of decanter on tumbler and a heavy sigh as Dr. Grayjoy pours his second Scotch. Jules sits across from me in the opposite wingback chair, her heavy-lidded eyes drifting closed from fatigue.

Maeve returned after seeing to an alibi at the estate and now lies curled on a bed in the corner.

She is speaking of returning to France, now. Her guilt drives her away—that and the fact she knows I shall not ever leave Jules's side. That someone else in the world now cares for Jules as much she does.

Jules's fingers drift to her neck as she fidgets. A tiny light flashes on the stone floor, catching my eye.

Her eyes pop wide open. "Jane, do you remember Mama?"

I bite my lip. "The sketches you have seen, that is all that remains of her for me. She is more a … feeling than a person for me."

She nods, her eyes horrified. "I do remember you. I always did. I used to endlessly bother Maeve about it, but she would lie, trying to protect me."

Maeve stirs, shakily sits, and allows her head to drop into her hands—as if it is simply too heavy from all these revelations.

We all sit without speaking for some moments, as if mourning the dead.

"Your mama … I think she knew he was unraveling. Your father was furious, as the police became involved, which made him even more anxious and nervous than usual. And then … then I overhead him on the phone one evening. And he was arguing with someone, though I had not heard anyone else announced that eve. Then you disappeared, my love." She turns to stare at me, a constant stream of wetness flowing as she blinks again and again, oblivious to it.

"Your mother stopped speaking then. She … could not do anything but sit and hum. Her music never left her. There was an incision … two dots on the tops of her eyes. And a few days later, he came to me, telling me she had passed. I was terrified. Your mama had been my very best friend. I knew, no matter what the cost, I had to protect Jules."

Anguish twists her mouth, and she chokes out between sobs, "I have no money, no connections. All I could do was keep Jules safe." Her eyes turn to me. "*Ma colombe.* I am so sorry. I wish I could've protected you. I should have looked for you. He did not know how much I knew, or I am certain I too would either be on Ward Thirteen or buried in the cornfield."

"Frost is powerful. You were no match for him, Maeve." I shake off the sentiment and stand. "But *is* she dead? I am alive. We need to find the truth."

"The truth to what?" Grayjoy finally breaks the silence.

I hurry to the window and point. "To there. The truth about there."

The cornstalks bend and shudder in the late fall wind.

"The birds," Jules says, her voice excited. "I dream of birds, most every night. Ravens and—"

"A bluebird." We say it in unison and stare at one another.

My heartbeats are wild as the night wind. I let the secret rush out. "I hear a symphony pour from their beaks. Embedded in it is a voice. A woman's far-off voice."

Jules's mouth pops wide, and her hands shake. "I hear the music and the voice, too."

Jules stands and closes the distance between us to kneel at my feet. She gathers my hand in hers. We are both shaking so hard, our gathered hands look to have a palsy.

"I am here now, Jane. And we shall never be parted."

My heart swells in my chest with reluctant gratefulness, but I manage to nod. "But whose voice is it? Is it Mama, or another? *How* could it be Mama?"

The thought of having not one, but two sisters, fills my chest, and it seems to expand like a child's balloon.

"I do not know." Jules stares at Dr. Grayjoy, and their eyes seem to carry on a silent argument. "We shall find out, however. No matter the price. I shall not be dissuaded."

She reaches into her skirt pocket to extract something dangly and silver.

"I believe this to be yours." She places a heart-shaped locket in my hand.

I cock my head and blink. "I don't understand."

"It is identical to mine." She pulls her necklace from beneath her dress for me to see. "It opens." She cracks it open to expose a tiny picture of Mother.

I fumble with mine, pushing too hard. It pops from my hand and clicks off the hard stone floor. "Oh, my."

I hurriedly bend to pick it up—and freeze.

"What is it?" Jules prompts, but she's instantly on all fours beside me.

The locket has popped open to reveal a false back. With trembling fingers, I pick it up, cradling it like a broken bird in my palm.

"I am afraid," I whisper.

"I am as well. It is your locket. Open it, Jane."

Jonathon and Maeve have rushed to stand behind us, neither moving, neither speaking.

My finger slides along the back, and it swings wide. Inside is the tiniest of braids. Three strands woven together.

Dark brown, stark white, and red.

Jules's hand flies over her mouth, and then her finger traces the braid lovingly. "That is you, that is me … " Her finger stops at the red. "Who is this?"

"Your hair is white," Grayjoy says, looking distinctly ill. "Your mother had to have seen you *in* the asylum. Our records say your hair went white the night you were admitted here."

Maeve hovers behind us, face ashen. "Zat locket."

We all stare, waiting.

"A bird. Ze massive, black bird brought it to me. Left it on my windowsill. I realized it was the match to your own, Jules. But I was so frightened. I … hid it."

"Preposterous!" Jonathon roars. "Birds merely love shiny objects," he suggests.

But he begins to pace before the hearth, his hands running over and over through his hair till it stands up in great, black spikes.

I stand, grasping at my chest, where my breath seems to have clogged my windpipe. "The words to the song. It says, *Find the red sparrow.*"

"Where?"

But we both know.

Her finger tightens on mine before she whispers, "In the corn."

"I must return to my room."

Grayjoy finally speaks. "You cannot."

"You cannot come with me. Any of you. It will draw attention. I have something I must see to." I cannot believe the words ready to come out, but I square my shoulders and say, "Before I can leave."

I hurtle out the door before they can stop me.

In my mind, I picture kind Miss Pinchok, a woman on Ward Four; I will tell her of Sebastian.

He was the first love of my life—he saved me really. I am

certain I am to leave where he cannot follow, but I shall not abandon him. Every soul needs a place to lay his or her head. To feel safe. To call home.

Chapter Twenty-Three

Mason

I hurry down the dank passageway as quietly as possible, keeping one hand on the wall, the other on the lantern. The passage heads due north, toward the patient rooms, as I suspected.

After some moments I stop, leaning against the stone wall to catch my breath, and extract my pocket watch. It has been ten minutes since I entered.

"*Caw-caw.*"

My heart catapults into my mouth at the sound.

I ease forward, my mind whispering the words I dare not say aloud: *These are not normal ravens. They think … and* act *upon intentions.*

The hair on the back of my neck rises. I have never been

one to believe in anything beyond what my eyes could see, but I cannot deny their actions any longer. *They are harbingers, but I know not of good or evil.*

I hurry forward, my chest tightening at the thought of him finding Jane once again. My footsteps ring like gunshots in my ears in the still tunnel.

I slide to a halt. The tunnel splits; one continues north, the other east.

I close my eyes, wishing for a compass, but below ground, I have completely lost my bearings. I haven't the foggiest idea where each would lead to on the asylum's grounds.

Fear for her safety tightens my throat, and I ball my fists.

"*Caw-caw.*"

In the northbound tunnel, the raven sits on the ground. Its black, beady eye stares directly at me.

I swallow.

It flaps its wings, as if waiting.

This is insane. I am following a bird.

"Why not? Nothing in my world is as it seems. A respectable physick is a bloody lunatic, I am in love with a patient, and now, I am following the advice of a raven."

Pictures of my former life flash through my head. On the plantation, when I was a younger man, I would've considered a tale such as mine, at best, tripe, at worst—I would've persecuted the storyteller as a fraud or lunatic.

I hold the lantern up in time to see black feathers fly round the corner.

Gritting my teeth, I hurry on.

In another few minutes, I am at what seems a dead end.

The raven sits, its twitchy head moving this way and that, as if trying to muddle a puzzle.

"What? Where have you taken me? It is a dead end. I am trapped."

Fear floods my mouth. *Perhaps the bird works for him. It is not trying to help. And I am now officially herded. A lamb ripe for slaughter.*

I spin on my heel, walking quickly in the opposite direction.

Tap-tap-tap.

I reluctantly turn back, staring over my shoulder.

The bird taps on something in the dark. Something decidedly not large, a hewn stone.

I jam my eyes closed, hesitating. I curse and turn back, hurrying toward the sound. I stoop to see ... a large square, hollowed in the stone, fashioned with a wooden, tiny *door.*

"I don't understand?"

Tap-tap-tap.

*Shuffle-shuffle-*step.

Merciful heaven. I am found.

"Hello?"

It's Jane's voice, just on the other side of the tiny door, sounding confused and sheepish.

"Jane, it's me."

"Mason? What? How?"

"Never mind. Does this door open?"

"Yes, just a moment." There are sounds of sliding objects and scrapes along the floor.

The tiny door cracks open, and a yellow column of light shines in the tunnel.

Shuffle-shuffle-shuffle. The creature's version of a run.

"Jane. Jane, I need to get out. Push it open further, alainn."

The bird, the ruddy bird, begins to sing, but it isn't birdsong. And it isn't music—somewhere between—as if an orchestra somehow flows out from its sharp beak.

Jane's hand, which was frantically pushing, is now still.

"Jane! He is coming!"

Her boot thrusts into the tunnel, jamming the door open as wide as it can go.

I slither into the too-small hole, wiggling and squirming till my waist halts my progress. All the while the bloody bird screeches a lunatic symphony behind me.

Footsteps, right in the corridor. "*Pull,* Jane!"

She grasps me under the arms, and I thrash to and fro—a *crunch.* A sharp pain in my side. But I shove harder.

The bird now *shrieks.* A flutter of wings. Many wings. As if the tunnel is now *full* of the birds. The creature *screams* in guttural pain.

I heave with all my might, feeling a *cruunch* in my side and a pain to match—but I scramble out of the hole to peer back inside.

They are attacking him.

"Aibhistear," I murmur.

I clutch my side, panting. My eyes flick to Jane.

"Ailleagan? Are you hurt?"

"We have to shut that door." I crawl forward, but she is quickly replacing the cut-out, miniature door. It rattles in her hand.

I lurch forward to help and grit my teeth as the pain shoots through my ribs. The door crashes in, Dr. Cloud's boot shoving its way in.

"No!" Jane howls.

Her face contorts with rage; lips drawn back, she nearly hisses. She whirls around, hauling the loose post of her bed free, crashing it down upon his exposed leg.

Another howl. Feathers float in, and a hand, pecked and bleeding, searches to find a hold.

I jam my boot against his fingers, and the same moment Jane swings the post again. The limbs retract, and I shove the board into place. I push my whole body against it, against the continued rattle as he tries to force his way in.

"Jane, in the nurses' closet, under the spare linens, are some tools. Fetch a hammer and nails."

She flies out the room and, in a moment, returns. I quickly nail the four sides of the rectangle in place. She shoves a strange square of stone on top of it. This escape was fabricated by someone or something. Jane was placed in this room for a reason.

My mind replays the overheard snippets of conversation between Grayjoy and Frost: *"But why can she not move to Ward One?"*

"Four is her home. To remove her from familiar surroundings would cause her to regress," was Frost's reply.

I help her jam the faux wall into place. *You would no longer have access to her if she was moved. Could no longer spy on her.*

She whimpers, her voice trembling. "The voice. The voice I heard. Whispering my name. It was him. Making me believe I truly, truly was mad."

We slide the bed in front of it for good measure, and I notice

Jane's face. Still flushed, enraged.

She paces back and forth across the floor, not seeing me. It reminds me of when she was in solitary, when she left me.

Fear causes my guts to shrivel.

"Jane, *mo cridhe*? It's alright. You're safe now."

She swings the post again and again against her bed, the coarse wood instantly bloodying her hands. "I am not safe. I will *never* be safe. *I hate him. I hate him. I hate him.*"

She collapses to the floor, shaking all over, sobbing into her hands.

I drop, cradling her to me. "Shh. Shh. *Mo cridhe.*"

"Fathers are to love their children. Why didn't he love me? *Why?* Am I so horrible?"

"You are wonderful. Magnificent." I place my hand across her cheek, pressing her closer to my chest.

Then I grasp her face, making her meet my eyes. "Singular. No others like you. He is sick, my love. Very sick. The side that is Isaiah Frost does love you." I take a deep breath and cannot believe I am speaking the words. "He cannot help himself. But it is not you, my pet."

Her large blue eyes flick up to mine. "The bird ... the music."

The hair on the back of my neck rises. "More words in the music?"

She nods. "It says, *It is time to go.* I ... believe that is my mother's voice in that music."

I wrap the shawl tighter about my shoulders and hurry through the freezing sleet, taking the asylum steps two at a time. After Jane departed, I hurried Maeve home and said my tearful good-bye.

The staff realized Father did not come home from his shift.

I replay the scene in my mind and shudder.

I had burst through the vestibule door, crashing directly into a ruddy-faced Willis.

"Jules, where have you been? Where is your father? I have been waiting near on two hours for him."

Fear contracted my gut. The time had come for utter honesty.

I grasped his hand and led him to the parlor, decisively shutting the door on a curious servant's face.

"Willis, we shall not be wed. I have found another, whom I love deeply."

Willis's hands balled into fists, and he paced, face as red as his curly hair. "I knew it. I knew it. I am such a fool."

I touched his arm. "You aren't."

"Do not touch me. I have had enough of your deception."

I nodded. "Too true. I have been a beast." I held up my hands, trying to still his constant pacing. "There is much you do not know about this house, and I refuse to involve you. The less you know, the better."

Although I at first thought him crushed, when I related the sad story of Nurse Ginny, her young husband lost overseas, and how she fancied him at the masquerade, he brightened considerably. A little too considerably. I was thinking Willis is in love with *love*. Not anyone in particular.

I give up on any pretenses and head directly for Jonathon's

study. The asylum is still and quiet, which makes my nerves strangely more on edge.

I have become accustomed to screams, moans, and shouts of joy. They are the language of this place. This silence is as if the very tongue of Soothing Hills has been extracted.

My footfalls echo down the hallway as I hurry past the faculty doors. I fling open Jonathon's door. He is bent over his desk, a massive tome cracked open before him.

"Jules, you're soaked." He stands, his ice-blue eyes tightening. "We have to talk, I—"

I silence him by flinging my arms around his neck, smothering his lips with mine.

At first, he resists, his entire body tense. My lips continue on, biting, pulling, stroking. His body softens, his arms grip me tighter, and his tongue invades my mouth, hot and velvety.

He pulls back, forcing our foreheads together. "It isn't right."

I meet his gaze. "I told him. Willis."

He nods. "Before we go further, I must confess something."

My heart drops to my knees, weakening them. "What is it?"

He takes me by the hand, out into the hall, walking towards his apartments.

He does not utter a word. The only sound in the cavernous hallway is the cadence of our steps, and I press my lips tight so as not to speak, to force him to answer me.

We finally reach the door, and he ushers me inside, closing and locking it behind us. We are in the room where first I met him. The study with all the pictures.

He stands, arms spread wide in the room's center. "All these … " His eyes dart around the room like an animal trapped. "All these sketches … are Jane's."

I cock my head, a hard knot of fear forming in my stomach. "Jane's?"

He walks slowly toward me. "Yes … I was … infatuated with her."

I open my mouth, but the words are suspended between my mind and tongue. I merely utter a small, astonished sound. "Were … Were you lovers?" Hot tears fill my eyes, along with the hot flush of anger. And jealousy.

But somewhere at its center is pity. And guilt. For the pampered, though sheltered, life I have led. Whilst my sister, my twin, lived here—with dunking tanks, and whirling chairs, and leeches, and vomiting tinctures.

He shakes his head. "She does not know. I never even held her hand. I felt it improper. That I was doing something wrong. Then I met you—and you drove away even the thought of her, Jules."

He reaches me, gently grasping my hand in his. He kneels before me. "I could not begin a life with you built upon a lie. If you no longer want me, I understand. But I had to confess—I just could not find the right time. And then you met … I am yours, if you will have me."

I blink, and the tears trickle down my cheek. I swipe them away. "I will not say it doesn't hurt, for it does. But—I want you Jonathon. I have never met a man like you. So honest. So brave. So bloody brilliant. I—"

I am in his arms, his mouth back on mine, our breathing a melody and harmony of wind and sound.

The siren blares.

We pull apart, and I see the fear in his eyes. "Another patient has gone missing."

"Jane," we both say together.

Chills erupt from my scalp to my bottom, and my teeth automatically chatter. "Father is gone. He did not come home for my meeting with Willis. He has never, ever missed a meeting."

"Good heaven above." Jonathon pulls me toward the door, grabbing his hat and overcoat.

"We must find her before it's too late."

"I'm frightened." I grasp Mason's hand tighter.

He doesn't break stride but does spare me a glance. "I know, my love. It will be alright. Get in, *mo cridhe*. I will be right here the whole time."

I step into the laundry cart, wiggling my way beneath the layers. Mason's eyes dart up and down the empty corridor. I slide under the covers and discover a tiny hole in the cart's fabric.

The siren begins.

"They know you're gone. I won't be talking now. Keep still and quiet."

The cart rumbles forward, and I struggle to keep my breathing steady.

We pass into the first corridor without issue. I flinch when I see the sentry for the next set of doors—Alexander.

"Where you off to, Mason?" His lips pull back to reveal blackening teeth.

"The pub."

For a minute, his great eyebrows pull together in confusion, then anger blackens his face. "Wiseacre. I could crush you like a bug, you—"

The voice of a feminine crone halts them both. "What are you standing around for, flapping your gums? A patient is loose. Alexander, head to the entrance and go to the admitting office." The nurse's gaze flicks to Mason's name tag.

"Mason, is it? Take this laundry down right quick and head back here. We need every hand on deck for the manhunt."

"I have never done a search. Where will we start?"

"The woods. We form a perimeter of the land, along the stone wall, a wall of people walking in a line to cover every inch. And that needs loads of warm bodies."

The cart shimmies and moves forward. "Alright, then."

We pass through the final set of ward doors, and the cart begins to fly, careening left and right as he bolts, pushing us toward the exit.

The cart halts abruptly, and my face smashes against the side.

"It's guarded," he whispers. We about-face, and I feel the cold seeping through the covers.

His warm hands find me in the folds and ease me out.

"Where are we?"

"The morgue." He takes my hand, and we are running again. "There is an exit here that may not be guarded."

Then I hear it. I halt so quickly, Mason is jerked backward by my still form.

The corn music plays, the strange symphony of words and music and pain.

"It says ... go to the corn."

Mason's eyes tighten with fear. "That is ludicrous. The corn is directly beside the asylum. We will be seen for certain."

I think I see it in his eyes then. The familiar pity. For the crazy girl.

He notices, his eyebrows shoving together as his reason wrestles with my words. His eyes clear, and he stares upward, as if speaking to an unseen host. "I hope your bloody music has the power of invisibility as well."

Shuffle-shuffle-shuffle. The world goes black and relights as I fight the swoon. *Cloud.* Cloud, Frost, *my father*, is near.

Mason pulls me out of the morgue and down the corridor, placing his fingers to his lips. He slips off his shoes and gestures for me to do the same.

We bolt soundlessly down the hallway. He stares left and right, panic pinching his face. He gestures, and we slide to a stop before the conservatory. The heat blasts our faces as we step inside, hurrying along the stone walkways.

"Why are we in here?" I whisper.

"He tracks by smell."

Every hair on my head stands at attention. *For the first time I fear ... What if somewhere deep inside, I, too, am a monster?*

"All these smells will confuse him."

Indeed, flowers and dirt and water fill the air.

We barrel forward, the door in sight. *Shuffle-shuffle.*

I dare to look behind. And like Lot's wife, I instantly regret my decision.

A froth drips from Cloud's lips, splattering his dirty waistcoat. His hair is wild and unkempt, and his teeth gleam in the night like a jackal's.

"Jane," he growls. "You are Patient Twenty-Nine. Jane is dead. She died long ago."

All my life I have wished to hear my real name from his lips, and now I shudder at the sound.

Mason squeezes my hand, belting forward. "Do not listen to him."

Mason wrenches open the door, and the deep, mournful call of a cello, layered and resonant, blasts so loud we cover our ears.

Mason forces me before him, and I pelt into the corn.

In the sky above the corn, the massive unkindness of ravens dives and pitches, their mouths open and closing as their bodies dart to and fro in time to the weaving, waxing notes.

Their black mass thins and thickens as the melody and harmony weave.

"Mama." I stop dead. "I hear Mama." I drop to my knees.

Mason's eyes widen as they dart from my face to the asylum and back. "You must run, Jane!"

I shake my head. "Mama. She's speaking in the music. I must listen."

His hands are under my arms, hoisting me up, dragging me.

"Twenty-Nine!" Cloud's voice thunders from behind.

Mason lifts me into his arms, running into the corn. The birds begin to dip in and out of the rows, nearly hitting us. But my mind is gone, lost in the notes and sound of my mother's voice.

"Jane."

I stiffen at the new voice.

"Jane. *You run this instant.*"

Mason sets me down. Jules stands before me, fire burning in

her blue eyes. Grayjoy at her side.

I nod, wiping away the tears. I go to her, and her arm tightens round my shoulders.

"Twenty-Nine!" Cloud breaks into the corn, loping forward like a jackal.

"No. Her name is Jane. And you are not even fit to speak it."

Cloud freezes, his eyes narrowing, coming to rest on Jules. He cocks his head, staring. Blinking.

"You shall not touch her. You monster. You ... *took* her from me. I wasn't alone. All the while, you kept her from me. *I hate you.*"

Cloud's face contorts, twitching and writhing. His hunched posture lifts, reaching skyward, till he stands ramrod straight. He moans, drops to his knees in the dirt, and then staggers to stand.

Frost has arrived. Back in his body. Back in his mind.

He blinks, as if confused. "Jules? What are we doing here? Grayjoy, what is the meaning of this?" He registers the screaming sirens, and his eyes rest on me. "You are helping her escape? How dare you—"

"You shall not touch her." Jules's body shakes where her arms envelope me. "How could you take an innocent child, place her here?"

Frost stiffens. "She is not my child ... You are my child. She is—"

"Cloud's child," Grayjoy interjects. "You are one and the same, Isaiah."

He shakes his head, fear clouding his features. "No."

"I have seen the journal, Isaiah. How your two selves battle, writing to one another. So that one understands what the other is doing."

Frost buckles, his knees sinking into the mud. His hand reaches out, fingers straining. "She would have been persecuted, she—"

"She was not perfect," Jules says. "You thought Cloud conceived her, put her in Mama's belly. Maybe he did. He *is you*, Father. Somewhere deep down, you are the same."

He shakes his head. "No. She ... heard the music, imagined the voices in—"

A blast of cello, so long and loud my ears ring, forces us all to the ground.

Jules stares up at him, eyes gleaming with defiance. "I hear the words, too, Father. Maeve made me swear to never, ever tell. So your girl, the one you conceived, hears those voices, too. You ... You took Mama's mind."

Tears stream down Frost's face. He shakes his head. "It cannot be."

The breeze blows hard, bending the stalks like mere blades of grass in the wind.

"Where is their mother?" Mason prompts. His eyes dart to the sky, where the unkindness undulates and flows like a black aerial river. "Jane, come to me."

I release Jules and hurry to his side. He tightly grasps my hand, pulling me slightly behind him in a protective gesture.

The smell of sulfur rides the wind, blowing across our faces.

My eyes stray back to Frost. His arms quake with a force that rattles his teeth in his mouth. Cheeks, chin, and brow quiver and twitch as a long, guttural, "*Rrrraaahh*," escapes his gaping lips.

"The turn. It's happening," Grayjoy says. "When Frost cannot deal with the pain, Cloud takes over. Begin backing away."

His hands slide to Jules's waist, pulling her closer.

Cloud's eyes are wide and wild, pupils small as dots of ink. "Twenty-Nine. It is foolish to try to find your mother. She is long gone."

I shake my head. "I hear her. In the music. She ... says to come to her."

He cocks his head, black curls blowing across his pinched face. "She's dead, girl."

"*Shut up, shut up, shut up*, you vile creature, or I shall shut that horrible mouth for you!" Jules darts forward, but Jonathon's hands quickly wrap about her waist, restraining her.

"No, Jules. He isn't worth it."

"We must follow the music," I cry.

Mason pulls a pistol from the waistband of his trousers to point it at Cloud's head. "I don't fancy using this, but I will if I must. Do not follow us."

We turn to go, Mason walking backward as we enter the rows of corn.

"You won't find her."

I whirl about, my heart hammering in my chest. "What did you say?"

"I said, you won't find her. I've taken care of that. You see, I have many names. Cloud. The Dark Man who makes people sign his book." He laughs.

"Who? What are you talking about?" Jules's arm, which touches mine, quivers in fear.

"If you go, you will end up like her."

The music rises, seeming to emanate from the dirt to swirl about us. The whispered words entwined in the notes: *"Find me, turtledoves, we are waiting."*

I look over at Jules, dread seeping into my heart, but she squeezes my hand, giving me courage. Tears flow in a steady stream from her eyes. "That voice. That is Mama."

Cloud bolts forward, body twitching all over, to alight in a flying lunge toward Jules.

The unkindness descends, squawking, pecking, ripping bits of flesh from his face and hands. "GAH!"

"Run!" Mason bellows.

We pelt into the corn, running in a single line, hands linked.

We follow the musical trail. On either side of us, the corn undulates, and visions fade in and out like the heat on a summer day.

A battlefield, cannon fire whistling, to the right.

"WHAT IS THIS? WHAT IS HAPPENING?" I scream.

Jules grips my hand tighter. "I do not know! Keep running!"

To our left, an image halts me in my tracks, so that both Jules and Jonathon plow into my back.

Another cornfield, through what seems a misty, undulating window.

A large, white farmhouse. And Cloud.

Cloud has passed through somehow. Cloud loping forward, toward the house.

Mother's voice calls in the music, and my heart breaks listening to it. But my eyes are drawn toward the limping, loping figure—and fear and dread seal the cracks in my heart. Fear for whoever lives in that house.

I see a flash of red hair on horseback flit past the window, unaware of us, unaware of Cloud.

"Jules." I stare at her. My sister. My eyes staring back from her face. "It's the red sparrow. We have to go. We have to save her."

She turns, staring in horror at the undulating picture. "But ... Mama."

I put my hand on her arm. "Wherever she is, he is there." I thrust a shaking finger at the misty window, which now shrinks, growing smaller.

I turn to stare at Mason. "This is not your fight. I cannot ask you to come with me. He is linked to us. That creature is my father."

Mason's face tightens with anger. "I am going. Where you go, I go, *mo cridhe*. There is no other option or argument."

Jonathon stares after the loping figure of his erstwhile mentor with a resigned expression. He takes Jules's hand. "We shall do it together. There are four of us, to one of him."

Cloud has almost reached the farmhouse. It is then I see children in the window. My heart freezes to ice and drops to my stomach. I point.

"Let's go." Jules stalks forward, hand tentatively outstretched to touch the shimmering surface.

An eruption of orchestral music drives us to our knees. My body trembles all over. I feel for Jules's hand in the dirt, and her grasping fingers find mine.

"He took my voice, but he could not reach the music. It is part of me. Part of you. It is the only voice I have, turtledoves. I need you— your music—to free me. Find the sparrow, bring her to me."

The voice of cello, violin, and strings all cease at once, as the unkindness of ravens takes flight, following Cloud in a spiraling tunnel of black feathers.

All that remains is the wind.

"Hurry, Jules." I rush forward to follow the flock. I rush forward into a stream of time.

Jules slides her hand in tentatively, and it blurs, then disappears. The air has *congealed*, it sticks to her fingertips. She eases one leg inside, and I rush forward to grab her hand. Mason grasps my hand, and Jonathon takes his other—and like a human chain, we enter the time door.

"Don't look back."

AUTHOR'S NOTES

Multiple Personality

Multiple personality is now called *dissociative identity disorder* in the DSM-5, the manual used in psychiatry to categorize disease states. One of the earliest mentions of Multiple Personality Disorder is Robert Louis Stevenson's 1886 novel, *Dr. Jekyll and Mr. Hyde*.

It is a hotly contested diagnosis as to whether it actually exists and each side, for and against, are vehement in their beliefs.

Later books published on the subject were The *Three Faces of Eve* (1957) and *Sybil* (1973).

Asylums in the 1800 and 1900's

All of the treatments mentioned in the book were used at one time or another throughout history. None is the product of the author's imagination. In addition to being a descendant of 1940's asylum workers, Brynn toured asylums to ensure historical accuracy. See her social media pages for photographs of the urban adventure.

Historical Forms of Address:

The phrase, "Your servant, mum." May be used for a woman who is not one's own mother. For more information on Georgian, Victorian and Edwardian Slang, visit Colonial Williamsburg website or any historical 'history comes alive' reenactment program.

Fraternal Twins Born Days Apart:
http://bit.ly/1PO73Id

Look in the annals of medicine; weird science abounds. Yes, it's possible. Two different eggs, two sperm, one difficult labor.

Ablation

Ablation was the Victorian/Edwardian term for the procedure which would one day become the lobotomy. The first were performed in 1836 in Switzerland on canines. The procedure severed the cortex from the rest of the brain, thus isolating emotion from intellect—at least that was the idea. More often than not, patients died during or after the procedure. If they did survive, they were passive, with no lingering trace of their former personalities. Lest we think it an ancient barbarism, it occurred as late as the 1950's—President John F. Kennedy's sister Rosemary was lobotomized.

ACKNOWLEDGEMENTS

For my agent Victoria Lea and editor Georgia McBride—who help translate the voices in my mind into the written word. I am grateful to be in your company.

BRYNN CHAPMAN

Brynn Chapman was born and raised in western Pennsylvania, and is the daughter of two teachers. Her writing reflects her passions: science, history, and love—not necessarily in that order. In real life, the Geek gene runs strong in her family, as does the Asperger's Syndrome. Her writing reflects her experience as a pediatric therapist and her interactions with society's downtrodden. She's a strong believer in underdogs and happily-ever-afters. She also writes non-fiction and lectures on the subjects of Autism and sensory integration and is a medical contributor to online journal *The Age of Autism*.

OTHER MONTH9BOOKS TITLES YOU MIGHT LIKE

BONESEEKER

THE MISSING

THE PERILOUS JOURNEY OF THE NOT-SO-INNOCUOUS GIRL

NOBODY'S GODDESS

Find more awesome Teen books at http://www.Month9Books.com

Connect with Month9Books online:

Facebook: www.Facebook.com/Month9Books
Twitter: https://twitter.com/Month9Books
You Tube: www.youtube.com/user/Month9Books
Request review copies via publicity@month9books.com

SHE WILL DISCOVER A TRUTH
THAT SHOULD HAVE REMAINED HIDDEN

BONESEEKER

BRYNN CHAPMAN

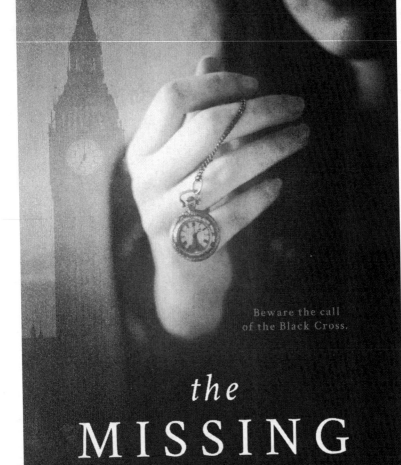

Beware the call
of the Black Cross.

the
MISSING

J.R. LENK

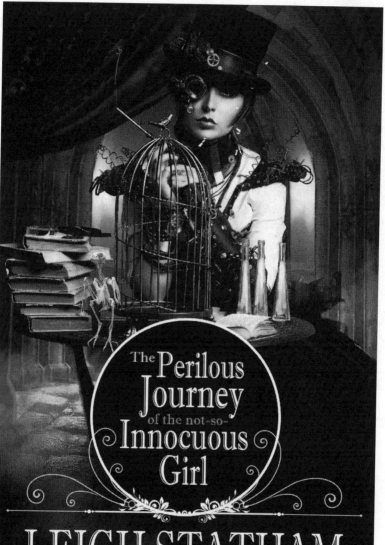

The Perilous
Journey
of the not-so-
Innocuous
Girl

LEIGH STATHAM

NOBODY'S GODDESS

NEVER VEIL SERIES BOOK ONE

Amy McNulty